"SAY NAUGHT," HE WHISPERED.

As if with his body flush atop hers it was possible to think? Emma scoured their surroundings for any sign of movement, tried to ignore the hard length of him, the feel of his entire body wrapped above hers.

And failed.

Footsteps sounded nearby.

A stick cracked, closer this time, followed by a muttered curse.

Patrik's calloused hand covered hers with surprising gentleness.

She stared at the tangle of scars battering his skin, the muscled hand atop hers. She should pull away, not feed this delusion of his protecting her. Instead, Emma savored his touch, his protectiveness in a world that offered none.

More from Diana Cosby

HIS CAPTIVE

HIS WOMAN

HIS CONQUEST

Published by Kensington Publishing Corporation

His DESTINY

Diana Cosby

ZEBRA BOOKS
KENSINGTON PUBLISHING CORP.
http://www.kensingtonbooks.com

ZEBRA BOOKS are published by

Kensington Publishing Corp.
119 West 40th Street
New York, NY 10018

All Kensington titles, imprints and distributed lines are avail-
able at special quantity discounts for bulk purchases for sales
promotion, premiums, fund-raising, educational or institu-
tional use.

Special book excerpts or customized printings can also be created to fit specific needs. For details, write or phone the office
of the Kensington Special Sales Manager: Attn. Special Sales
Department. Kensington Publishing Corp., 119 West 40th
Street, New York, NY 10018. Phone: 1-800-221-2647.

Zebra and the Z logo Reg. U.S. Pat. & TM Off.

ISBN-13: 978-1-4201-0992-4
ISBN-10: 1-4201-0992-8

First Printing: October 2011

10 9 8 7 6 5 4 3 2 1

Printed in the United States of America

At times in our lives we are blessed to meet those incredibly special people, those who take time out of their busy lives to make a positive difference in ours.

This book is dedicated to two such men, Dr. Gregory K. Moffatt and Jim Street, both truly amazing men whose selflessness have made an immense positive difference in my life as well as so many others.

My sincere thanks to you both; you each are truly heroes.

ACKNOWLEDGMENTS

I am truly thankful for the immense support from my family and friends. My deepest wish is that everyone is as blessed when they pursue their dreams.

My sincere thanks and humble gratitude to my editors, Alica Condon and Megan Records, my agent, Holly Root, my critique partners, Shirley Rogerson and Michelle Hancock, and to Mary Forbes for the extra brainstorming, all of which made Patrik and Emma's story breathe life and allowed the magic of story to infuse their journey. A special thanks to Sulay Hernandez for believing in me from the start.

And a huge thanks to my children, Eric, Stephanie and Christopher, the Roving Lunatics (Mary Beth Shortt and Sandra Hughes), as well as the Wild Writers for their friendship and continued amazing support!

Chapter 1

Scotland, July 1297

A woman's terrified scream rent the air.

Sir Patrik Cleary MacGruder whirled. Sweat from his grueling pace this summer morning soaked his skin as he scanned the gnarl of elm, ash, and fir.

"No, do not touch me! Please!" a woman begged.

Men's crude laughter echoed nearby, rough, ugly, and thick with menace.

A muscle worked in Patrik's jaw as he touched the writ secured beneath his tunic. He must reach Bishop Wishart without delay.

Her next scream, raw with the terror of the brutality yet to come, pierced him as if a well-aimed sword. Nae, it struck deeper, into the pit of his soul.

Silence sheathed his steps as he wove through the woods toward the woman's desperate pleas. With Scottish soil crawling with the English bastards, only a fool would rush in alone to aid the lass. Yet, here he was.

"Look at her, she would be wanting us," a gruff English voice stated.

Another man's harsh laughter sounded nearby.

Bloody bastards! Patrik tamped down his fury and edged closer, scanning the forest for any sign of a trap.

Shadows flickered ahead.

He ducked behind a fallen tree. Pulse racing, he peered around the mossy tangle of weathered bark.

Caught between two English knights, a slender woman kicked and twisted to break free. Her chestnut hair, wild with the struggle, obscured her face.

Patrik's anger shoved up a notch.

"A fighter she is," a burly Englishman laughed. "And a good bedding she will be."

She lunged forward in an attempt to break free. "No!"

With a lewd smile, another knight reached out, ripped her gown. Bare flesh rippled beneath the flutter of cloth. He jerked the ruined garment free.

Naked, the woman fought harder. "No, I beg of you!"

Memories of watching his mother being raped scalded Patrik's mind. Darkness consumed him, a blackness so thick it smothered his soul. Hand trembling, he withdrew his blade, edged forward. They'd not touch the lass, or draw another breath. He scoured the area for any other men, then refocused on the knights.

Four of the bastards.

Odds he'd take.

Sword raised, Patrik shoved to his feet, sprang into the clearing. "Release the lass!"

The tattered dress sank to the ground as her closest attacker whirled, drawing his blade.

At the English knights' distraction, the woman tugged a hand free. Without hesitation, she whirled and kneed the other knight in the groin.

Face distorted in agony, the man dropped.

The woman clawed at him as Patrik charged, drove his sword to meet the closest knight's blade.

At the blow, the Englishman stumbled back.

Patrik slashed the knight's throat. At the spurt of blood, he spun to face the three remaining warriors. Fury pounding hot, he withdrew his dagger, hurled it at the nearest knight. His blade sank into the knight's chest.

Shock widened the man's eyes. Blood spewed from the wound. The man stepped toward him, crumpled.

The knight the woman had attacked cursed, staggered to his feet, outrage carved upon his face.

Nostrils flared, Patrik drove his sword into the Englishman's chest, then spun to face the final warrior. "The odds are even. As they were not for the woman you tried to rape."

"You will die for this," the Englishman spat.

Patrik arched a brow, scanned the knights sprawled around them. "'Tis English blood that stains the earth."

"Once I carve your worthless arse, I will find the Scottish whore. Scum, the lot of you." The English knight angled his blade. "If she pleases me, mayhap I will allow her to live the night."

Patrik tamped down his fury. His opponent wanted him angry, wanted his thoughts blurred with reckless emotion. Nay, too many battles lay behind him to make such a critical error.

With a roar, his aggressor drove forward.

Patrik dropped and rolled. Steel whooshed a hairsbreadth above his head.

Shock that he'd missed twisted to outrage upon the knight's face as he whirled.

Patrik shoved to his feet and swung. His blade met flesh, slashing the man's throat, the spurt of crimson satisfying.

Knees trembling, the knight sank to the ground, his words mutilated within a gurgle of blood.

"Die, you bastard," Patrik hissed. "Rot in Hades where one day your English king will lie!" Chest heaving, he ignored the groans of the dying men as he scoured the thick of green for the lass. She'd run. Curse it!

Steel hissed against leather as Patrik secured his blade. He jerked his dagger free of the dying man, scooped up her tattered garment and followed the soft indents of earth that betrayed her passing.

With her screams of terror, the clash of blades and the woods cluttered with the English, 'twould be but a matter of time before more of the bastards arrived. He had to find the lass before they did. Given the graveness of his mission, the thought of abandoning her flickered to mind, a thought he abandoned as quick. As long as he breathed, never would English scum touch a Scottish woman he could protect.

Leaves rustled in the dense thicket ahead.

Patrik halted. He scanned his garb, grimaced. His

tunic and trews splattered with the Englishmen's blood would far from ease her fear.

"Lass," he called, keeping his voice soft as he listened for any sign of approaching men. "I know you are in there. And afraid."

Silence.

He stepped closer. "You know me not, but the woods are thick with English. With the scuffle, more knights will come. We must go. Now."

A leaf shook. "How do I know I can trust you?" Her soft, trembling words held courage.

He held out her tattered gown. "I give you my word, that of a Scottish knight."

Long moments passed. He sensed her silent scrutiny, struggled to bank his impatience. His mission was crucial; the sooner he saw to her safety, the faster he could deliver the writ.

"Place the gown near the bush."

With slow steps, Patrik moved forward, laid the battered garment into the shadows as she'd asked.

"Move away."

He eased back.

A slender arm reached out, snatched the torn garb, then disappeared. Leaves shook. Hints of creamy skin against shadows slipped into view as she dressed.

He scanned their surroundings. "We must hurry."

The leaves stilled.

A fresh wind stirred, etched with the warmth of the oncoming day, thick with the tension infusing the moment.

"Lass—"

The woman stood.

Patrik's breath left him in a rush. Though garbed in a torn gown tied in hurried knots, her face marred by bruises from the knight's rough handling, caressed within the fractured light she appeared as if crafted by the fey.

Nay, a paltry description for the beautiful woman who stood before him.

Thick chestnut hair with hints of bronze framed softly carved cheeks, a full mouth that would tempt a saint and emerald eyes that held naught but distrust. Her eyes. As if a spell cast, he couldn't look away. They held him, mesmerized him, drew him as no other.

Embarrassed to catch himself staring, he cleared his throat. "Lass, I will not harm you," he said, keeping his words soft. "I swear it."

"Your name?"

The soft sweep of her burr wrapped around him like a dangerous luxury. He gave a brief bow. "Sir Patrik Cleary at your service." Regret touched him. Not Sir Patrik Cleary MacGruder, the latter a name he'd lost the right to speak.

In a nervous sweep, she took in his garb. "You are loyal to Scotland?"

The doubt in her voice he understood. "Aye."

"The English knights?" She shot a glance toward where her captors had stripped her a short time before.

"They are dead."

If possible, her face paled further.

"They chose their fate," he stated, unapologetic.

She rubbed her thumb over her fingertips in a hesitant slide. "They did." Her breath trembled. "I thank you for rescuing me. Had you not . . ."

"Our present worry is to leave. We must be as far away as possible before the English find their comrades slain."

"Of course." Nervous fingers tugged on a ragged tie as she assessed him.

What did she see? With the Englishman's blood staining his tunic, did she wonder if he was as merciless as the men who had tried to rape her? Did doubts crawl through her as to why he would come to her rescue?

"My name is Cristina Moffat."

Her soft words erased his dark thoughts. A strange warmth touched him that after the violence of this day, she offered a sliver of trust. In this war-ravaged country, a name wrongly given could mean death.

He extended his hand toward her. "Come."

With hesitant steps, she moved from the bush. Dirt clung to her gown, the knots far from shielding the luxurious sweep of creamy skin, nor the bruises left by brutal hands. She stared at Patrik's hand, then looked away.

He dropped his hand. "Never feel embarrassed. The shame is theirs. May they rot in Hades."

Thick chestnut lashes lifted. "They did not rape me."

Given moments more they would have accomplished the deed, a fact they both knew. He remained silent, understood her battle against the terror clawing her mind, allowed the lass to focus on her innocence retained.

"They have been slaughtered!" a man's voice roared nearby.

"Blast it!" Patrik caught her hand and pulled her

with him. Sticks cracked beneath their feet, limbs whipped his body as he pushed her before him, then followed at a run.

"Their blood still runs," another man called. "Whoever killed them is nearby. Find them!"

A horse whinnied.

"They have mounts," Cristina gasped as she leapt over a tumble of low brush.

He cleared the thicket, close on her heels. "Aye." And would easily catch up to them. Familiarity with the land was their only hope. Turning to the right, he led her through the tangle. "Hurry."

The leather of their flat-soled shoes slapped against the earth as they ran. After several moments, the dense foliage of the forest gave way to a field dotted with tufts of fresh grass, brave buds of flowers, and sweeps of heather.

Cristina jerked her hand free.

Patrik whirled, his breath coming fast. "We cannot stop."

She stared at the roll of hills leading to the formidable ben, the mountain but one of many to the north. "The brambles before us would not hide a field mouse."

"And what the English will be thinking as well," he agreed. "But I know of a place to hide. Trust me."

Trust him?

Sir Patrik's piercing hazel eyes held hers. He was a warrior, from his muscled arms to his carved cheekbones and deep baritone voice. A man used to giving commands. A man many feared.

A man she, too, would be a fool to dismiss.

She turned in the direction they'd come and scoured

the concealing woods. Shadows littered the dense foliage, numerous places where they could hide.

A shiver crept through her. Why was he exposing them? If anyone scanned the field, they would be seen. No, it was too late to question her decision. She'd committed herself to the journey long before this day.

She turned toward the handsome Scot, a man as intriguing as he was dangerous. A man who, if he learned the truth—that her real name was Emma Astyn, a woman acclaimed as one of England's top mercenaries—would kill her.

Chapter 2

Rebellious sandy hair framed the eyes of a warrior as Sir Patrik watched her, those of a man confident in his decisions, those of a man who killed without hesitation. The beard shadowing the rebel's face lent another layer to his dangerous aura, that of a man unbending, a man served many an injustice, and a man who had sent many an opponent to Hades. The blood spilled upon his sword this day but a pittance to the legendary Scot.

Dubh Duer.

A dark hero indeed if half of the legends detailing Sir Patrik's exploits proved to be true. Emma shuddered at the stories told, at the tales of his complete ruthlessness when he set out to achieve a goal.

Dubh Duer's real name had eluded the English, but the man who had hired her, Sir Hugh de Cressingham, King Edward's treasurer of the English administration in Scotland, was a man as determined as viciously inventive in achieving his goals.

After losing many a knight to *Dubh Duer*'s blade,

Sir Cressingham had publicly declared he would catch, torture, then kill his Scottish foe, a man other Scots admired, a man whose name was sparking rebellion in addition to that of another formidable Scot, Sir William Wallace.

On an attack against another powerful Scot, Sir Andrew de Moray, English knights had captured several followers of the rebellious Highland leader. To Sir Cressingham's delight, one of the rebels had broken beneath his cruel torture. On the promise of sparing the man's family, he had revealed with his dying breath that *Dubh Duer* was Sir Patrik Cleary. *Dubh Duer*—a Scot who hid in the shadows, a rebel who had integrated himself with Sir Andrew de Moray and the Bishop of Wishart.

Distrustful of the bishop's loyalty to England from the start, a man who was one of the original Guardians of Scotland, Sir Cressingham had made it his personal task to catch Sir Patrik, as well as unveil proof of Wishart's perfidy.

King Edward believed Scotland's resistance was but mindless spurts of resentment, easily quelled, and had turned his attention toward the war with France and the development of the Flemish alliance. The king offered little response to Sir Cressingham's warnings of Scotland's growing unrest.

Furious with the English king's dismissal and learning someone close to the king was smuggling military information to Wishart, Sir Cressingham had employed Emma. Then, he'd learned that the runner used for the covert messages was *Dubh Duer*.

With gleeful malice, Sir Cressingham had ordered

her to befriend Sir Patrik, retrieve the writ he carried as well as discover who was sending traitorous information to the bishop. Once she'd gained the information, she was to ensure the rebel's capture.

Confident in her abilities, lured by the amount of coin offered, Emma had credited the viciousness of *Dubh Duer* to fable and accepted the mission. She had learned the hard way never to let emotion sway her. After crafting the Scottish name of Cristina Moffat along with her character's tattered past, she'd used her secret contacts to discover Patrik's whereabouts. Now, faced with the daunting man whose life she'd chosen to infiltrate, the enormity of Emma's task slammed home.

A challenge, but not an impossibility.

She nodded. "You lead, I will follow." Never must he learn that Sir Hugh de Cressingham had hired her or her true identity. Once Sir Patrik lowered his guard, she could discover where he hid the writ, and with cloaked questions, the name of the traitor to England who'd spawned the missive.

With confidence, the dangerous Scot turned and led her up the steep incline at a brisk pace. They topped the crest; then he guided them toward a large rock jutting from the wash of green.

She stared in disbelief. "We are to hide behind this boulder?"

"Nay."

Sounds of the English knights moving through the forest grew closer.

The man was mad. "Then where? We will never make it across the field without being seen."

"We will." The rebel knelt and parted the sturdy tufts of grass edging the massive stone. A narrow slit appeared. Shadows fell into blackness.

No, not blackness, but a hole large enough for a man to crawl inside. Surprised, Emma looked up. "An entry?"

"Aye, to a cairn."

A grave site. She swallowed hard. Darkness, enclosed space, weathered bones, and decaying flesh.

"I do not see anyone," a man's voice boomed from the edge of the forest.

Sir Patrik caught her shoulder. "Go!"

Emma half climbed, half tumbled into the darkness, the ancient steps having long since eroded into a slide of stone. She refused to think of the uneven narrow walls on either side, blackness so dark it smothered any light, or the press of the earth, a cold welcome for the bodies within.

"Use your hands to guide you and keep moving forward," he urged from above.

As if it was that easy. Dirt trickled over her. Behind her, in the spew of broken sunlight, she made out Sir Patrik's half-bent frame.

"Keep moving," he said. "I will be right behind you."

Half crawling, she edged forward. When the light eroded, Sir Patrik's steady voice guided her; her each step into the vat of blackness a major victory. The walls on either side fell away. Emma shoved down her fear as she entered the cavern that held the graves.

The thrum of hooves grew closer, and the ground

above began to tremble. Loose rock clattered to the floor.

A whinny echoed nearby.

She whirled, opened her mouth to scream.

Sir Patrik clasped his hand over her mouth. "'Tis the knights approaching."

With effort, she nodded.

The rebel released his hand.

"They are scouring the field."

"Aye, prodded they are," he said, his words rich with pride. "And mad as a badger stuck."

With their four comrades slain, the knights would be furious. God in heaven, if they captured her and Sir Patrik now, it would destroy the fragile bond gained.

A bond formed only after weeks of careful planning.

Anger touched her that the men involved had died. She'd weighed all of the factors, had plotted out the specific details of the supposed rape. Like her, the knights who'd volunteered for this task had believed the chance of harm slight, the dangers ahead hers to face.

And they'd all been wrong.

Sir Cressingham would be furious when he learned of the loss of his men, but no more than she was at herself. She prided herself on her expertise, on the skill that those who hired her paid well for. However much she'd prepared, she'd underestimated Sir Patrik Cleary. A misjudgment she wouldn't make again.

Emma started forward.

"Hold, lass."

She stumbled to a halt, steadied herself against

a rock; her hand was shaking. Focus on the mission. Naught but that mattered. "What is it?"

"I am going to take the lead."

Frustrated at her wash of emotions, she smothered the upsetting thoughts, the kernels of feeling that made a person weak. She backed against the cool rock. Well she knew the choice in war, the risks taken, as had the knights.

The rebel edged past her, the hewn muscles of his body brushing her arm.

Warmth swept her.

She gasped, moved aside.

He reached over, caught her. "Do not fear me."

At his soft burr, another burst of warmth swept through her. No, not warmth, awareness. Heart pounding, she froze, stunned. When he'd jumped into the clearing to rescue her, of all the descriptions she'd received, none had prepared her for the impact of the man.

Emma quelled her nerves. Did she not thrive on the tasks others feared? Did she not rush forward when others would retreat? She held not the weakness of caring, or believing that anything but her own decisions guided her life. Too many years had passed since she'd entertained the notion of believing in others.

Or given a damn.

Warm flesh slid over her hand. She tried to ignore the strength in Sir Patrik's fingers as they curled around her palm. He believed he aided her. With her hatred of closed-in places, in this he did. But no more.

"Come." He tugged her forward.

"The grass is flattened over here," a distant voice called with anger.

Hooves rumbled above.

"They will catch us!" she whispered.

"Nay."

"How can you be so sure? Our footprints on the grass will be seen and followed."

Ahead of her, Sir Patrik halted. "Wait." He released her hand. Stone grated. With a grunt, the scrape of stone again fractured the silence.

"What are you doing?"

"A tunnel lies beyond. When they find our entry, we must be within and the entry secured."

A rebel hideout? A detail she would pass on. "How long is it?" She allowed nervousness to ride her voice, needing him to believe unease inspired her question, which in part was the truth.

"Worry not. I will lead you through it." Dirt and small stones clattered into the distant opening. Sir Patrik hauled her forward.

A tremor slid through Emma as she half tumbled after him. She refused to think of the spiders or rodents inside, and whatever else lived within this blackened crypt. Thank God they would soon be out of the mind-numbing blackness.

"Wait here," Sir Patrik whispered.

Stone scraped; he was closing the entry.

Leather padded against earth. Cloth shifted as he moved beside her. His body's heat enveloped hers. "Say naught."

"Do you see anything?" a muted voice called from the other side.

Emma jumped.

Patrik laid a calming hand upon the lass. Even if the English searched the burial mound, they would find nothing but stones and the bones of those once loved.

The knights knew naught of the secret rebel passage, a tunnel hewn through the earth into a maze of natural chambers leading to the other side of the ben. By the time he and the lass had reached the northern exit, the knights should be far away, and once he'd left her with friends in a nearby village, he could return to his mission.

He touched the writ secured beneath his tunic and again cursed their delay. Too many lives lay at stake for him to fail.

"Sir Patrik?"

At the fear in the lass's whisper, he set aside his worrisome thoughts. "'Twill be fine." He drew her against him, found her shaking. After the horrific events of the day, she would be in shock.

Although the situation was dangerous, he tread upon familiar ground. Too well he knew the twisted entertainment of the bastards. Anytime he drew English blood 'twas a day to celebrate.

Men's voices on the other side of the stone grew louder.

She stiffened against him.

"They have but entered the cairn," Patrik whispered to offer assurance.

"They will see where you have slid the stone."

"Nay. The entry to the tunnel is well hidden. After a quick check within the blackness, they will believe that if we indeed hid inside, we remained but a short time."

Long moments passed. The murmur of angry voices echoed from the other side, a muted curse, grumbles of dissent, then finally, blissful silence.

Patrik released a sigh.

"They are gone?"

"For now. When they find no other tracks leading away, they will return. By then, we will be long gone." And the rebels' secret passage would remain safe from English eyes. He hesitated. After saving the lass this day, would she expose the escape route? Under the circumstances, he believed not. Still, he would watch her.

Patrik released her and stood. "Wait here."

"What are you doing?"

"If the knights return with torches, I must ensure that any trace of our passage within the cairn is erased." With quick, efficient movements, he slid his hands up the wall until he felt the candle and the mound of dried grass placed there. He withdrew his dagger and flint. In seconds a flame sprang to life. Patrik lit the wick.

Yellow light from his candle flickered, then grew in the blackness, exposing the time-worn walls, the layer of uneven dirt around them and the tunnels beyond.

She gasped. "There are numerous tunnels."

"Aye." He smothered the fire, then replaced the remaining tinder for future travelers. "Anyone entering must know the route or they will become lost."

Beneath the flickering light, her face paled.

"Do nae worry, lass. I am well familiar with the

passages." She appeared far from convinced. "Stay here. I will be but a moment."

He shoved the stone aside, quickly retraced their steps and swept away any sign of their passage. Thankful to have finished the task, he slid the stone into place.

Candlelight flickered in the gloom, the soft, pungent scent of the tallow melding with the musty air. He extended his hand. "Come." Cristina stared up at him, the wariness on her dirt- and flame-smeared face easy to read. "Unless you wish to remain here?"

She scrambled to her feet. The tattered gown hung on her like a crude joke, a harsh reminder of her perils this day, and a sober warning to be gentle with her.

Well he knew of the hurt within, of the time needed to find stable ground when one's life lay destroyed. Memories of the MacGruders, whom he'd once claimed as family, of a surname he no longer used, to keep hidden, rose to the forefront of his mind. He stowed the hurt, the ache of three brothers lost, fellow rebels who for the year past believed him dead.

A belief for the best.

His thoughtless actions had severed their tie, had destroyed a bridge that could not be rebuilt. But that knowledge did not end his desire to be with his adoptive family. Bedamned. Why did he think of his past, or wish for bonds lost? The memories would invite but further misery.

Patrik focused on the woman, on what for this moment he could control. "We are safe."

Skeptical eyes studied him. "Why did you save me?"

He frowned. "Is the reason not easy to understand?"

"The English roam Scotland, butchering in the name of their king. No one is safe to interfere in their actions, regardless of the brutality served." She hesitated. "You could have easily ignored my situation."

"Why would I have left you at the mercy of those who have none?" Patrik studied this woman who looked as if created by the fey, but viewed the world with a warrior's eye.

"I assure you, not every Scot would have cared about a woman alone. Not all men live with honor."

Eyes as angry as cynical watched him, searched his as if seeking a sign of deception. Saint's breath, someone had hurt her terribly, beyond that of the violence served this day. "Any who would turn from a woman in need is a coward, or in bed with the English. Neither of which I tolerate."

At his words, her body relaxed. "I share your dislike of traitors to our country."

He nodded. "Aye, they will soon learn they have made a grave error. Those true to Scotland will fight until our country is free."

A smile flickered, then faltered upon her face. Cristina lowered her eyes, then looked up from beneath thick lashes. "Without your aid . . ." Her body trembled. "I am sorry."

"Do not be. You have suffered much this day."

"I—" She shook her head.

Bedamned! Patrik stepped over and drew her against him, the touch, the softness of her body a foreign luxury, one he'd long denied himself. He ignored the awareness, the needs she inspired and held her close. The lass needed comfort, to find belief in good, to understand that not all men were bastards driven by carnal lust.

He stroked her hair. "Let the tears come, lass. They need to be shed."

After a long moment, on a shaky sigh, Cristina stepped from his hold. Tears glistened in her eyes, but none shimmered upon her cheeks. "I am sorry. Long since have I learned crying solves nothing and betrays weaknesses held."

A belief of his as well. Then again, she was a lass. He gave her a gentle smile. "It has been a trying day." Aye, the lass had endured much, but before him she held her own. Who was this woman? Though she was a lass, she reminded him of himself.

Neither could he understand why she was alone in a forest thick with the English. "Come." Patrik started forward. His questions would be answered. Too much lay at risk to allow them to go unasked.

They strode by a rough column of stone that speared the low ceiling, one of many cluttered within the maze of caverns. The uneven splay of dirt upon the floor played accomplice to the time-worn cylinders, awkward pillars that crafted eerie shadows in the candle's flickering light.

He inhaled the cool air, infused with the faint scent of tallow. "Once we depart the tunnel, I will take you to friends."

Her steps at his side slowed. "Friends? Can I not go home?"

His chest squeezed tight. Of course. With her beauty, Cristina would have long since wed. "Worry not, my friends will ensure you are reunited with your husband."

In the muted light, the flicker of flame exposed her distress. "My hu-husband?"

"What is it?" From the fresh pain within her voice, the stiff set of her frame, he knew.

And prayed he was wrong.

Chapter 3

"The English knights mu-murdered my husband."

The angst of Cristina's admission wrapped around Patrik like a blanket thrown, her whispered words but a punctuation of pain. "Saint's breath, lass."

She crossed her arms, a defensive measure that shielded naught of the turmoil within.

"When?"

A thick second passed. "Two years ago while Gyles and I slept, the English torched our home. We awoke to crude laughter and the stench of smoke." She closed her eyes, then slowly opened them, her expression haunted by the nightmares ravaging her mind. "Gyles yelled for me to escape." She shook her head. "I refused to leave him. As he pushed me from our bed, the English smashed the door and cut him down. So I ran."

Hatred welled, built upon fury as Patrik imagined her brutal shock at witnessing her husband murdered. Though two years had passed, she'd far from recovered. A fate he well understood.

"I am sorry," he said.

"After the knights almost . . ." She dragged in an unsteady breath. "My focus is on that of making it through this day. Tomorrow and its decisions will come soon enough." She turned toward the loom of darkness. "How long will it take us to reach the other side?"

"More than a day." He lauded her fortitude, courage he'd rarely seen in a woman.

Except for Nichola.

Regret streaked through him at thoughts of the English noblewoman his brother, Alexander, had abducted. Of a time when he'd chosen to protect his family, of a decision ill made, and a decision too late to repair.

Through sheer will, Patrik purged the dark memories, potent reminders of his family lost. One would think with a year past, the pain would ease.

He took in the beautiful woman before him. 'Twould seem Cristina shared his sorrow. And what of her feelings for her husband lost? Was her love so great she might never recover?

Jaw tight, he turned toward the blackened tunnels ahead, thankful she was ignorant of his musings. The image of her full lips and emerald eyes filled his mind, but it was the pain in her eyes that captured him most.

He frowned. Never had a woman incited in him more than a desire for a lusty romp. But with Cristina, he felt more. Something about her drew him.

Unease filtered through him. Nay, his protectiveness bolstered his feelings, made him aware of her as of no woman before. Both of them had suffered loss of family at the hands of the English. How could he not feel a connection to the lass? Still, the intensity of the emotions Cristina inspired left him on edge.

His mission had not changed. He must deliver the writ to Bishop Wishart with news that John de Warenne was preparing to depart for Berwick to rejoin forces with Hugh de Cressingham before the end of July. Each day lost stole another the rebels needed to prepare for the impending attack. As for Cristina, he must keep his feelings for this woman whom he'd rescued in perspective.

"This passage takes us beneath the ben?" she asked.

"Aye." He grimaced. At least one of them had their mind on reality.

"You have but the single candle."

The worry in her voice had Patrik glancing over. "Others are hidden along the way." He explained no more. Regardless of the circumstance that had tossed them together, he knew naught of her. Though she professed to be a Scot, a woman whose life had been torn apart, she was a stranger and his country's freedom as well as countless lives lay at stake.

After he'd recovered from his supposed death a summer past, he'd ridden to Glasgow to speak with Bishop Wishart, had confessed his sins and asked for forgiveness. Then, on trembling knees before one of Scotland's two remaining guardians, he'd begged to remain an integral part of the rebel movement to reclaim his country's freedom.

Sage eyes had studied him, the bishop's grimace a dark omen. Then, as if a gift given, Wishart had granted him both. After informing Patrik of secret rebel hideouts, those known only to a select few, the bishop had asked him to be his special liaison between himself and

Sir Andrew de Moray, a rebel leader in the Highlands. That had been his life, except for a few trips to receive missives from their informant within King Edward's walls, a task that kept him well north of his brothers.

At the bishop's suggestion, he'd agreed 'twould risk being exposed to continue using the surname Mac-Gruder. The name *Dubh Duer* had been created by Wishart as an added cover to ensure no connection was made between him and the MacGruder brothers.

Patrik exhaled. Little time existed to ponder the past or poor decisions made. He could change neither. "Come, we should be safe within the caves, but I want to put more distance behind us."

Relieved by Sir Patrik's lack of questions, Emma followed. He'd accepted her story as truth. Neither had she missed the fury on his face at the tale of her supposed husband's murder. His mention of family had inspired her tale as well as the false tears. More important, the story explained why she was in the woods alone.

And unprotected.

As for traveling to his friends, she must find a way to delay their journey. She needed time alone with the rebel, time to build more trust, and time to cull as much rebel information as possible to pass to Sir Cressingham. As well, she needed to find where Sir Patrik stowed the writ.

Still, the Scot's compassion caught her by surprise. The man Sir Cressingham had described held none, the rebel naught but a cold, harsh warrior whom few dared to cross. Though the man was both formidable and withdrawn, she caught shadows within Sir Patrik's eyes, those of a man who'd witnessed too much, those of a man who refused to allow himself to care, to risk emotions that fate could destroy.

An outlook they both shared.

Emma shoved the twinge of apprehension aside. Their similarities changed naught. As with every other mission she'd undertaken, she refused to become personally involved, to allow feelings to break through her emotional barriers.

His handsome face held great appeal. With his honed muscles, agility and certitude, she had no doubt his deftness with a blade matched his intensity as a lover. Intimacies she'd overheard other women discuss. Intimacies she refused to allow within her life.

Allow? No, accept. Well she knew a man's touch, the brutal taking. Well she remembered the rape during her youth, how she'd lain in the narrow alley afterward, damp with the stench of sour rain, wishing for death.

However drawn she might be to Sir Patrik, she doubted he could erase the demons haunting her mind.

Candle held before him, the Scot moved with a cat-like grace, that of a warrior, his body taut, his hand clasped upon his sword, readied for danger. She understood his kind, the iron will with which warriors like he pursued their every decision.

Memories of him attacking the English knights smothered her admiring thoughts. Never could she forget his merciless assault. Beyond the skill, she'd witnessed his anger. An animosity long nurtured.

No, with him she must keep up her guard. Neither would she be foolish enough to kindle any emotion toward him. To foster feelings for Sir Patrik on any level would invite risk.

Yellow light wavered upon an unending labyrinth. Ahead, the cave began to narrow. Uneasy, Emma followed the fluid outline of the half-gutted taper's glow, too aware of the embracing blackness. If the flame died they would be lost in unending darkness.

"How much farther until we reach the next candle?"

"A ways yet," he replied, his deep burr offering little comfort.

"How long will it take?"

The rebel halted and turned. Yellow light cast hard shadows against eyes that saw too much. "We are safe."

Mouth dry, she yearned for light. Warmth. A sign of life. Not this terrifying blackness that eroded her calm. "I know."

"Do you?"

"I was but curious."

Curious? The lass was petrified, but determined not to show it. But, as long as they traveled together, she would nae face her demons alone. Patrik turned and started forward.

Hours passed as they trekked beneath the ben. Though he caught her quickened breaths, never did the lass cave to panic.

Rock curved. Ahead, the tunnel sloped down to a narrowed opening wide enough for only a single man to pass. Candlelight exposed time-worn walls smeared in colors of brown and gold and in places hints of red.

"We will need to crawl through," he said.

"Cr-Crawl?"

He glanced back. In the play of light, her lips grew

tight and her eyes widened with fear. "It is the only way through. You can do it."

Cristina angled her chin. "Of course I can. I was but waiting for you to go first."

He turned away before she caught his smile. Saint's breath, the lass was a woman to admire. A waft of fresh air hit him as he knelt, then crawled through the narrow opening. Candlelight flickered in a mad dance. He edged forward, the blackness fading as the dim glow ahead grew brighter.

"I smell fresh air?"

Patrik inched forward. "Aye, we are nearing the center of the ben."

"The center? Why would we find fresh air so deep within the mountain?"

A smile touched his face as he remembered his first time through the complex tunnels, his shock when he'd reached this cavern. "You will see."

"See? Our escape is no riddle."

"Nay, lass, that it is not." Somber, he pushed forward. The tunnel fell away. He blew out the candle, then stood.

The shuffle of clothing echoed behind him as she crawled. "How can I see when—" She gasped. "Oh my . . . it is . . ." Cristina stood in the soft spray of shimmering light, like a child catching sight of a gift unveiled. "'Tis wondrous."

The awe in her voice touched him. And as he'd suspected, her fear was forgotten in her wonder at this magical place. "Aye, when I first viewed this cavern, I felt the same."

"There is . . ." She slowly turned as if to try to take

it all in, then halted, her face filled with amazement. "It is as if—"

"As if we have found the secret passage to the Other-world." At her frown, he realized he'd spoken aloud of the fey, of things like wishes that he would be a fool to believe in.

"The Otherworld?"

He frowned. The lass was Scottish, her soft burr a testament to her heritage. How could she not have heard of the home of the fey?

At Sir Patrik's confused glance, Emma froze. With her ignorance of the Otherworld, she'd made an error. The last thing she wanted was to invite doubt. She made her body tremble, then her knees give slightly.

Sir Patrik caught her. "What is wrong?"

With shaky fingers, she touched her brow. "'Tis nothing. A wave of dizziness came upon me."

A grimace tightened his mouth. "'Tis no wonder, after all you have endured this day. You need food and rest."

Guilt wove through her at his sincere concern for her false claim. "My thanks," she said, too aware of him, of the strength behind the man, and that for the first time in her life she'd met someone who challenged her on every level. With gentle strength, he guided her forward. However much she wished to break away, she must keep up the appearance of dizziness.

Fragmented rays of sunlight streamed from a frac-ture within the immense ceiling and spread out in a magnificent shimmer, exposing a huge cavern punc-tured by spears of rock arching to the ground. Color infused the grand stones, from the deepest brown to a myriad of oranges.

Along the edge of the cavern lay a pool, a mirror to the magnificence, its stillness reflecting an identical image of the immense beauty above.

"The water is warm."

Sir Patrik's soft burr rolled over her. She turned to find him standing at her side, and heat swept her cheeks. She was too aware of his presence, drawn to a man who invited naught but danger.

"Warm?" she repeated, the nervousness within her voice very real.

"Natural springs lie below the pool. No one knows the why of it." Patrik paused. "After this day, you would be wanting to bathe." In the soft light, he saw that red flushed her cheeks. Embarrassment? Of course. He released her hand, stepped back. "You will have complete privacy."

The flush on her face grew. "My thanks."

"Should you need me, call. I will be nearby standing guard."

Cristina's expression grew serious. She stared at him a long moment. "I am not sure why, but I believe you will protect me."

Touched by her words, more so than was wise, he nodded. "Take the time you need. I will set out some food. You will not see me, but I will be nearby."

"But—"

"Lass, we are both tired and hungry."

She searched his face. "What about you?"

"Me?"

"This day has been a trial to you as well. You should bathe first."

He stiffened, disliking the warmth her thoughtfulness infused in him. Too long had passed since anyone worried about him. "I will bathe once we have eaten." Patrik stepped back.

"My thanks," Emma replied, analyzing the myriad of emotions flickering through his expression. Surprise. Retreat. Coldness. She focused on the latter, intrigued by the rebel's complete withdrawal. His shifts of emotion were slight, so faint, had she not watched for them, she would have missed them altogether.

A complex man indeed. When she believed she was beginning to see the real man, to understand him a bit, he withdrew. The violence he'd experienced as a boy, hiding as he'd watched his family slaughtered by the English, may have crafted the hatred blackening his soul, but something more had deepened the hurt within.

The information she'd gathered about Sir Patrik, though helpful, was far from complete. Logic assured her the gaps in his latter years would yield the insight she sought.

Discovering what haunted him wasn't part of her task. Yet she found herself curious to know, drawn by the complexity of this intriguing Scot. On the outside a warrior who held his own, a man who intimidated the fiercest competitor, yet deep within, a man of intense passion.

Sir Patrik turned on his heel and strode around a large pillar.

Emma glanced at the still pool, then toward the ceiling spiked with enormous hanging rock, shimmering in the wash of light. Drawn, she walked over. At the edge, she turned. Along the outer fringe, the wondrous expanse of sunlight faded into complete blackness.

Silence.

Anxiety flickered through her. Had he left her alone? "Sir Patrik?"

"Aye?" His deep burr echoed from behind the pillar.

"Naught." Embarrassed, she turned toward the water. It seemed to beckon her, lured her to enter and relax. As if for her being at peace had ever been possible? She removed her gown. Water rippled as she waded into the mirrored pool.

Warm, silken luxury embraced her with each step, the sand a soft balm against her aching feet. Emma eased into the velvet depths and a sense of complete relaxation swept over her. It was as if her troubles were cleansed from her mind and nothing existed but this moment.

On a sigh she savored the sparkles of the sunlight on the rock around her, the shards of colors cast from their play like magic.

Magic?

A smile touched her lips. The thoughts fatigue spun. Never had she held any belief in magic or anything so whimsical. Life within an orphanage had taught her that neither hope nor magic existed.

With a sigh, she scooped a handful of sand and rubbed it against her skin, doubting she would ever feel truly clean. However incredible, the beauty of this chamber could not erase reality. This was yet another day, one to achieve a goal and once it was accomplished, to walk away.

Somber, Emma finished, then waded to shore. She pulled on the tattered gown, a stark reminder of her role, of the dangers she had yet to face, and of the penance for a poor decision made.

"I am finished," she called out, her voice revealing none of her inner turmoil.

Solid steps echoed in the cavern. Sir Patrik walked into the swath of scattered light. He halted, his expression dark.

She tensed. "What is wrong?"

Wrong? Patrik smothered the unwanted surge of desire. The lass knew not that she stood with the prismed light as a backdrop. The rays framed her slender outline with lust-stirring clarity. And her damp garment clung to her full curves, a body that would make a grown man beg.

"I have placed oatcakes and cheese on the other side of the rock. Eat while I bathe." He ignored her surprise at his abruptness as he strode past. With his body hard and aching, he was not fool enough to remain by her side and allow her to notice his interest. She'd endured enough this day without adding to her worries.

Irritated at his unexpected desire, he strode to the merge of sand and water and stripped. Tossing his garments in a tumbled heap, he dove into the deep end of the pool. Warmth churned around him, embraced him as he swam the entire length. He surfaced, turned and swam hard toward the opposite bank. The lash of water and burn of muscle did little to lessen his body's need.

Reaching the end, he stood, cursed as Cristina's alluring image remained emblazoned in his mind.

Warmth touched his chest.

Surprised, he glanced down. The halved malachite hanging around his neck glowed. He frowned and strode from the water. Was nothing to make sense on this blasted day? Why was he even wearing the gemstone? 'Twas not as if he still belonged to the MacGruders. With his betrayal a year past, he'd given up the right to use their name or to be called their brother.

Except the memory of a proud day long past stirred in Patrik's mind. A time when he'd stood beside Seathan, Alexander, and Duncan. Seathan, who was now an earl. Lord Grey. A smile touched his face, faded. Proud he was the day Seathan claimed the title. But the day was bittersweet because their father, the man who had adopted him, now lay cold beneath the earth.

A hard passing. He knew their middle brother, Alexander, carried guilt for it because the arrow that downed his father had been meant for Alexander.

Neither could Patrik forget the youngest brother. Duncan had lost both parents, his mother dying during his birthing, but he hid his grief behind a veil of cheer.

Patrik gripped the gemstone, a gift presented to him, as it had been to each of the brothers by their grandmother when they were knighted. Each halved gemstone was unique, each a badge of honor. After his betrayal, it was an honor he no longer deserved. Bedamned. He should toss it into the water.

His fingers squeezed tight; then he let his hand fall away. He could nae sever the final tie to his past.

Exhausted, he dried himself, tugged his tunic over

the gemstone, then, as if a man sentenced, strode toward where the lass was eating.

He rounded the corner and halted. On the blanket he'd spread out, with the food he'd left for her gone, Cristina lay curled in a ball, asleep. Gentleness washed through him. 'Twas not her decision to appear in his life, to be forced along this dangerous path, or to have spawned the uninvited attention of the English knights.

Instead of lusting after her like a randy ass, he should remember she was scared, alone, and needed his protection.

Patrik sat at her side. In silence he ate, ignoring the silken wash of chestnut hair spilling around her face and the lingering urge to draw her against him. Once he'd finished eating, he stowed the remainder of the oatcakes and cheese within his leather sack and set it aside.

Fatigue washed over him. Aye, rest would serve them both well. The morrow and hard travel ahead would come too fast. With one last glance at the lass, he laid another blanket nearby and closed his eyes.

The body lay slumped before her. Vestments cloaked the lifeless figure like a macabre shroud. A scream built in Emma's throat, but it would not come.

She tried to step back. As if weighted by stones, her feet refused to budge.

Blood spilled from beneath the finely spun cloth to curdle against the dirt and grime staining the ground.

Of its own volition, her trembling hand reached out and lifted the vestment.

Unseeing eyes stared out of Father Lawrenz's pale face. Grotesque bruises marred the skin of the priest, the only man she had ever trusted, the only man who had ever shown her compassion, the only man who had taught her of faith.

No! She stumbled back, looked down. His blood smeared her hands, dripped through her fingers to pool at her feet.

She screamed.

"Cristina!"

"No." She fought to break free of hands that held her tight. "Let me go!"

"Wake up. You are having a dream."

A man's concerned voice beckoned to her from a distance. Panic riding her hard, she struggled against the pull and jerked her eyes open.

In the murky light, Sir Patrik stared down at her.

Chapter 4

Another tremor rolled through Emma as she stared up at Sir Patrik. Beneath the flicker of candlelight, she glanced over and studied her fingers, which moments before within her mind had dripped with blood. 'Twas a dream, naught more.

"Are you all right?"

Mouth dry, she turned toward the Scot. The worry on his face stole her breath. "Yes, I . . ." Emma stiffened, withdrew from his touch, shaken to find she missed the gentleness of his hands, a quiet strength that promised protection. God in heaven, she could tell him nothing.

"Your husband?"

"My husband?"

"You dreamt of his death?"

Of course Sir Patrik would think that. A husband who didn't exist. Deception tasted ill upon her tongue. No, not deception, a fable crafted to gain his trust, a fact she must remember. Her time here was but a job to be done, a mission to be accomplished. After, she would move on to the next job, never to think of this rebel again.

And if she believed she could simply erase this intriguing Scot from her thoughts, she was a fool.

Sir Patrik slid the back of his hand over her cheek, his gaze tender.

Emma steadied herself, fought to smother the awareness, sensations no man had ever inspired. 'Twas the plans gone askew yesterday that yielded these unwanted feelings, and learning that however cold or dangerous, Sir Patrik was a man loyal in his beliefs. A way of life she well understood, a path she ruthlessly followed. Except his loyalty was to a country he loved, while hers was only to herself.

What would it be like to have passion for what you fought for? To care for those you loved so much that to protect them, you would sacrifice your life?

"Cristina?"

Cristina. A woman who didn't exist. A potent reminder this was but a farce. Damn Sir Patrik for making her wish for other than what she had. Her life suited her. Each decision was of *her* choosing. And when she was done, she would walk away. No loss. No regrets.

At the thought of leaving him, an ache built inside, a yearning of unexpected force. "Go away."

"Ignoring the hurt but prolongs it like a fire banked. 'Tis opening the door to the pain, working past the hurt that makes it fade."

His thoughtful words left her feeling more of a fraud. "Can you not see that I do not want to talk? That I wish to be alone?" Alone she was good at. Alone was safe. Alone she spoke no more lies.

"Aye," he replied, "and I see the hurt, that of a lass who holds her misery too deep, mires herself in grief and forgets to live."

Emma cast him a hard look. "Leave me alone."

"And if I did, I would be like everyone else."

The sincerity in his voice sliced to her soul. Her anger faded. Damn him for being so noble. He believed her grief was due to a husband lost, a family destroyed, when it was her realization that her life held naught but the promise of emptiness.

"I am tired." Her quiet words echoed between them.

A muscle worked in his jaw. "I never took you for a coward."

She angled her jaw. "You know me not."

"Nay? I know you are a woman alone, a woman afraid, and one who sleeps with troubled thoughts, but also a woman brave enough to hold her own when most would crumble."

Uneasy, she rubbed her thumb against the tips of her fingers. He saw too much, made her feel more than was wise. "Do you always interrogate the women you save?"

A hint of a smile touched his mouth, one too alluring, one that should have seemed out of place with the brutal life he led. Instead, it made his all too handsome face more appealing.

"Nay. 'Tis not my normal lot to save a lass, nor to care. 'Twould seem with you, I have done both."

"You cannot care for me." Panic kicked in her chest. She'd not meant to speak aloud.

"Why?"

Because I am not the battered Scottish woman you

*think, but one of England's top mercenaries, a woman
whose real name you would know—and hate.*

At his sharp glance, a shiver stole through her, one
that had little to do with the coolness of the cave and
everything to do with this dangerous Scot.

Emma rubbed her arms, wanting distance, to be
away from a man who possessed the ability to read
her so well. "Why would you care?"

A fair question, one that confounded Patrik as well.
Yet, when he'd awoken to her cries, her face twisted in
grief, a part of him had wanted to hold her, to save her
from whatever demons tormented her mind.

Save her? An ache built in his chest as he studied
Cristina against the backdrop of the blackened cavern,
the weak flicker of flame upon her face like a golden
caress. His body hardened with need.

Frustrated, he shoved the desire aside, the urge to
touch her, taste her, everywhere. She was not his to
keep, nor could ever be. His life was dedicated to win-
ning Scotland's freedom, not to musings of after the
battle, of laying down his sword and walking into the
arms of a lass. His belief in permanence had died a
year past when his brothers stood beside his grave at
Lochshire Castle. Yet, 'twould seem with this woman,
logic fled.

Nay, his feelings for Cristina were born of more
than a face so beautiful it could have belonged to the
fey, or a body that would make a man weep. Within
her eyes lay sadness, the same torment reflected back
at him whenever he looked within a calm pool.

Regardless of the reasons, the trouble brewing
within her drew him. Patrik grimaced. As if he needed
to be heaping more onto the burdens that toppled his

life? In addition to delivering the writ, he yearned to reclaim a family who believed him dead. Remorse weighed upon him. Was such a feat possible? Could he ever find forgiveness from the MacGruders?

He should tell the lass to go to sleep, then lie upon his pallet and push her from his mind. Their time together was but days. Once he left her with his friends who lived within a nearby humble village, they would ensure she was delivered to a safe haven. Then she would go on with her life, as would he.

With her face, her tempting lips but a handsbreadth away, the lass watched him expectantly, awaiting a reply. One he should not give.

He blew out a rough breath. "I care because I understand what it is to hold on to things we cannot change, and to do penance for poor decisions made."

The anger within her expression ebbed to curiosity.

Blast it, why had he added the latter? He did not wish to speak of his past or become further involved with the lass. Both were unnervingly easy to envision.

She searched his face with fragile sincerity. "What happened?"

The image of his brother Alexander's captive filled his mind. A captive who was now his brother's wife. "I allowed the bitterness of my past to skew my judgment."

Emotion flickered on her face, understanding, pain, and acceptance. "'Tis easy when life offers you naught but hurt to guide your decisions."

Saint's breath, what had the lass endured? Aye, her husband's loss had devastated her, but from the wisdom of her reply, more than the pain of his death carved her words. "And what hurt has life offered you?"

"I told you of my husband."

He caught her hesitation, the flare of uncertainty a split second before she spoke. Cristina rubbed her thumb over her fingertips, a trait he noted when she grew nervous or upset. Instinct flared. She withheld something. As if he, too, did not conceal secrets?

Patrik stood. "Go to sleep. We depart at the break of dawn." He turned away. The scrape of leather against sand alerted him that she stood.

"Sir Patrik."

He stopped, but didn't look back.

Emma's heart pounded. She didn't want the Scot to go, but neither did she wish to lie to him anymore. So she would give him truth. Or, as much as she could.

"I was raised in an orphanage."

The rebel turned.

Beneath his intense gaze, she struggled to find the right words. "Few want to care for a child abandoned."

Silence.

"When I was ten and two summers, I ran away." At the sadness in Sir Patrik's eyes, she stiffened. "I need not your pity. I made my way just fine. Then I met Gyles." Her voice broke as her thoughts went not to an imaginary husband, but to Father Lawrenz. "I did not want to care. I was a tough one, but he ignored my bluster, took time to help me, and incredibly, made me laugh." And he had died. Murdered for a pence. She swallowed hard. "So yes, I understand bitterness and hate. I know the Bible says to forgive, but for the English who took Gyles's life, I cannot."

Images of that fated day rolled through her mind. Of having finished her studies, and her excitement to share with Father Lawrenz her lessons learned. Of how she'd run from the chapel to meet the priest as he returned from his daily round of prayers with the elderly.

She'd taken a shortcut through an alley, and had stumbled upon a heap of black cloth. Then, she'd realized it was a man. In horror, she'd stepped closer. Instead of a drunk sleeping off a long night of drink, she'd recognized Father Lawrenz.

Horrified, she'd seen the blood.

The assignment of faith she'd penned with pride had tumbled to the ground, the page blown away by the stench-filled breeze.

And the fragile hope the priest had given her that she might live a normal life had shattered.

No, never could she forgive whoever had murdered Father Lawrenz.

Or forget.

Sir Patrik remained silent, the understanding in his expression urging her to continue. For the first time in her life, she wanted to share her tragedy, relate her pain to another who'd survived such torment.

"After Gyles's death, I hurt so much. I ran away, wanted to be alone, wished never to see anyone who reminded me of Gyles or the life we had." The grief of finding Father Lawrenz murdered filled her, backed her words. "I swore never to care for anyone again. With each passing day, I have grown stronger. More important, I have kept my promise."

Until now.

"There comes a time," Sir Patrik said, "when we must look back if we are to heal."

"Why?" she asked, stunned that after everything he had endured, the rebel would offer such advice, but also intrigued. Never had she expected such depth from the brutal man Sir Cressingham had described.

Doubts of Sir Cressingham's claims that Sir Patrik was a cold-blooded killer swept through her. As if she should be surprised the Scottish treasurer would lie to achieve his goal? Sir Patrik was no murderer, but a man haunted, an intelligent man who yearned to be whole.

"Why must we look back?" Sir Patrik asked, dragging her from her thoughts. "Because hatred kills one's soul, denies one the healing time offers."

"Healing?" Anger crept into her words. "When broken, does one's heart ever truly heal?"

"I believe it is possible."

"Then you are better than I. Never will I forget, nor let go of the hate." He sighed, a long, lonely sound, but Emma held firm. In this she would give him truth. If he turned away from her, so be it. Already he made her feel more than was wise.

"And what has hate served you?" Sir Patrik asked.

"The ability to live, to go on each day."

"And what of happiness?"

"Happiness? Our country is ravaged by war, those we love butchered beneath the Englishman's blade, and you dare ask me of happiness?" Emma paused. "Tell me, are you happy? Is anyone?"

Sadness flickered in his eyes. "My questions were asked to guide you from your grief."

"I want not your help."

But Patrik caught Cristina's tremble, and the hint of need that never quite left her eyes. She was afraid. God knew what she'd endured during her time as an orphan, or since her husband's murder. The English knights' attack was only the latest of the atrocities she'd survived.

They shared a battered past, each given a second chance. He, the MacGruders who'd adopted him and raised him as their own. She, a husband to heal her soul.

And both had lost the people they loved.

He took in the web of darkness within the cavern, his heart aching. He was nae the person to guide the lass from her misery while his own was still so raw.

"What are you thinking of?"

The gentleness of her voice lured him to reply but he'd reveal no more. He'd known the lass but hours. Well he understood the dangers of giving trust. What he'd exposed about his personal life disturbed him. Never had he shared such intimacies with a woman.

"We both need to be finding our pallets," Patrik said. "Dawn and the leagues we must travel will come soon enough."

She hesitated. "Will you be able to sleep?"

"A question I should be asking you."

A faint smile touched Cristina's mouth, and he found he liked knowing he'd put it there. As he watched her, her eyes softened.

The moment shifted.

The blackness surrounding the meager flicker of flame seemed to embrace them, to heighten the fact they were very alone. The golden shimmers of light caressed her face, lured him to trace her skin, to sample the lush fullness of her mouth and discover whether it would fulfill its silent promise. He could all but taste her, a potent sensuality that beckoned him for more.

Unsettled by his musings, Patrik stepped back.

"Rest, I will be nearby." He strode off, damning his amorous thoughts.

As Sir Patrik's figure faded in the darkness, Emma exhaled. What had just happened between them? Nothing. Everything. She'd witnessed his desire, an emotion the warrior stirred within her as well.

God help her, she'd wanted him to kiss her. Since her rape at twelve summers, never had she yearned for a man's touch. But something about the Scot made the horrific memories fade, left her wanting.

Go to sleep. Leave him be. 'Twas safe.

Yet, he was hurting, tormented by a past he, too, had weathered. A past he believed her ignorant of. Emma stood, needing to talk to him, to help him. Not because of her mission, but because he was a man who under different circumstances she might have called friend.

Friend? Laughable truly. She made not friends, only contacts.

Or enemies.

She turned from the candle toward where Sir Patrik had faded into the gloom. Gathering her courage, she walked into the darkness. Her eyes slowly adjusted. Within the faint spill of candlelight, she caught hints of shapes within the cavern.

A soft splash echoed in the distance.

She caught the rebel's faint outline. He sat upon a boulder, his feet dangling in the water.

Loneliness. It radiated from him as if a man sentenced. A feeling she knew too well. A feeling her harsh comments had inspired.

In silence, she walked over and sat.

He stared straight ahead. "You should be asleep."

"I should." Emma removed her slippers, set them aside, and then slid her feet into the warmth of the water. "I am amazed at how the distant candlelight still plays upon the columns of stone."

"Why did you come?"

The roughness of his question alerted her that he battled against his wanting her. Warmth flooded Emma. "You asked me questions, questions I struggle with. My frustration made me lash out when you were but trying to guide me from my grief."

"You were honest."

"I was, but it does not make my curt manner right."

"Right?" Sir Patrik asked. "Is there such a thing?"

"I do not know." A sad smile touched her mouth. "Do not think too deeply; you will sound like me."

Within the wisps of candlelight, a hint of humor touched his face, and then fell away. "Aye, a sad lot we are."

She trailed her foot through the water. "So where does that leave us?"

"To go on, to believe our lives can be better."

"Is that what you have done?"

Sir Patrik drew a circle in the water. "I am trying."

"How can you be so positive?"

He looked at her then, his face a play of shadows and determination. "To be otherwise is to give up hope."

Was that what she had done? Given up hope to avoid hurt? It made sense, but never had she considered her withdrawal as anything but avoidance of pain.

The heaviness of her thoughts overwhelmed her. "I was wrong to come." Emma made to stand, but the rebel caught her wrist.

"Stay. Sit for a while. With me." The soft pad of his

thumb skimmed the sensitive skin at her inner wrist. "It would please me greatly."

Heat spilled through her at his touch. "Sir Patrik, I—"

"Patrik."

"What?"

"Call me by my given name."

She swallowed hard, fought to feel nothing. Failed. "'Tis unseemly."

His thumb stilled. "'Tis my wish."

"Patrik," Emma breathed, testing the familiar use of his name on her tongue as if to taste the forbidden.

In a gentle move, he drew her against him, brought her head against his chest and slowly began to stroke her hair.

She gave a shaky exhale. "I thought you were going to kiss me."

"I would be wanting to, but right now, 'tis not what you need."

At his thoughtfulness, tears burned her eyes. No, she couldn't feel this much for him. For *Dubh Duer*. It mattered not that for this moment her task was but a blur within her mind, that right now it was only him and her struggling against the sorrows of life.

"Is that why you left the pallets," she asked, "because you wanted to kiss me?"

His fingers paused within her hair, then he slowly continued to stroke the unbound length. "Aye. A thought I am not proud to admit. You have known enough anguish."

"As have you." She snuggled closer, savoring the sense of protection, humbled by his honor, traits absent from her life since Father Lawrenz. Except the priest's thoughts were of God, of educating her and helping her find a path to stability and faith. Patrik was dedicated to war, but a warrior who wanted her as a man did. "Thank you."

In answer he pressed a chaste kiss upon her brow. "We should both get some rest."

"We should." But she lay against him saddened that this fragile moment, like her excursion into normalcy, would all too soon end.

The soft pad of footsteps upon dirt echoed in the silence as Emma followed Patrik down the tunnel, his candle held high. Since they'd departed the cavern this morning, he'd said little, which suited her fine.

Better than last eve when she'd made an error in dredging up the emotions of her past. Yes, they lent credibility to her supposed near rape yesterday, and had earned Patrik's protection, but they'd unleashed horrific dreams throughout the night.

She must gain Patrik's trust, but other ways existed besides exposing her weaknesses, emotions the Scot might use against her. Had her years as a mercenary taught her naught?

Thank God he'd not tried to kiss her as they'd sat beside the pool. Had he reached for her . . . No, 'twas better not to ponder how his mouth would feel upon her own. Except, her body warmed at the thought, her mind welcoming the intimacy of his embrace.

Ahead, a faint wisp of light fractured the blackness. Hope ignited. "Have we reached the other side?"

"Aye," Patrik replied.

Her relief to be free of this godforsaken complex of tunnels fell away. How close were they to his friends? She needed to discover who was the traitor to King Edward before they arrived.

As they neared the exit, sunlight scraped the uneven walls, exposing translucent spiderwebs woven within crevices above. Fresh air, infused with a hint of flowers and earth, blended with stale.

Emma exhaled. Mired in darkness for so many hours, she reveled within the sanity of light.

At the hewn opening, Patrik blew out the candle, stowed it within a carved hole in the wall, then peered through the shield of leaves and branches. "I see no one."

She nodded, studying the meticulous weave of limb and leaf shielding the tunnel. With the entry so well hidden, it would prove difficult to find for the untrained eye.

"We have two days of travel before we reach my friends."

That answered the question of how long she had to complete her task.

Patrik pushed aside a limb and stepped into the sunlight. "Though I see no one about, we must travel with caution. English knights could be nearby." He strode forward.

Emma followed, shielding her eyes against the glare of the afternoon sun. She glanced back, scoured the thick foliage in her wake. Except for the rise and fall of the land, she discerned no sign of the entry. Incredible.

"Cristina?"

"Coming." She stole one last glance toward where, somewhere within the dense tangle, the tunnel's opening lay. Sir Cressingham would be pleased. The English treasurer could advise John de Warenne, Earl of Surrey, to set up his forces at either entry to ambush the rebels.

Guilt edged through her that in the end, she would betray Patrik. She shoved the emotion aside. A year had passed since King Balliol had abdicated his throne at Brechin, resigning his Kingdom of Scotland to King Edward. Regardless of the Scots' wishes, an English king ruled their land. It was the rebels' decision to continue this fruitless war, not her guilt to bear.

If Patrik hated her when he learned her true identity, so be it. By then she would be gone, her mission long since completed. Nor would he ever find a Scottish woman named Cristina Moffat.

A shout echoed in the distance.

Patrik caught her hand and hauled her beneath the dense brush. "Stay!" With his body close to the ground, he inched up the embankment to the trail they'd walked moments before. After a quick search, he jumped to his feet and used a branch to erase any sign of their passage. Tossing the limb aside, he hurried beneath the shield of leaves, then covered her body with his.

"Say naught," he whispered.

As if with his body flush atop hers it was possible to think? Emma scoured their surroundings for any sign of movement, tried to ignore the hard length of him, the feel of his entire body pressed against hers.

And failed.

Wind rattled leaves overhead.

A raven flitted in the tree above, then flew away.

Footsteps sounded nearby.

A stick cracked, closer this time, followed by a muttered curse.

Patrik's calloused hand covered hers with surprising gentleness.

She stared at the tangle of scars battering his skin, the muscled hand atop hers. She should pull away, not feed this delusion of his protecting her. Instead, Emma savored his touch, his protectiveness in a world that offered none.

Patrik's body tensed, his unruly sandy hair tangled within the mash of leaves, but his hand upon hers held steady, the dagger in his other hand held readied.

"They found the four of them dead," a gruff voice said.

Through the twist of brush, she made out an English knight, his garb smeared with dirt, evidence of hard travel. Another warrior appeared. The steady pad of steps exposed several knights in the contingent.

"The bastard rebels," another man cursed. "Not even a king to back, yet they fight on. And for what?"

Another man grunted. "Wallace stirs the pot."

"He killed Sheriff Heselrig as if 'twas his right," the first knight spat with disgust. "And Sir William Douglas running with the traitor."

"They will be stopped," the second man said. "Sir Cressingham is not a man to infuriate."

Their voices faded as they passed, but Patrik remained still. He'd counted five men. Had he been alone, he would have slain the lot.

Precious seconds passed.

Silence.

Convinced the knights had left, he sheathed his

dagger, his body hard from the intimate contact. He grimaced. Focus on the danger, lad.

Patrik shifted to her side. "They are gone."

Emerald eyes turned on him, dark, etched with concern. "Will we go back to the cave?"

"Nay." He understood her worry, but he knew the land about them. Nor would he be fool enough to linger and be tempted to touch her further. "We will travel deeper into the woods before turning north."

"North? Your friends live in the Highlands?"

He shook his head. "'Tis a safer route."

Cristina hesitated; then her hand relaxed within his, her eyes brimming with trust. "When will we leave?"

He watched her mouth, the subtle movement, imagined plundering the soft depths. "Now." Patrik pushed to his feet, helped her stand, his blood racing hot. Bedamned, he ought not to think of the lass, but the danger at hand.

Her eyes met his. Awareness flared.

Heat sliced through him.

"Are we not leaving?"

The huskiness of her burr drew him. "'Twould be wise."

She didn't move.

Blast it, did she have to stare at him with that destroying mix of need and innocence? Innocence? Nay. Married she'd been and lain with a man many a night, tasted the pleasures of the joining.

So why did he hesitate? They needed to leave, to go before he did something foolish—like kiss her.

Sunlight slicked the soft glisten of her mouth.

Bedamned! As if guided, his hands cupped her face. "Tell me you want me to stop."

Her lower lip trembled. "And if I did, 'twould be a lie."

On a groan Patrik covered her mouth. Heat, it poured through him at her sultry taste. He drew out the kiss, savored the searing intensity. At her shudder he pulled her against him, trailed his hand from her face to the curve of her neck, slanted his mouth and took the kiss deeper.

She moaned as her body pressed against him, shuddered.

"Ah, lass," he murmured as he nibbled along the curve of her jaw. However much he wanted to make love with her, this was neither the time, nor the place. Blood pounding hot, Patrik lifted his head.

A blush heated her face. "I—" She glanced to the side. Frowned. "What is that?"

Patrik looked over.

A pace away, sprawled within the tangle of grass and leaves lay the writ.

Chapter 5

Saint's breath! With his blood pounding hot, the haze of need still searing his blood, Patrik pulled away, grasped the leather-bound parchment and shoved it out of sight.

Cristina sat up and glanced toward where he'd stowed the writ with a frown. "What is that?" she repeated.

"'Tis not of your concern."

Hurt etched her face. "I see."

She didn't, but that could not be helped. Well he knew of his responsibility, the importance of his delivering the writ to Bishop Wishart. He'd lost over a day of travel, time he could ill spare, but he had no regrets.

He held out his hand. "We must go."

She ignored his offer, stood. Leaves and twigs littered her hair and if possible, made her more alluring. "Please, tell me what is going on."

Silence.

"Patrik?"

Her soft plea prodded him further. 'Twas his penance for kissing the lass. What had he been thinking? Nay, thinking was exactly what he hadn't been doing. If he had, he would have led her away untouched. Neither did her taste lingering in his mouth help a wit.

"Come." Patrik turned and headed north.

The rustle of leaves echoed as she followed. "What is in the bound leather?"

"Leave it." He despised the coolness of his tone; his anger was at himself.

"Have I somehow upset you?"

He spun on his heel.

Cristina halted, her face pale, at odds with her lips swollen from his kiss.

God, how he wanted her. "I should not have touched you. 'Twas wrong."

Her brow dipped in confusion. "What does your kissing me have to do with the missive?"

"Naught." He drew in a slow breath, released it. "I am making a mess of this."

She hesitated. "You did not enjoy kissing me?"

Blast it. "Nay, lass, I took great pleasure from the kiss. Far too much."

"As I." Wariness crept into her eyes as she cast a glance toward where he'd stowed the leather-bound document. "Are you wanted?"

Patrik gave a rough laugh. "As a rebel, aye. Longshanks wishes my head upon a pike."

Red slashed her cheeks. "I—"

"Cristina, the missive I carry is of great import. Should it fall into the wrong hands"—he shook his head—"God help us all. 'Tis why I must see to your safety posthaste. As long as you are with me, you are in danger, more than you could ever believe."

"Is that why you were nearby yesterday when the knights almost . . ." Her breath hitched and she looked away.

Patrik turned her to face him. "I will protect you."

Emotion swamped Emma at his selfless offer of protection. Sir Cressingham would be pleased. 'Twould seem she had earned Patrik's trust, a necessary accomplishment to fulfill the remainder of her task.

"Your vow is unnecessary," she said.

"I wish I could do more." He pulled a twig from her hair, tossed it aside. "But you cannot matter to me, lass. I have secrets, more than those within the document I carry. I can make no promise to any woman. Yet with you I have. More unsettling, I find no regrets in my heart."

She ached at his tenderness. He spoke from his soul, while she wielded naught but lies. "I ask for no promise."

A sad smile touched his face. "Not with words, but I see the question in your eyes."

She tossed her head, a move for a role played, and despised her deception. "'Tis arrogant you are."

"Am I?" He stroked the pad of his thumb over her lower lip. "Tell me, lass, do I matter naught to you?"

Her carefully chosen words fell away. "Patrik—"

"Blast it. My feelings cannot be of import. I have a duty."

As did she, but her role as a mercenary lay in shameful tatters. Somehow, within the tangle of a day, they'd connected far beyond what she could have ever imagined. Their troubled pasts, both blackened by tragedy and horror, had bonded them in a way that breeched their defenses.

Emma remained silent as he turned and strode forward. Patrik didn't understand 'twas her he would hate. No, hate was too kind a word. After their kiss and supposed exchange of trust, he would curse her to Hades and bid her soul burn for an eternity.

Regret churned within. She had given her word to complete this mission. If she were to walk away, Sir Cressingham's fury would know no bounds. A cold and vicious man, he would find her, whatever it took. For the rest of her life, she would be on the run.

In silence she followed Patrik, trying to lose her worries in the blur of green, the rich scent of forest etched with pine. Flickers of sunlight lit the path ahead, lending innocence to this day.

Innocence? As if she or Patrik could pretend such.

The rush of water echoed in the distance. With each step the tumble increased until it was a thunderous roar and the air grew heavy, rich with the taste of moisture.

As they rounded the next bend, several large boulders came into view. Mist hung above the stone, embracing the time-worn rock in a slick sheath.

Emma shielded her eyes as she looked up. "A waterfall?"

"Aye."

Intrigued by the vertical rush and the cloud of resultant mist, she moved to his side. "How long will it take us to walk around?"

"We will not." He stepped up on the nearest boulder, held out his hand.

Emma hesitated.

"Do you trust me?"

Did she really have a choice? Emma laid her hand within his, savoring his touch, wishing her reason for being with him was different.

"Watch out, the rocks are slippery."

With care they picked their way up the slick tumble of rock, over the tree limbs daring to weave amongst the rough stone.

"Hold on." He hauled her onto a ledge.

The roll of white below collided with the black, the angry churn potent in its force. "It is magnificent," she yelled into his ear.

Patrik gave her hand a gentle squeeze, then led her toward the massive downpour. Water sloshed near her feet and mist billowed around her like a cloud. With her in tow, he moved parallel to the rushing water, then angled toward a smaller curtain. He halted and lifted a nearby thin, flat stone the size of a cauldron and held it over their heads.

"Hold on," he shouted.

Was he insane? They would be washed over the side! "I—"

He tugged her with him as he stepped into the spewing rush. Water pounded, muted all but her panic. She closed her eyes as she stepped forward and braced herself to be swept away, to plunge down the sheer cliffs to her death.

Instead, with his grip steady against hers, her foot settled upon dry stone. Pulse racing, she opened her eyes. Water poured before her in a thunder of white, a powerful curtain racing past.

"It is the back of the falls!" she yelled with delight.

A smile widened his face. He nodded and set the flat stone aside.

Emma turned. Sunlight poked through the edge of the falls, the mist splintering the light into a rainbow of colors that splashed upon the jagged rock. She laughed out loud. It was truly amazing.

And another rebel hideout.

The magic of the discovery fell away.

Ignorant of her turmoil, Patrik led her toward the back of the gouged rock to where the pound of water echoed as but a soft rumble. "We will rest here for the night. In the morn, we will depart on the other side. We should reach my friends before the sun sets."

"So soon?" Embarrassment touched her face.

Patrik remained silent, finding himself conflicted about reaching their destination. The hint of shadow against the waterfall's soft color was a reminder of the oncoming night, the last one he and Cristina would share.

With a somber expression, she scanned the surrounding stone. She stiffened. "Someone else has been here."

He followed her gaze. Charred remains of a fire lay near the back of the cavern. Patrik walked over and with his boot, nudged the coals.

Red flared within the embers.

On alert, he set down his pack and withdrew his sword. "Wait here."

Cristina nodded.

He crept along the path leading to the other side of the falls. Bedamned. He was so caught up in the lass, he'd neglected to ensure the pathway behind the falls was safe. Only the rebels knew of its existence. Still, 'twas foolish to let down his guard.

After a thorough sweep of the entire hideout, he was confident no one was about. "Whoever built the fire is gone."

Worry carved her face. "Do you think they will be back?"

"I am not sure. The only ones who know of this place are the rebels. If anyone should return, it will be a Scot."

She shot a nervous glance at the opposing entry.

"Trust me."

Emerald green eyes settled upon him, then softened with belief. "I do."

Warmth touched him at her faith in him, and he found himself wishing she could be more to him than a brief interlude, another desire he must allow to pass.

"Come," he said, "I have more oatcakes."

"You are a man prepared."

"Always." Except she didn't smile at his teasing, but watched him, her chestnut hair mussed, her tattered gown worthy of a beggar. To him she looked beautiful.

"While you were away, I found this within the ash." She held out her hand. A length of carved wood lay on her palm.

With a frown, Patrik lifted the whittled, smooth length of wood into his hands. Where feathers had once existed, there were naught but charred lines.

"'Tis the remainder of an arrow." He started to toss the useless shard into the embers, then hesitated. Cut into the shaft, a thumb's length apart, sat two notches. The technique seemed familiar. Indeed, he knew many a Scot who crafted arrows and left his unique mark upon each.

"What is it?"

"Naught I—" Saint's breath, 'twas Duncan's arrow, the notches Alexander's brand.

Pain rolled through him as he stared at the charred fragment. Time rolled back to when he and Duncan had followed Alexander to the loch near Lochshire Castle. Concerned for a man he considered his brother, he and Duncan had watched him from behind several bushes.

After ensuring Alexander needed not their help, Duncan had produced a bottle of wine. While Alexander had gone for a swim, they had stolen Alexander's clothes. Hidden and with their minds blurred by drink, they'd convinced Alexander he was surrounded by the English. A fact he'd believed, until Duncan had shot an arrow nearby and Alexander had recognized his brand within the shaft.

The same two notches carved into the charred wood cradled in his fingers.

He glanced toward the other entry. Was Duncan still nearby? And what of his other brothers?

"What is wrong?"

Patrik tossed the arrow into the coals. "We need more wood." Unable to shake the unsettled feeling, he turned and walked away.

Emma noted his stiff gate. As he rounded the corner, she took a stick and freed the half-burned shaft. She cradled the warm wood within her palm. From his reaction, this fragment belonged to someone he knew. It would belong to another rebel, so why would that leave him upset? At least the arrow didn't indicate a woman.

Wood clattered nearby.

She started, glanced to where he stacked the wood. "I did not hear you return."

Patrik remained silent as he knelt before the warm coals, his face taut. With care, he inserted moss, twigs, and other dry tinder. Then, he leaned close and gently blew upon the embers. Red flickered, dimmed to black. He blew another steady breath at the center. Embers glowed beneath the gray ash. Moments later, a wisp of smoke sifted through the moss. A flame ignited.

With care, Patrik fed the fire, small bits at first, then angled limbs that would easily catch, and finally, larger pieces that would burn the entire night. On a sigh, he sat back.

She settled beside him, his tension palatable. "You recognized the arrow shaft?"

A muscle tightened in his jaw.

Emma hesitated to push him, but something important had just occurred. She set the charred length before him. "This person means something to you, do they not?"

For a long moment, he remained silent. Then, fingers trembling, he picked up the carved wood and set it within his palm.

A part of her regretted the pain the memories invoked. God in heaven, look at her, allowing emotions to affect her mission? Shaken, she fought to deal with the realization that somewhere in their time together, Patrik had become too important to her, even more than her mission.

"Who does the arrow belong to?" she asked, her voice shaking.

Hard eyes, eyes like a wounded animal, met hers. He tossed the charred wood into the ash. "My brother."

A brother? Irritation flared. No one had disclosed that Patrik had a brother. Sir Cressingham, as well as another man in his employ, had explained how English knights had murdered *Dubh Duer*'s family. A resultant hatred guided his hand within battle, a savageness that had led to the legends of the merciless Scot, *Dubh Duer.* But nothing about another sibling who'd lived.

Why?

Had Sir Cressingham set her up? That made no sense. The treasurer of Scotland hated Patrik, salivated at the idea of watching the Scot gutted, then making the rebel's death an example to all who dared defy him.

So why had neither his man nor he told her about Patrik's brother? Mayhap his sibling had played little or no role in the Scottish uprising? Or, his fealty lay with King Edward. What if neither man knew Patrik had a brother who had lived?

From the raw grief on Patrik's face, he struggled at the thoughts his brother inspired. If his brother was indeed loyal to the English king, that would explain Patrik's strife.

His strife, but not her increasing distaste for her mission.

"I am sorry. I have upset you." More so than he would ever know. He'd lowered his defense, a trust she now would shamefully exploit.

Scarred fingers picked up a stick to shove an ember

free. Then he buried the heated wood within the dirt. Angst-stricken hazel eyes lifted to hers.

"The arrow belongs to your brother?"

"Aye." A muscle worked in his jaw as he lifted the stick. Against the cheerful pop of the fire, he nudged aside the mound of ash, exposing the remnants of the arrow. He again lifted the shaft, rolled it slowly within his fingers. A charred line of soot remained. He stared at it, closed his eyes, then opened them. "At times a man is a fool and cannot see the precious gift he holds until it is lost."

The intensity of his words unnerved her. Well she understood the pain of losing someone you loved, the emptiness and the loss. Except life cared naught for your pain, or hurt, but moved on. 'Twas you who chose to step forward or to remain buried within your grief.

"Was your brother killed?"

Patrik laid the charred shaft at his side. "Nay. But to them I am dead."

Them? He had more than one brother alive?

Cristina's eyes widened with questions, but Patrik remained silent. A fool he was for telling the lass anything of the MacGruders. He barely knew her. But as he'd held the arrow, emotions had stormed him, the pain immense. And he'd found admitting the truth to her had brought a wisp of relief.

Blast it, he wanted his brothers back, he wanted to use the surname MacGruder, desperately so. With their love and support during the years when he'd struggled to find stability after his family's death, how could he not?

Grief washed through him as he studied Cristina. A stranger? Mayhap, considering the amount of time he'd known her, but something about her drew him, had from the start. Her beauty he couldn't deny, nor the desires she inspired, but what lured him was more than the intrigue of the flesh. From the bits of her life she'd shared, he sensed she carried enormous hurt, pain carved by years of suffering, emotions only those who had survived similar ordeals understood.

A stranger?

Mayhap, but not to his soul.

But could he trust her?

An ache tightened his chest at the thought of leaving her on the morrow. It could be no other way. What she made him feel, want, made little sense. Yet, for the first time since he'd awakened from his brush with death, he found himself wanting to share with someone the dark secret of the family he wished to reclaim.

No, not someone, Cristina.

Yet, however she moved him, to give into his yearnings would further complicate an already muddled situation.

"But what about—"

He handed her an oatcake. "Eat."

After a brief hesitation, she accepted his offering, her eyes darkening with understanding. Cristina leaned back against a large boulder and took a bite.

Patrik followed suit, the soft thunder of water a fitting echo of his mood. Through the break at the end of the falls, darkness stole the last fragments of day. Too soon the dawn would come, and the realities of tomorrow would unfold.

He studied Duncan's arrow. Given the ember's warmth, his brother had stayed here but hours ago.

What had made him pass through? Had the English seized Lochshire Castle?

Nay, his eldest brother, the Earl of Grey, held a significant force. His knights combined with Lochshire Castle's strategic location, surrounded on three sides by a loch, made a strong defense. Still, something significant must have occurred to send Duncan this far south. Not that he would be discovering the why of it now. When he met with Bishop Wishart, he would learn the reason.

The lass finished the last of her oatcake. Patrik handed her the water. "Here."

"My thanks." She accepted the leather flask. After a long drink, she passed it back.

Patrik quenched his thirst, secured the top and set it aside.

She cast a nervous glance at the entry. "Do you think anyone else will seek shelter within this night?"

"Mayhap, but only once has anyone entered while I rested here."

"So, are you telling me not to worry?"

"I am. Any who would enter this hideout are rebels. Unlike the English, we change not our loyalty beneath threats."

Guilt tore through Emma at the thought of the men tortured to gain Patrik's name and identity of *Dubh Duer*.

"Here." Patrik handed her another oatcake.

Sickened, she shook her head. She did not deserve to be in the company of such an honorable man. "I am tired." Tired of the lies, of the betrayal she intended for a man who gave naught but courage and loyalty to those he loved.

Sir Cressingham had lied to her about Patrik, about

his being a heartless man necessary to destroy. If anyone fit that description, 'twas Sir Cressingham, a man even the English despised. What else had the treasurer deceived her about?

"Cristina—"

"Where will I sleep?"

He frowned. "What is wrong?"

Everything. How did one confess to being a liar, to hurting the person who'd made her aware of wishes and desires she'd refused to believe could ever exist.

She stood. "I am tired."

"You are." He shoved to his feet and stepped toward her, his eyes never leaving hers.

"Do not—"

"What?" he said, taking her hand. "Touch you?"

She closed her eyes, her pulse racing too fast. "I cannot do this."

"Tell me."

Aching, she opened her eyes, stared at the man she'd sworn, if necessary, to kill. As if she could raise a blade against Patrik.

She despised her emotional defenselessness, had since she'd watched the last pile of dirt tossed upon Father Lawrenz's grave. A child of twelve, she'd sworn never again to be placed in such a position. A vow she'd kept.

Until now.

Until Patrik.

Overwhelmed, Emma tried to pull away.

Patrik's grip held firm. "Lean against me."

"I-I cannot."

"You can. Try. For me."

"You do not understand what you ask." Nor the dangers he invited. Against all logic, against what her mind ordered, she stepped forward and laid her head against his muscled chest. Too aware of him, comforted by the steady beat of his heart, she closed her eyes.

"You scare me."

He gently stroked her hair. "I know."

"Arrogant, too." But she didn't look up, didn't dare.

A chuckle rumbled in his throat. "Aye, I have been called that a time or two."

"'Tis not funny."

He drew back, the humor on his face fleeing. "Nay, lass, I find naught amusing about what you make me feel."

As if his admission helped anything. "Patrik—"

He gently cupped her face, lifted her chin until their eyes met, until it was as if he could see straight to her soul. "I have tried to understand the why of it, to figure out what about you intrigues me, and have told myself I am wrong to want you when you still grieve for a husband lost. And at every turn, I fail." He shook his head. "My feelings for you make little sense, especially considering the meager time I have known you." He paused. "However wrong, I want you, want to make love to you."

Her body trembled at his confession while her mind screamed for her to break free. Already she'd crossed lines she could never repair.

He stroked his thumb across her lower lip. "I have no right to ask, to want you this much, but damn me, I do." Patrik searched her face. "Tell me you do not want this and I will leave you alone."

Tears burned her eyes. After being raped during her youth, Emma had believed the only man she would ever care for was Father Lawrenz. Now, she understood her feelings for the priest were those of a girl searching to be accepted. Nothing compared to the depth of a woman wanting Patrik's touch.

Long moments passed. Still, he held, waited, giving her every opportunity to step away.

And if she did, if she allowed her assault of ten and two summers to guide her decision, smother what he made her feel, she would never know the joy of being with a man who made her feel desire.

She was wrong to consider intimacy, especially when it would be tangled in lies. But the desire in his eyes, his need for only her, filled an emptiness inside she'd never believed any would touch.

Bedamned the consequence. However wrong, for this one night, she would hold what destiny would deny her.

On a shaky breath, Cristina reached up to kiss him.

Chapter 6

Patrik met Cristina's mouth halfway, soft, steady, firm with intent. He gently backed her against the smooth wall and pressed his body flush against hers. Heat exploded inside, poured through him, engulfed him until it was as if his body was on fire.

He groaned as Cristina's body molded against his. God in heaven, their earlier kiss had but hinted at the breadth of the woman within, of her desire. She was a woman crafted by the fantasies of many a man.

With his blood pounding hot, he drew on her tongue, savored her taste. Would even this night be enough? Aye, he would make it so.

He took the kiss deeper, wanting her whimpers of need, her mews of pleasure as he slowly made love to her.

The force of his need left his fingers trembling as he slid his hand down the silk of her throat. With slow enjoyment, he unbound the first tie, and then cupped the curve of her breast.

At her gasp of pleasure, desire ripped through him.

He ignored the urge to strip her, to take what his body demanded. He'd wanted to make love to her, but their joining would be more than finding release. More than he'd ever expected.

As if life ever gave you what you expected?

Now, he'd been given the gift of this woman, a woman he must let go on the morrow.

With infinite care, he teased her bud, skimmed his fingers over the taut flesh as he claimed her lips. He savored the softness of her mouth, amazed at how she gave back, more than he could have ever believed.

Her body trembled, shifted restlessly against his.

He hardened, painfully so. Patrik cupped the back of her neck, turned with her until his back pressed against the wall. He caught her hand and laid it over his hard length to show her how she pleased him.

Cristina stiffened, jerked her hand free.

Stunned, Patrik broke their kiss. Within her passion, he caught a hint of fear. "You are safe with me." He kept his words soft, gentle so as not to alarm her further.

Her mouth swollen with his kisses, she stared at him, her nerves easy to read. "I-I thought you wanted to make love to me?"

Damn him, he'd pushed her too fast. "I want you, never doubt that. But what we share this night is your decision. We are both tired, our desires tangled with fatigue." She wet her lips; his body trembled with wanting her. "Neither can I forget the attack of two days past, nor the loss of your husband, a man you loved. As much as I want you in my bed, never have I taken advantage of a woman, neither will I begin now."

"I . . ." Cristina looked away.

With his entire body aching, he released her. "I will retrieve the blankets to make a pallet."

"Patrik—"

He stopped, did not face her. "Say naught unless you mean it. I am but a man."

Shaking with what she'd almost allowed, aching with needs unfulfilled, Emma struggled to admit what her body desired, what her heart yearned to feel. How did she explain that the shock of an intimate touch ignited flashes of the rape during her youth? And of the endless hours afterward, when she'd lain abandoned, bleeding in the shadows upon the cold, filthy stone.

At her silence, Patrik nodded. "So be it." He strode to a shield of rocks, withdrew blankets hidden behind them. In the clearing, he spread them out.

He was upset, how could he not be? She'd believed herself strong enough to be with a man and was wrong. "I am sorry."

Storm-filled eyes met hers. "Do not be. My wanting you does not make the time right."

"As if there will ever be a time right for either of us?" The words spilled out before she could stop them. "Forgive me. I should not have spoken."

"Why? On the morrow we will part, never again to see each other. I should not have pushed you to choices you are not ready for." He nodded. "For that I am sorry."

He referred to her supposed rape by the English knights. Guilt swept through her.

Patrik walked over, placed a gentle kiss upon her lips. "Go to sleep, Cristina. If you should want to talk, I have been known to be a good listener." He walked to the fire and sat before the flames, his back toward her.

Damn him and his honorable ways! "I want you as well."

He tensed.

"Never has a man kissed me like you." At his silence, anger trampled over caution. "I want you to make love with me, but I know not if I can."

Patrik shoved to his feet. With quiet steps he walked over. Dark eyes assessed her, softened. "Tell me."

She wanted to, desperately. Emma wrung her hands and studied the flicker of flames.

"Look at me."

Emma lifted her eyes. The sincerity of his gaze stole her breath. If she told him of the rape during her youth, it would explain her hesitance, yet raise questions about her husband's touch. But she needed him to understand.

And offer yet another lie?

No, in this she would give him truth. "After my husband was murdered—" She struggled for the right words. "—one of the English knights caught me and I was raped."

Fury burned his eyes.

"The man . . ." She stared at the distant rush of water, the years rolling past, seeing the merchant's greedy hands, feeling the pain of his assault. "I tried to run, to escape. I could not get away." A sob escaped, then another. Emotions she'd withheld, had never shared with another, broke free. Hands, strong and tender, caught her, drew her against him, held her as if she was something precious.

"God, lass," he whispered, "I am so sorry."

Her tears fell harder, in part at the memories, in part

that even in her horror she invited deception. She shook her head. "I no longer cry."

Patrik wiped her cheek. "Tears do not make you weak, but alive."

"It hurts to feel." She sniffed. "I swore never again to care."

"'Tis an unreasonable vow," he said, his words without censure. "Our feelings are not for us to dictate."

She fought to give him a smile, failed. "I was doing well until I met you."

His mouth opened as if to say more. Instead, he drew her close, the steady beat of his heart reassuring, making her want to stay there forever.

"You need to rest." His quiet words held an edge of tension, and of need as well.

Emma looked up. "But I want you."

Instead of heat, tenderness filled his gaze. "As I do you, never doubt that. But with your emotions so raw, you are not ready."

"I—"

He pressed a finger over her mouth. "On this I will not budge."

At his thoughtfulness, fresh tears threatened. Though he might never admit it, they both understood that after the events of this moment, the bond between them had changed, had deepened.

"Come." He led her to where he'd made a pallet. "We are both tired and need sleep."

She nodded, emotions storming her as she walked by his side. They halted before the fire, but she found herself unable to let him go.

"Patrik?"

"Aye?"

"Will you hold me?"

Tenderness creased his face. "'Twould be a fine thing."

Shyness touched her, ridiculous to feel after asking him to make love to her, more so after their heated kiss when he'd touched her, made her body come alive.

He helped her settle, then wrapped his hand around her waist and drew her against him. Warmth surrounded her, a contentment she'd never expected to feel.

Emma snuggled against him. "Thank you."

He kissed her brow. "Go to sleep."

His muscled body pressed against hers, inspiring desire more than sleep, but within his arms, she felt safe, protected, feelings she'd never experienced. She closed her eyes and allowed herself the luxury of drifting off.

On a sigh, Patrik shifted, and the writ within his trews bumped her.

Guilt severed the warmth of the moment. She closed her eyes and prayed that when Patrik learned the truth, somehow, he could find forgiveness.

At the soft brush against her cheek, Emma shifted closer to the warmth and fought to reclaim the haze of sleep.

A soft scrape tickled her ear.

Frustrated, she swatted at the pesky irritant, but a firm pressure stayed her hand. Confused, she opened her eyes and stared into Patrik's face.

Amusement warmed his hazel eyes.

"I was asleep."

"So you were." He claimed her mouth, soft, warm, seducing her until her sleep-jumbled mind collided with thick emotion.

On a groan, he rolled her onto her back with his body atop hers, his weight upon his elbows while his mouth continued its amazing foray. Heat poured through her, hot, seducing, eroding her thoughts.

Patrik lifted his head, gave her a tender smile. "A kiss from a beautiful lass is a fine way to begin the morning."

"'Tis pleasing," she replied, fighting to keep the tumble of reality from stealing this fragment of bliss.

"Pleasing?" A wicked smile touched his face as he settled himself more intimately against her. "If my kiss is merely pleasing, I am doing a poor job of it. Neglect I will be fixing."

"Patrik—"

He smothered her words, destroyed her thoughts with mind-stunning intensity. He used teeth and tongue, taking, tasting, his hands caressing her until her mind tumbled into a blissful haze.

Patrik nipped along the curve of her jaw. "Tell me, lass, was that merely pleasing?"

Breathless, her body alive from his touch, Emma trembled. His smug expression assured her he knew exactly how his kisses made her feel. Would it be so wrong to enjoy this time with him, to take what could not be? Never had she wanted a man or believed she could find desire. But Patrik, with the depth of his caring, with his sincerity and passion, had changed everything.

Guilt tore through her. If he learned of her deception,

he would hate her. But how did his hatred weigh against loneliness? Tears burned her throat. God in heaven, however wrong, she would take this moment, store it in her mind to keep. If her actions damned her to hell, it was a path too well trod.

She stared at the fire burning nearby, the darkness beyond, a blackness that for too long coated her soul. Too soon she would reclaim the bleakness she called her life.

A life alone.

"Your kiss is a touch better than pleasing," Emma said.

Hazel eyes narrowed with roguish delight. "A touch better? Wounded I am."

"Mayhap your ego, but little more."

"You make fun of me, lass."

"No, I adore you." Her playful words fell out in a husky whisper, far from the teasing she'd intended.

The smile on his face sobered. He stroked her cheek with the pad of his thumb. "We are making a muddle of this."

"We are," she replied, aware of exactly what he meant. Except, he didn't understand that the Scottish woman he believed her to be didn't exist. No, she couldn't do this. "I must get up."

At her gentle shove, Patrik eased his grip, but he didn't let go. When he'd awoken with Cristina curled at his side, he'd meant to steal a kiss before they began their journey this day. Instead of his lighthearted intent, he'd made her think of her rape.

"I will not harm you," he said, keeping his voice calm despite the violence battering his heart against a man who would attack a lass.

"I know."

But he saw the fear, the nerves she fought to hide. With the paltry time remaining between them, if he waited for her to come to him, she might never dare. "I want to kiss you."

"I—"

"Trust me." And he found her response important, wanting, no craving that she would give him her trust. In mere days the lass had become important to him.

Emerald eyes darkened with emotion. "I do."

The enormity of the responsibility she'd given him weighed heavy on his mind. The rape after her husband's death had left her with nightmares, yesterday's near brutality another harsh reminder.

His irritation built. With her faith in him, if he left her with fear in her eyes, he would be far from the man she needed him to be. He tamped down the ire. By God, he would purge the bastard's vile act from her mind, leave only memories of the beauty of a lover's touch.

On edge, wanting her with his every breath, Patrik gently claimed her lips. Awareness sparked in her gaze, grew, trampled upon the nerves shadowing her eyes. Pleased, he caressed the curve of her jaw as he slowly moved his mouth again over hers.

"Kiss me back," he whispered.

Cristina hesitated, and then complied, her cautious movements stoking the heat within him. But he allowed her to set the pace, endured the nervous press of her mouth, her fumbling passion as her lips hesitantly explored his own. Then, as if the demons haunting her mind fell away, she took his mouth in a hungry demand.

The intensity of her kiss stormed him. His body

hardened with fierce intent. His breathing grew uneven, but he curbed the urge to strip her and sink deep within her warmth. Now was a time for her to heal, a time to rid herself of the darkness seizing her mind.

Patrik made love to her mouth, taking, giving, savoring her each little sigh, her every gasp of pleasure. When her body softened against his, he slid his hands along her curves, appreciating her every tremble, the awareness he evoked, the need his touch had invited.

On a whimper, she shifted restlessly against him.

Careful not to push her too fast, he skimmed his fingers across her silken flesh, releasing the ties of her gown. He nudged the cloth aside and exposed her to his view. If she made any attempt to cover herself, however much he wanted her, he would stop.

Instead, she continued to kiss him, her mouth demanding, ruthlessly taking. So he sank into the kiss, savored the swell of her breast against his hand, enjoyed her every shudder as he toyed with the sensitive nub.

At her moan, he pressed kisses against her cheek, then moved lower, allowed his teeth to scrape the curve of her jaw. He nipped her gently, enjoying her shudder of surprise, the sensual flush that slid up her throat.

"I am going to make love with you," he whispered, her heat, her scent, driving him wild. "I want to see you, touch you all over."

Worry flashed in her gaze.

He steadied himself, tamped down the flash of anger. "No," he said, his words soft, "do not think of anyone but me. No one else is here but you and I."

"I know."

"You are safe with me. Never would I harm you."

Tenderness softened her expression, her delicate blush striking. "I am being foolish."

"Nay." He stroked her cheek with his thumb. "If anything, you should be angry, furious that a man dared touch you, scar your mind against what should be amazing."

Cristina turned away.

"Look at me, watch me while I make love to you."

Fear fluttered in her eyes, but she met his gaze.

With care, he wove his way down her tempting flesh, lingered along the sleek curve of her neck, then at its sensitive base. "You are an amazing, beautiful woman."

Her blush deepened.

She must know. Had her husband not told her many times over? If not, then he was a fool. Or, mayhap she'd refused to think of herself as pretty since her attack?

Gently, he cupped her breast.

"Patrik!" she gasped.

Pleasure shot through him at how her body tightened beneath his touch. Slowly, he stroked his finger across the silken skin, savoring her surprise, then the sheer wonder upon her face. As he continued to stroke her, her breathing grew faster. Never had he met a woman as sensitive as she.

He leaned down and drew her nipple in his mouth. She moaned as he continued his sensual assault, and he enjoyed her lush taste, the slide of his mouth against skin. He caught her other nipple within his finger, squeezed.

Without warning, her body began to quake.

Stunned, he pulled back, watched the flood of emotions wash across her face. God in heaven, he'd hardly touched the lass and she had almost come apart. Had he not known of her marriage, he would think her a virgin.

His mind clasped upon the thought, the idea of her supposed innocence. In a sense she was virginal; with her mind afraid, Cristina was unsure, nervous of what lay ahead. Beneath his touch, she was relearning the intimacy of a man's caress.

Excitement built inside, a heat so hot it threatened to fracture his control. *Slow, lad, if you take her now, you will destroy the trust you've won.*

The flat of her stomach trembled against his hand. She closed her eyes.

"Cristina."

Hesitant lashes fluttered open.

"You are beautiful." Slowly, he caught her breast within his mouth, suckled, capturing the tip with his teeth. "I am going to touch you," he said, preparing her, needing her ready for him in every sense. "Everywhere."

She wet her lips, nodded.

Patrik eased his hand lower. Wetness greeted him, a slick warmth that had his body aching. He focused upon her pleasure, on the building of need, on watching her as he took her over the edge.

With slow strokes, he caressed her soft folds, enjoyed the way her body shuddered at his every touch, her gasps becoming broken whimpers.

"Let go, lass. Let your mind follow your body's needs." He slid his finger into her wetness.

Panic slid across her face. Her entire body stiffened.

"'Tis me," he soothed, "no other." He waited, understood her nerves, her remembered terror. With excruciating slowness, he stroked her, gritted his teeth at how her slick walls clasped him tight. As her body began to relax, he increased the pace. When she began to arch into his touch, he edged lower.

Eyes wide, she stilled. "What are you doing?"

"I am going to taste you."

Distress paled her face as she jerked back. "No!"

"Shhh, lass." He edged back up. "Never would I do what you would not wish."

Eyes wide, she watched him, the pulse at her throat erratic. "Why do you want to . . ." She closed her eyes.

What in Hades was going on? "What?"

She edged open her eyes. "You wanted to . . ."

"Taste you?"

The blush on her face deepened. "Yes."

Her husband was a complete fool. "Many men enjoy a woman's taste."

Disbelief flickered on her face. "Truly?"

He drew a steadying breath. "Aye. If you let me, I swear it will bring you only pleasure."

She gave a hesitant nod.

With his body aching, he lowered himself, her woman's scent luring him. He took a slow taste.

Cristina shuddered. "Yo-You enjoy that?"

He gave a silent groan. "Immensely." Patrik ignored her skepticism. After her torment, that she allowed him such an intimacy left him humbled, and aroused. With slow, savoring strokes, he suckled, his tongue slowly keeping pace with his finger in her slick sheath.

A whimper spilled from her lips, but this time instead of nerves, her eyes shimmered with pleasure.

Pleased, he focused on his sensual task, enjoyed the way her trembling grew beneath his touch.

"Patrik!" she moaned.

"Aye." He increased his pace. "Let go, give yourself over to me."

A shudder tore through her, then another. On a cry, her body stiffened against his, then slumped back.

After one last taste, he positioned himself above her, poised himself at her slick entrance. On a sure stroke, he sank deep, her body snug around him.

Cristina froze.

Blast it, he would not lose her now! Patrik seduced her mouth with his tongue, taking, demanding, touching her in the places he knew would leave her aching. When she began to kiss him back, he set a steady pace. Her slick warmth pulsed around him, fresh from her own release, a mixture of heaven and hell. He kept his strokes slow, his kisses hot, and slowly, so slowly, she responded to him. On his next stroke, she arched her hips to meet him.

Finally.

He increased the pace, leaning down to catch her breast as he drove into her. Her body tightened around him, her gasps changing to cries of need. Lost to all but her, he reached down, stroked the nub hidden within her woman's folds.

Cristina cried out as she again slid over the edge.

Already close, with his body raging hot, Patrik slammed into her. The power of his release stunned him. His body shaking, he laid his head beside hers.

What had just bloody happened? He'd made love with many a woman, but never had he experienced a joining that made him feel so complete. He stroked her hair. Then, never had he met someone like Cristina.

At her sigh, he nuzzled her neck, pleased by her release, that he had brought her such satisfaction.

"I think I have died," she groaned.

He chuckled. "'Tis the best way to go."

"You are arrogant."

"Aye."

"And shameless," she said with a sated smile.

"With every right." Her earlier claim echoed in his mind. "Now tell me, was that kiss a touch better than pleasing?"

A rough laugh fell out threaded with happiness. "Yes, it was amazing."

"Aye, it was at that." He slowly pressed himself deeper within her slick walls, his body already growing hard again. "And but the first of many such amazing moments."

Hours later, Emma shoved aside a low-hanging limb and followed Patrik as he continued to climb up the wooded path. Ahead, early afternoon sun filtered through the swath of leaves, and sprinkled light upon the land. A smile edged her mouth, warm with the memories of Patrik's touch, the amazing way he had made her feel. Heat slid up her cheeks at the intimate things he'd done, at what she'd allowed. They'd spent but this morning making love. How would it feel to have days, or more?

Sadness wilted her thoughts. In a few hours they would arrive at the home of Patrik's friend. Days before, she'd been determined to learn what traitor within King Edward's close circle had given him the writ.

Now, she had no desire to betray Patrik, or to leave him behind. All because she'd foolishly allowed herself to care, because damn him, in addition to being an amazing lover, he had shown her what it was like to have a friend.

"Cristina?"

Emma glanced ahead, startled to find Patrik watching her. "Yes?"

"You had stopped," he said, watching her with fierce intent.

"I am fine."

"Why do I find myself not believing you?" He walked back, drew her to him and set his mouth over hers in a fierce kiss.

Heat poured through her, and she gave in to his every demand, aching for him, for what could never be.

After a long moment, he lifted his head. "Think only of me, of the love we made this morning."

Emotions choked her throat. How could she ever forget?

He stroked her cheek. "Do nae let that bastard's touch soil what is beautiful."

The warmth fell away. Of course, he believed her withdrawal was due to her remembrance of the man who'd raped her. Except that man had raped her as a child, not a woman.

"I will never forget you." Her words spilled out with passion, a sadness she couldn't stop.

He caught her face within his hands. "I want—" His

breath hissed through clenched teeth. "I want what I can never have, what I can never give you."

Pain touched her heart at the dreams he offered. To allow him to feel them was wrong. "We both have our own lives, different paths to take."

"We do." But he sounded far from convinced. "After my friends see you to safety, what will you do?"

His question caught her off guard. "Do?"

"What are your plans? Will you stay with your husband's family?"

Family? She searched for an answer, floundered. Never could she tell him that once she'd delivered the writ, disclosed the rebel hideout, she would seek the next task for hire. But, for the first time in her life, the idea of facing another dangerous mission brought no thrill.

"I have not decided yet." She couldn't answer his questions. "And what of you?"

Disappointment shuttered his gaze.

"What is it?"

Patrik stared at her, the turmoil storming his mind easy to read. "We must go."

After everything they'd shared, that he could close her off so completely hurt. "You are avoiding the question."

"Are you not doing the same?"

Coldness seeped through Emma as she stepped back. "Nothing has truly changed between us, has it? We are strangers, really. You saved my life, and for that I am grateful." She exhaled. "But soon, we will part. It is best this way."

"For whom?"

His anger surprised her, nudged her own. "You said

this morning you could offer me nothing. Has that changed?"

Patrik's face tightened. "Nae."

"I thought not." She gentled her words. He deserved not her anger. She had wronged him, more than he would ever know. "Neither can I promise you anything in return."

"You have nowhere to go." It wasn't a question.

"I did not say that."

"Nae," he replied. "You said you were unsure, the answer is the same."

In this she must tread with care. "Patrik," she said, unable to keep her voice from trembling, "this is not about me or you."

"I disagree."

Damn him. "Do not make this harder than it already is."

His gaze darkened, hardened to that of a predator. He caught her face in his hands. "It is already too late."

Chapter 7

Cristina shook her head.

Furious she'd deny what existed between them, Patrik caught her mouth in a demanding kiss. When she finally kissed him back, he pulled away, his blood pounding hot.

"Regardless of what either of us wants, this *is* about us." He spun on his heel, strode up the narrow path and muttered a curse. Aye, he should have said naught. She was right, he could offer her nothing, a fact that grated upon him.

Throughout the day, he kept their pace steady. The roll of the rugged terrain was demanding, the summer heat forcing them to halt to refill his water pouch in nearby streams many times over.

Hours later, the rough path they followed narrowed, the slide of land to his left making the way treacherous but not impossible. Once they passed this narrow gap, naught except a field lay between them and his friends. After he explained the situation to them, he'd immediately depart to deliver the writ.

A fact he'd withheld from Cristina.

The slap of the impending loss stunned him. Focus, lad. Now is not the time to be thinking of the lass, or of what never can be.

An overhang of trees shaded the path ahead, the shadows a cool relief from the late afternoon sun. Wind tumbled in the forest as sunlight spilled through the leaves like gemstones.

A quiet thump sounded nearby.

Patrik halted, held up his hand.

"What is it?" Cristina asked as she worked to catch her breath.

He scoured the trees and rocks ahead. "I heard something." He gestured to a clump of bushes. "Hide behind them. Once I am sure no one is about, I will return."

She hesitated. "Be safe."

"You worry for me?"

A blush touched her cheek. "Mayhap."

He caressed his thumb across the smear of dirt upon her chin, too aware of the day's passing, the short time left before he must depart and never see her again.

On a sigh he dropped his hand. "Go."

She gave a solemn nod, then slipped into the thicket.

Patrik took in the sky, the wash of orange smeared by hints of red. Soon the sun would set. If someone was up ahead, he needed to hurry while he could still see.

Accompanied by the rattle of the leaves, he crept forward.

A low murmur echoed ahead.

Were the bloody English holed up for the night? Or

was it his brothers, who knew these hills and might be on a rebel mission?

Regret squeezed his chest. If his brothers indeed lay ahead, however much he wished to see them, he would take Cristina and backtrack to another route. He refused to allow her to witness what surely would be an angry confrontation.

Angry? Nay, after his trying to kill Alexander's wife, Nichola, his brother would want him dead.

This time for good.

With one last glance at where Cristina hid, he edged closer. Limbs shivered above him, the rich scent of earth and forest thick in each breath.

A horse snorted in the distance. Another man's voice reached him, this time closer.

Patrik scanned his surroundings. In the distance, he caught the outline of a man hidden within the fold of trees. Blast it, he couldn't make out whether the guard was friend or foe. He knelt. Using the brush as cover, he crawled forward.

Firelight flickered ahead.

A sinking settled in his gut. No Scot would dare light a fire. Several paces closer, he peered through the shadow-dredged leaves.

In the clearing a campfire burned. Cast in the flicker of yellow light, he made out several English knights.

Blast it. Of course the bastards would make camp in the open, a fire of no concern. They believed the rebels but a few Scots, easily quelled. They knew naught of Bishop Wishart's secret orchestration of events, of his covert meetings and correspondence with skilled strategists such as Andrew de Moray and James

Stewart, or of the bishop's garnering of support for Wallace.

Patrik counted ten men. Too many for him to kill in a charge. Neither did time allow him to wait and take them out one at a time. The only way around the knights was to backtrack. That was the reason the Englishmen had chosen this position on the trail, to prevent any rebels from moving past.

Patrik scoured the darkening skies. Some ways back lay another trail. It would take them leagues away from his friend's home, but closer to reaching the bishop.

On a muttered curse, he crawled back. At a safe distance, he stood and ran. As he neared where Cristina hid, she stepped from the bush. As always, her beauty stole his breath.

"What did you find?"

"English knights are camped ahead. I saw one sentry and suspect there are others positioned about."

She rubbed her thumb over the tips of her fingers. "What are we going to do?"

"We will take another route." He paused. "You will have to remain with me."

"I see."

But he heard the worry she tried to hide. He took her hand. "I had not meant to keep you with me. 'Twill be dangerous." However much he wished her safe, a part of him cherished the extra time they would have.

He carefully led them back, using the last of the light to follow the path. As they made their way around a massive boulder, he caught sight of four English knights striding up the path. He grabbed Cristina, covered her mouth and pulled her behind a tree.

"English knights," Patrik whispered.

"You there," a deep voice boomed. "Step from the trees."

Mayhap they had only seen him.

Cristina turned to him.

"Come out, now!" a rough voice demanded.

The bastards wouldn't touch her, he vowed. But with the knight's demand echoing around them, 'twould be moments before the other men at the campfire heard the commotion.

Patrik signaled for her to remain, freed his blade and stepped into the clearing.

The English warrior closest to him shot a glance at the tree. "There is another."

Blast it, he'd seen Cristina. No, mayhap in the gathering darkness, he believed a man hid there. "We seek but to pass through."

The warrior's eyes narrowed. "Whoever hides within must come out."

Bedamned, once they saw Cristina, they would want her. He tightened his grip upon his blade. The bastards would never touch her. Against four, surprise was his only hope. Before the knight closest to him realized his intent, Patrik sank his dagger deep into the warrior.

On a gasp, the knight stumbled back as he withdrew his blade, his legs collapsing beneath him.

Withdrawing his sword, Patrik turned. Blades clashed. Patrik cursed each scrape, each echo of steel.

A knight strode toward where Cristina hid.

No! Patrik drove his sword deep in the closest Englishman's chest, yanked, and whirled to meet the next attacker. With two quick stokes, he delivered the man to his fate. As the knight slumped to the ground, Patrik kicked the injured man back, bolted to head off the warrior striding toward the boulders.

Steps pounded in his wake.

As Patrik started to turn, the injured knight tackled him from behind. His sword clattered to the ground near the knight's weapon. Fury drove him forward, the primal urge to protect Cristina burning his mind.

"Come out," the fourth man ordered as he neared the trees.

Patrik slammed his fist into the injured knight's face, kicked him away, then grabbed his sword and jumped to his feet.

In the murky light, Patrik caught Cristina emerging from the shield of trees. Bedamned! "Get back."

She held, her focus riveted on the guard.

The knight bore down on her.

Damn her, she was going to get herself killed!

The knight was but two paces away, yet she held. "Leave her!" Patrik yelled.

The warrior spun toward him.

Thankful, Patrik raised his blade and willed the lass to hide.

"Patrik, behind you," Cristina warned.

He whirled as the injured knight he'd kicked away charged. In a deft maneuver, Patrik rounded his blade, served him a deadly blow. He turned.

The knight towered over Cristina, blade raised.

Panic ripped through him, the distance between him and the knight was too great. "No!"

As if in slow motion, the knight attacking Cristina glanced at Patrik.

With the knight's back toward her, Cristina raised her blade and drove it deep with methodical precision.

The knight's eyes flared in shock. He stumbled forward, collapsed. Face twisted in agony, he clawed at the dagger shoved in his lower back, a location skilled warriors used for a quick, sure kill.

What in Hades? Patrik lifted his gaze.

With stunning control, Cristina walked forward with a calm step and withdrew her blade, its tip slick with the man's blood. She turned toward Patrik, and stilled.

Their gazes clashed. Hers dark, unreadable.

The entire event had taken mere seconds, her action delivered with deft sureness. She'd never faltered, never betrayed the terror she must feel.

He opened his mouth to ask her what the bloody hell was going on.

A branch cracked. The angry sounds of men echoed in the distance as well as the pounding of steps.

The English approached! He secured his weapons as she stowed hers. He caught her hand. "Run!"

The slap of leaves whipped him, the tangle of stones threatened to take him down as he hauled her alongside. He pushed on, using every wisp of light to guide them, Cristina on his heels.

The sound of the men's steps echoed behind them as if a curse.

Gasping at his side, Cristina began to falter. At this pace, it was only a matter of time before the knights caught up to them.

They started up the next incline. In the dim light, a shield of brush and boulders rose to their left.

Patrik pulled her up the incline, helped her hide behind the largest rock. "Do not move."

Pulse racing, Emma caught the shadows of the English knights racing down the path.

"They went this way," a man yelled.

"How can you be sure?" another snarled, "I can barely see."

"We will split up," the first man said. "Sir Henry, take four of the men and follow the path south. They could not have gone far."

Footsteps echoed as the men hurried past, then the slap of leather upon earth faded.

Silence echoed like a tomb as the events of moments before replayed in her mind. She'd meant to stay hidden. But when she'd peered out and saw the knight striding toward her, she'd exposed herself with the intent of distracting the warrior to give Patrik time to finish off the other three knights. But the knight had come too close, the bloodlust in his eyes assuring her of his intent to kill her.

Then, the other knight had attacked Patrik, and she'd been left without a choice. Her years of being a mercenary had taken hold. No thought, pure reaction.

Except, she'd never meant for Patrik to see.

Questions. He would have them. How could he not? He'd witnessed her killing a man with deft precision. How would she answer them?

Patrik shifted at her side, his dagger ready if they were discovered. Little did he know that with her honed skill, her blade was just as lethal.

Slowly, his body relaxed. "They are gone."

Unsure what to say, Emma remained silent.

He glanced over. "Are you well?"

"Yes."

"We must remain hidden until the knights have returned to their camp," Patrik whispered, "then we will backtrack and take a different path."

His body vibrated with tension, and she could well imagine the questions in his mind. It would behoove her to dictate the direction of their discussion.

"I learned to handle a knife as a child." Her quiet words fell into the night, the moon slipped into the sky, filling the forest with an eerie glow.

"I did not ask."

"I know, but I need to explain." She found his acceptance of her more important than she would ever have believed. "Growing up in an orphanage teaches a child many things about life, including the dangers."

"Who taught you how to handle a blade with such skill?"

"Father Lawrenz."

"A priest?"

"He was worried about me."

Patrik turned toward Cristina, finding only hints of her face within the shadows. "What happened to cause a man of God to teach you to wield a blade?"

Silence grew around them, broken by the cry of a distant owl. "Few care what happens to an unwanted child. The safety of those cast within an orphanage is but an illusion."

The image of Cristina as a child came to mind. A girl without a family, without anyone to love her. She'd found salvation within the teachings of a priest.

In his youth, Patrik had had his family, his early years rich with warm memories. And when his own family was murdered, he'd known the love and support of the MacGruders, men whom he had once called brothers. But Cristina had known naught but cruelty and loneliness.

And soon, he too, like everyone else in her life, would leave her to fend for herself.

Still, the image of her sinking the dagger into the knight's lower back haunted him. Few held such expertise with a weapon. A priest may have taught her to use a knife, but Patrik wondered whether a man of the cloth had imparted such skill.

He took in the woman before him, a woman who at every turn proved herself not the person whom he believed her to be. But then, she knew not the truth about him either. Whatever her secrets, he doubted they could be as dark as the actions of *Dubh Duer*.

Chapter 8

With a seasoned eye, Patrik scanned the blackened path beyond the trees. The moon offered but meager wisps of light.

"We have seen no one in a long while," Cristina whispered.

"Aye, but no doubt they have left guards hidden along the path. The question is, how many and how far down? However arrogant, the English are not fools."

"No," she replied, her voice on edge, "though their methods are at times crude."

Fury trembled through him. She referred to her rape. "I would not err in underestimating the English, but neither will I or other rebels allow them to take a country that is ours."

"And how will you or the other Scots stop them? King Edward's army is tremendous."

Sadness echoed in her words, revealing the exhaustion of a woman who had endured too much.

"Tremendous mayhap," Patrik agreed, "but an army without a heart."

"And what of the Welch archers and their infantry reinforcements? Many Scots, those who have not pledged fealty to King Edward, are poorly trained and fight out of sheer determination." She shook her head. "And more. 'Tis not merely a formidable army the rebels face, but deception within."

"You speak of whom?" he asked, surprised by her claim as well as her knowledge of English defenses.

"The Earl of Carrick. Rumor has it that the rebels' hope of him becoming their future king may be in vain, for he is considering abandoning Scotland's cause to again swear his fealty to King Edward."

Anger brewed at her mention of Robert Bruce, Earl of Carrick. "No matter the whispers, Robert Bruce's heart is true to Scotland."

"And this is shown how, by the numerous times Lord Carrick has switched his loyalties to whichever country he perceives has the most to offer him?"

"Strategy is Lord Carrick's strength. Though he is the rightful claimant to the Scottish crown, 'tis denied him. So, he engages in becoming Scotland's king as if playing a game of chess. With our forces severely diminished, he considers whether it is prudent to lie low within the enemy camp." Despite his explanation, Carrick's behavior ate at Patrik like a festering wound, and was the reason he and other Scots supported William Wallace, a man whose loyalty to Scotland never wavered, regardless of danger.

"By the many times Robert Bruce has switched his support between England and Scotland," Cristina said, "I doubt the English king believes in Lord Carrick's loyalty."

"Indeed," Patrik agreed. "And that is the reason the king no longer appoints Lord Carrick to oversee anything of great importance." Again the lass surprised him with her understanding of Scottish politics, but her sincerity and the frustration in her voice assured him she struggled with Robert Bruce's decisions as much as he.

"So why would King Edward make such a pretense of accepting Lord Carrick's fealty? Why has he not charged Robert Bruce as a traitor and order him hanged?"

Patrik scanned the moonlit sky, then their surroundings for any sign of the English. "With Lord Carrick a strong competitor for the Scottish throne, such a bold move might invite greater dissent toward King Edward. Many of the Scottish nobles have sworn fealty to the English king under duress. Longshanks accepts Lord Carrick's fealty to keep an eye on him."

"Longshanks—I am unfamiliar with the term?"

Unfamiliar? How? 'Twas a nickname known by many a Scot. He blew out a sigh. Having lived on her own, she must have missed the term. A fact at odds with her insight on Scotland and England's political state; her knowledge was enormous compared to most commoners.

"The name is given to the English king because of his height."

"Not too pleasing a nickname."

Though she spoke quietly, he heard her nervousness. Why? "There are others the English king has garnered, but they are unfit to speak before a lass."

"That I can believe. Though King Edward tolerates

Lord Carrick, I doubt he would find such leniency for Sir Wallace."

Patrik gave a rough laugh. "Aye, with the disruption Wallace has served the English king, if our rebel leader was ever captured, King Edward would make an example of him." A shudder rippled through him. "A day I pray never comes." Seathan, his oldest brother, was a trusted advisor to Wallace, and courted danger by the mere connection.

"How long do you think Wallace can evade the king?"

"Until Scotland is free." A question popped into Patrik's mind. "Where did you hear that Robert Bruce is again considering swearing fealty to King Edward?"

Though Patrik had asked with ease, Emma caught the dangerous curiosity beneath his question. Curse her tired mind. What he must never learn was that she'd acquired the fact while she was briefed for her mission by Sir Hugh de Cressingham.

Unease shuddered through her. Her meeting with the treasurer of the English administration in Scotland seemed as if a lifetime ago. A time when her heart lay dead and her greatest desire was to face the next challenge. A mission that would bring the coin that allowed her to exist.

But, in a few short days, because of Patrik, everything had changed.

"A week ago, I entered a tavern to buy some bread and smoked meat," Emma lied, hating every word. "Several English knights were at a table nearby, drinking and talking loudly. Not wanting to draw their attention, I kept to the shadows. I overheard them boasting that Robert Bruce was again considering abandoning the rebels."

Patrik remained silent.

Did he believe her? To remain here would only allow him more time to think, and her more time to slip and reveal something to further raise his suspicions.

She rubbed her arms as if chilly. "Will we be leaving here soon?"

He hesitated. "Aye. We will remain near the path, but I dare not use it." He stood. "If you see or hear anything, tap my shoulder."

Relief swept over Emma. Each foolish slip was minor, but if Patrik began to piece them together, he might begin asking more questions, requiring answers she could never give. Worse, if he learned Sir Cressingham had hired her, Patrik would believe their lovemaking was naught but another tool to deceive him.

Ashamed her deception had tainted the intimacy between them, she reminded herself that if he learned the truth, Patrik would use every means at his disposal to find her.

And he would soon discover the Scottish woman named Cristina Moffat didn't exist.

However much she wished to remain with Patrik, she could not linger. This night, once he'd fallen asleep, she would take the writ and leave. After she met with Sir Cressingham and passed him the writ, along with information she'd gleaned, she could wash her hands of this damnable situation.

God in heaven, she'd made a fine mess of it. However much Patrik made her feel, never could she forget he was a man who had given his heart to the Scottish cause.

Coldness swept through her as she pushed aside another branch. "How far will we go tonight?"

"A bit more. We cannot risk traveling to my friends. This detour has gained us a day's time together if not more."

She glanced at him. "Where are we headed?"

"A rebel camp." Patrik kept his answer vague. She would be safe while he met with Bishop Wishart, and his friends would keep an eye on her.

That he believed it necessary to have her watched left him restless. She was a stranger, a lass he'd known but days, despite the bond that had formed between them.

If they'd shared naught but sex, he could have dismissed it, but the lass had given him her trust. He'd witnessed her discovery as he'd touched her, her genuine surprise as she'd fallen apart, which confirmed what she'd shared about her life. Many a woman could act, but a lass could not fake her body's first time.

Her body's first time? Nay, not her first time with a man, but her first time with a lover who cared.

A rock shifted beneath his foot and the earth gave away. He grabbed a limb, caught himself from slipping back.

"Patrik?"

"I am fine." 'Twould teach him to be mulling over the lass. He scanned the sky. The moon loomed overhead. "We have traveled a fair distance west and should be well away from the knights, but we will continue a ways farther. I will take no chances."

"Do you think the English forces we came across were sent to search for us after they found the four knights you killed when you rescued me?"

"Mayhap." But he suspected another reason. In preparation for the main English force pushing northward to seize Stirling Castle, smaller bands of knights were being sent ahead to weaken the opposition. Then, when the main force arrived at the castle gates, the Scots would have naught but the fortress walls and rations as their defense.

And as Cristina had noted, with Welch archers in tow, if the Earl of Surrey led the knights up to the drawbridge, the walls would be burned if not destroyed. This was the reason rebel forces must turn them back at Stirling Bridge.

A sliver of moonlight cut through the forest, weak against the stubborn darkness, but enough to outline the shadows of exhaustion lining Cristina's face.

The angst churning inside him softened. "We will rest, and then continue tomorrow."

"Where?"

"To our right is a large boulder, the top flat."

She studied the mix of shadows and light. "'Tis a long drop from the cliff."

"Aye, but height gives us the advantage to hear anyone approaching."

"And to see their outlines in the moonlight."

He nodded, impressed by her calm. After this day's strife, most women would have shuddered at the idea of remaining in the wilderness. Then, most women would not have been able to kill a man with such skill.

"Come." Somber, he strode toward the swath of

stone. At the flat expanse, he cleared away any foreign debris. "Without a blanket, we will be cold."

"At least it is not winter."

"True." He paused. "And we can use each other's bodies for warmth."

"'Tis a possibility."

The sensual heat in her voice made thoughts of the knights and this day's confrontation slide away. He walked over to her and stroked her cheek with the pad of his thumb.

"I am going to miss you, Cristina Moffat." He'd expected a soft smile, a look of tenderness, not for her to try to pull away. He held her against him, suspecting the reason. "You think of your husband."

She stiffened.

"Your husband is dead, that I cannot change. And I regret that my words made you think of him. It was not my intent."

"I know." Her body sagged. "I am tired."

And troubled, still haunted by memories of her husband. He could tell by the sadness within her eyes when she believed he wasn't watching. How would it feel for a woman to think of him so, for a woman to long for him, and when the time came, to mourn his passing?

"Cristina, look at me."

After a moment's hesitation, she turned.

He stroked his thumb along her moonlit cheek. "Two years have passed since your husband's death. You cannot live in the past forever. It will steal the time before you and strip away the happiness yet to be found."

A lesson he'd learned only after his brothers believed him dead. A death he'd allowed them to believe was real. A fitting penance for his attempt to kill his brother's wife, Nichola, when her only crime was that of being English. If only he could take back that day.

For too long he'd allowed his hatred for the English to taint his life. Through the months as he'd recovered, he'd had time to think, time to regret.

A sad sigh spilled from her mouth. "Do you believe anyone truly finds happiness?"

He thought of his parents, the remembered laughter of his youth. "Aye, but you do not?"

"No."

The simple conviction within Cristina's reply disturbed him more than if it'd held vehemence. Questions of how much her husband had truly loved her resurfaced. The more Patrik learned, the more he was convinced her marriage had been crafted for protection, her tenderness toward Gyles that of appreciation, not love. The thought pleased him.

"Tell me about how you met your husband?"

At Patrik's question, Emma tensed. "I do not want to speak of him." An understatement since there was no *him*.

"It has been two years since he died."

Heart pounding, she struggled for words. What should she say? Already she'd made up more than she could keep straight.

He sat on the stone, drew her to sit beside him, and then guided her head against his chest. "I wish to know."

"If it was only so simple."

She recalled a beggar on the streets nearby the orphanage in her youth, a man who had one day disappeared. Not disappeared. Murdered. The fact that his body had never been discovered meant one of two things. The killer had been crafty, or most likely, no one cared enough to try to find him.

But she would give the beggar a role in her life, or, at least speak of him as if of someone who had truly mattered. "I met him on the street one day."

"When you lived in the orphanage?"

"No. I had run away. He offered me food and a smile. I trusted neither."

Patrik remained silent.

Spinning the options in her mind, she chose the dream she'd never dared to speak, a notion that would never be. "He remained in town several days. With each one, he'd come to where I worked and talk to me. Nothing more. Just talk."

"About?"

"The day. The scents coming from the market. Where the ships in the port would travel." A wisp of her dreams crept into her voice, the longing for them to somehow come true.

"You wished to travel?"

A cold laugh fell from her lips. "At the time, my vision was more to escape."

"Because of your life in the orphanage."

The bubble of her imagination burst. "Yes."

"So you married him?"

Emma hesitated. "What?"

"When the stranger asked you to be his wife, you agreed?"

"Yes," she lied.

"But you never loved him?"

That answer was simple as a husband didn't exist. "No."

He exhaled. "I am glad."

Confused, she turned. Within the moonlight she found him watching her. "Why?"

"Love is something one should not easily give."

Mouth dry, she stared at him, too aware, wanting him too much. "Have you ever loved a woman?" Why had she asked? This night, once he fell asleep, she would steal the writ, then leave, break the trust she cherished. Still, she found his answer important.

Patrik stared at the sky, but she caught the shadows of sadness on his face. His gaze met hers. "Never has a lass made me feel a heart's tender yearnings." He lifted her chin with his thumb, gave her a gentle smile. "But then, never have I met a woman like you."

His breath, whisper soft, teased her, his gentle hold as if a caress. Emma shuddered.

"You are cold?"

"No."

Satisfaction shimmered in his gaze. "Tell me what you feel."

"You know."

"Do I?" He skimmed his mouth along the curve of her jaw. "Tell me."

Her pulse raced. "I want you to kiss me."

Slowly he lifted his head, his gaze hot and his mouth but a breath away.

God in heaven, he'd not kissed her lips, but Emma's

body burned as if tossed into a fiery pit. As he stared at her, the desire in his eyes fed her own.

"Now," he whispered, "I will taste you." He covered her mouth, his kiss, hot, hard, erasing all coherent thought. In a deft move, he lay back and pulled her on top of him, drawing her body flush against his.

Heat pulsed through her as he pressed intimately against her. "Patrik, 'tis indecent!"

"Aye," he said, laughter in his eyes. "Because we are both dressed. A fact I will be taking care of post-haste."

"What if I do not wish you to?" she asked, the sheer wantonness of his intent seducing her further.

His expression grew serious. "Then I would be leaving you untouched."

"And I would ache terribly from the wanting of it," she confessed.

"Ah, lass." On a groan, he stroked his thumb over the curve of her face, then drew her against him for a soft kiss, a slow, easy melt, a soul-tearing kiss that had her wishing for the impossible, one that left her aching for this one last joining, for memories to take, to cherish in the barren years ahead.

"Make love to me, Patrik," she murmured against his mouth. "I need you desperately."

Dark eyes searched hers, raw with desire. "Do you now?" he teased, the hardness of his body evidence he played no game.

"Yes."

Challenge sparked in his eyes. "What would you be wanting me to do?"

He was giving her control. She shuddered at the gift. "Touch me."

"Where?"

Memories of where his hands and mouth had made love to her filled her mind, the easy kisses, the frantic need. "Everywhere."

He groaned, but she caught the edge of a smile on his mouth. "Sounds like this might take the entire night."

A smile touched her mouth. "It very well could."

Chapter 9

A soft mouth skimmed across her skin, tasting, nibbling, lingering until her body ached with need. "Patrik," she breathed, her eyes fluttering open.

"Mornin', lass."

His deep burr curled around her in a sultry cloak. Emma sank into the warmth, then froze. Morning? It couldn't be! She tried to sit, impossible with Patrik's muscled body atop her.

"Do nae move," he murmured as his mouth skimmed along the column of her throat, lower, along the sensitive swells of her breasts. "You are interrupting a warrior laying siege."

"Patrik—"

He covered her nipple with his mouth.

Sensations exploded within, her words lost in a soft moan. He used his hands and tongue, stroking her, sliding wave after wave of delicious heat over her already sensitized skin. She gasped, arched against his erotic play, fighting for coherent thought.

He didn't understand. She'd planned on taking the

writ and leaving last night. Except, with the darkness blanketing them, he'd touched her, tasted her, had savored her more than she would have ever believed possible. Sated, exhausted, and content within the safety of his arms, she'd fallen asleep.

Even now, her body hummed with the heated memories. "After last night," Emma said half in a moan as he angled himself more intimately against her, "you should be dead."

"A warrior I am."

Soft laughter tumbled from her mouth. The hard press of him assured her he was more than prepared for his erotic intent. "I am not a battle."

"Aye, but you are. As worthy to claim as any stronghold to be seized."

"You are comparing me to a castle? I am not sure if I should be honored or insulted."

"'Tis my belief that you are thinking over much, an error I will be fixing." He covered her mouth a split second before he sank deep within her, again sweeping her into heady bliss.

A long while later, Patrik rolled to his side, drew her against him, her body still trembling from her release. The gentleness of his embrace, as if he held a precious gift, tore through her soul. Never had anyone treated her as something cherished.

Unbidden, tears came to her eyes. A traitorous drop slipped and fell upon his chest.

In the flicker of dawn, worry roughened Patrik's brow. "I have hurt you?"

"No."

He shifted back, took a full look at her, lifted the

salty drop with the pad of his thumb. "What is wrong?" At her silence, he gave a soft scowl. "Tell me."

"'Tis embarrassing."

"After we made love most of the night, with me touching, tasting your body everywhere, you are embarrassed?"

Heat stroked Emma's cheeks. "You make me sound foolish."

"Nae." He tilted her chin with his thumb. "I am but trying to understand what has upset you."

Her heart ached. "What we shared was so beautiful. Never had I imagined being with a man could be like this."

Male satisfaction etched his face, but tenderness as well. "The joining is not always so intense, or steeped with so much emotion or satisfaction."

She frowned. "What do you mean?"

"When making love, if you care for the other, the act is more than bodies joining."

It's a joining of the soul, she silently finished. Emma remained quiet, thankful when he didn't say more. Tears threatened. Through sheer will, she pushed them back.

Patrik glanced at the heavens where hints of gold crept through the sky, then sighed. "We have lingered too long." He shot her a playful wink. "Something we seem to be making a habit of."

"I—"

He silenced her with a hard kiss, and then he pulled away. He frowned; his body had hardened with desire.

"You will be the death of me."

She laughed despite herself.

He scowled, except naught but wicked delight lingered on his face. "Come, lass, we must make haste."

Emma quickly dressed, took one last look at his muscled body before he shielded it with trews and a tunic. Another day. One more they would share together. A day she'd not planned. Somehow, before the next dawn, she must take the writ, then leave.

Throughout the morning Patrik avoided any sign of a trail or clearing regardless of the extra travel it caused. Leaves whispered overhead as he glanced at Cristina. A pace away she pushed on in silence.

The lass was a mystery. Four days with her had but whetted his appetite to learn more, her each action but reshaping the woman he believed her to be.

After her near rape, when she'd first climbed from the bush and stood before him wearing her tattered dress, she had seemed emotionally strong, though scared. But at times since, within her confident eyes, he'd caught shadows.

Her recounting of her past explained a portion of what had put the darkness there, but questions as to what else she hid lingered. He still could not understand how Cristina had never heard of the fey or the Otherworld, the fairy's magical homeland. Her explanation that no one had cared enough to take time to explain such whimsy rang true. Still, after she'd struck out on her own, how could she never have heard talk of the fey?

And though the priest may have instructed her on how to wield a knife, instinct assured him another had taught her the skills he'd witnessed during the fight.

More unsettling, where had she gained such in-depth military knowledge of both the English and the Scots?

Patrik thought of Bishop Wishart, his immense influence as well as his knowledge of the military struggles throughout the world. Aye, her priest could have held extensive military insight, but by her account, he had died years ago. The information Cristina shared of Lord Carrick's floundering loyalty was recent. Doubts she had indeed overheard guards discussing Robert Bruce crept through Patrik.

Saint's breath, with the important writ he carried, the lives it affected, he could allow no doubts of anyone around him. So what was it about her that lured him, made him step past boundaries he had no right to break?

Heat pulsed against his chest.

He glanced at the halved gemstone and frowned. It had warmed, as it had within the cave when he'd struggled with his feelings toward Cristina. An image of the MacGruder brothers' grandmother gifting him the halved malachite upon his being knighted wavered in his mind as did the whispers of her having the second sight.

Unease trickled through him. Nae those were but whispers. Regardless, she was dead, her abilities long since passed.

A stick snapped in the distance.

Patrik withdrew his dagger as he glanced toward the sound.

A wash of brownish red flickered through the brush. A fox.

His body eased, and he secured his blade.

At the next rise, Patrik took in the sun sliding from

its zenith. He paused within the shadows, scanned the roll of woods ahead.

Cristina halted at his side. "There is smoke to the north."

He scanned the tree-lined sky. Cursed.

"An English encampment?"

"I doubt they would halt this early in the day."

"Do you think the English have torched another Scot's home?"

"Aye. Likely so." Anger welled inside him at the image of a scene he'd too often beheld. He drew a calming breath. "If 'tis the English knights' doings, I must see if anyone still lives."

She cast a somber glance. "And if no one survived?"

"Bury the dead." He started forward; she fell into step at his side. "Once we are near, you will hide until my return."

"I am going with you."

He cast her a cool glance. "You will not. If I know you are safe, I will not worry."

She angled her head. "But you will not always be here to protect me."

"Nae, but I am here now."

Emerald eyes darkened, but she said no more.

He damned the image in his mind of her killing the knight. Did the confidence in her voice hint that yesterday's act was but an example of her skill? If so, exactly how well trained was she? Or were his doubts feeding complications that didn't exist?

Still, she'd had a weapon, one she'd kept hidden until yesterday. "Where is your dagger?"

Her stride never faltered. "Secured at my thigh."

"You hid it from me."

"I will not apologize for having learned to protect myself nor for concealing a weapon."

"When I first saw you encircled by the English, I saw no sign of a strap."

"Before you arrived, the men had found and relieved me of my weapon. When you attacked, I used the distraction to grab the dagger before I fled."

That she could think so clearly despite her panic impressed him, but also deepened his suspicion. "Where was your weapon when we made love? I stripped you and should have found it."

"Behind a nearby rock. And just barely." A smile edged her mouth. "You, Sir Patrik Cleary, are a man who moves very fast."

Though she teased him, he couldn't shake the feeling that there was something about the lass he was missing.

A man's voice echoed ahead.

Patrik hauled Cristina behind a clump of brush. Blood pounding, he scanned the dense forest. "Stay here."

"Let me go with you."

"Nae. I will be back in a trice. Once I see who is ahead, I will return."

Worry shadowed her face, and she nodded.

He slipped from the thicket.

At the next knoll, he glanced back. The dense wash of green hid Cristina. Keeping to the shadows, using the thick bushes as a shield, he made his way forward.

Ahead, a break in the trees exposed an open field. Amidst the sea of green, interspersed with patches of heather and broken by wildflowers, stood a crofter's hut. The smoke they'd seen came not from charred remains, but swirled out of the chimney.

Still, he would take no chances. Though normally a home to Scots, he knew neither to whom they swore their fealty, nor whether English knights lay within.

A solid thunk had him glancing east.

Another had him slipping along the edge of the forest toward the sound. A short distance away, a burly man wielded an ax upon a felled tree. By the man's garb, he was a Scot. Still, he'd assume nothing.

Patrik remained hidden a while longer to ensure the man was alone. Then, with his hand on the hilt of his sword, he emerged from the woods.

The burly man made to take his next swing, halted. Eyes narrowed, he lowered his ax, but he didn't let go. "Ho there." Caution sounded in his words.

"Good day to you," Patrik said.

The red-haired man made a quick scan of the words behind Patrik, then studied him with a wary eye. His gaze flicked to his sword. "You a Scot?"

"Aye."

"A contingent of English knights rode through this morn. They were seeking a man and a woman."

So, the English still pursued them. Not surprising since he'd left four of their men dead. "What did you tell them?"

He capped his hands upon the top of the ax. "That I had seen no one."

"And now?" Patrik asked.

"The same."

"Are you loyal to Scotland?"

"Aye, though the English believe otherwise." Hard eyes watched him. "And you?"

"Until my last drop of blood stains the earth."

The Scot scanned the edge of the forest, then met Patrik's gaze. "And the lass?"

"Hidden."

He grunted. "As well she should be. My name is Fergus. Bring her to sup. My wife would be enjoying another woman to talk to. And I have a daughter as well."

"The English have left you unharmed?" Patrik asked, stunned.

The burly man crossed his arms, grunted. "With each visit, I have kept my family out of sight. So far, the knights have only watered their horses and taken a sheep or two when they pass." He paused. "But I fear for my family's safety."

The red-haired man went on. "Bring your lass, you both can stay the night."

"My thanks. If your wife can spare it, she will be needing a gown."

The Scot arched a brow.

A muscle worked in Patrik's jaw. "English knights tried to rape her. I killed them."

"The bloody bastards deserved to die." He nodded. "A gown she will be given."

"My thanks." Patrik turned and slipped into the cloak of trees.

Heart pounding, Emma eyed the sturdy woman at the doorway of the crofter's hut, her pale golden hair braided down her back, her weathered skin at odds with the smile in her eyes. She'd found no solid reason to give Patrik as to why they couldn't remain with the Scots overnight.

"Welcome to you. My name is Marie," the woman said, but the warmth in her voice far from put Emma at ease. This night, she had intended to escape. Surrounded by a family 'twould prove a near impossible feat, especially since she must first relieve Patrik of the writ. Curse the entire situation.

The woman tsked. "Sorry I am at hearing about the English curs who attacked you. I have a gown for you."

Emma nodded. "My thanks." A movement from the edge of the doorway caught her attention.

Red hair, bright like a flame, tumbled across the cheek of a young girl she guessed to be five summers. Wide green eyes stared out, a mix of curiosity and shyness.

Emma's heart melted.

At the bump against her leg, the woman glanced down and smiled. She caught the child's hand, drew her forward. "This is my daughter, Joneta."

Clutching a bedraggled doll, the girl stared up at Emma in awe. "Are you a fairy from the Otherworld?"

Unused to children, Cristina fumbled for an answer.

"Aye she is, lass," Patrik stated as he strode past Emma and knelt before the child. "And who might this bonny lass be?"

Delight sparkled on the girl's face, overtaking her shy smile. "Joneta."

He winked. "And a bonny name to match."

She giggled, and then peered at Emma. "Did she indeed come from the Otherworld?"

"I am not sure," Patrik replied, "but I suspect so. I found her beneath a lily."

Her eyes widened further. "Truly?"

"Aye," he said in a conspiratorial whisper. "And now that I have found her, I am thinking of keeping her."

Patrik's eyes met Emma's. The truth in them stole her breath.

The girl squirmed in her mother's hold. "Can I see the fairy?"

"Her name is Cristina," Patrik said as he stood. "She is a shy one." The panic in Cristina's eyes caught him by surprise. The lass had taken a man's life without hesitation, yet when confronted by a mere child, she stood frozen. His heart softened. 'Twas shame of her tattered gown. Except through the eyes of a child, the torn bits of gown indeed appeared like the magical dress of the fey.

"Joneta," her mother said. "Go and finish sweeping the floor."

The girl pursed her lips. "Are you staying the night?" she asked Patrik.

"If you will be having me," he replied.

She clasped her hands behind her back, rocked to and fro. "And her?"

The imp would steal the stoutest man's heart. "Aye."

With a squeal of delight, the lass rushed inside, her flame-red hair bouncing in her wake.

Marie laughed. "Never do I know what my daughter will say." She turned to Cristina and her expression grew somber. "These days, rarely do we see anyone aside from the English. 'Twill be nice having another woman to talk to. Come inside when you are ready." She entered her home.

Cristina's fingers worried the side of her tattered gown. "Do you know them?"

"Nae." He caught her hand, rubbed his thumb along the soft curve at her palm.

She pulled away, shot a nervous glance toward the doorway. "Then how can you trust them?"

He caught her hand again, held firm. "They are Scots. 'Tis our way to help each other without question." A fact she should know. Then again, Cristina had said she'd never heard of the fey. Saint's breath, the lass was a confusing mix. "Come." He drew her with him as he entered the crofter's hut. The rich scent of simmering venison greeted them as did the fragrance of onions and herbs.

The woman smiled. "We are having stew. Fergus killed a roebuck yesterday. Lucky you are."

"Aye," Patrik agreed, but Cristina's face had paled. Why? Outside, he'd believed her withdrawal was due to her embarrassment at the ragged state of her gown as well as his having informed Fergus and Marie of the English knight's attack. But then, she'd floundered beneath the attention of the little girl.

Until this moment, they'd traveled alone. Now, he suspected there was more to her awkwardness. After the fractured life of the orphanage, had Cristina's husband kept her secluded, not allowed her to meet or befriend others?

It would explain much. 'Twould seem her husband's attention was little more than that of a rutting boar. Her innocence in the art of making love proved he'd neither given her proper attention, nor ensured that she found her pleasure.

What other cruelties had the lass endured beneath her husband's hand? 'Twas fine with him that the bastard lay rotting beneath the earth. A man who treated a woman so poorly deserved no better.

They would remain here but one night. Another gown would give her confidence, but mayhap the next few hours around a family would show her another side of life, one with laughter, sincerity, and kindness. He wished he could give her more, but on the morrow their time together would end.

The thought of leaving Cristina left an emptiness in his heart. His heart? Nae, that he could never give. Too many challenges lay ahead. Even without the uncertainty of war, his personal life remained a mire.

He grimaced. Mire was an understatement when he thought of his relationship to the men he desperately wished to reclaim as brothers. Did the possibility of rebuilding a bond with the MacGruders exist?

Patrik gave an inner shake. Now was not the time for such musings. "I will go and help your husband with the wood. 'Tis thankful we are for the night's lodging."

A blush spread across Marie's cheeks. "The pleasure is ours."

With a nod, Patrik left.

The woman wiped the sweat from her brow, set the cloth on a nearby peg to dry. She shot a worried glance at Emma. "How fare thee?"

She spoke of the supposed near rape. "I am fine." The lie twisted in Emma's gut.

Marie nodded. "Come, let me give you the gown."

"I appreciate your generosity."

"Nonsense, 'tis an offer I am happy to make." The sturdy woman dug through a stack of gowns folded neatly within a trunk. "Here is the one I was searching for." She withdrew a soft green gown embroidered with gold threads at the neck. "My mum gave this to me when I was younger." A smile curved her mouth as she laid her hand upon her stomach. "After several babes, it no longer fits, nor do I believe it ever will. I was going to use scraps of it to begin sewing a blanket, but I would much rather see it worn."

The beauty of the garb stunned Emma. Never had she owned anything so regal. "I will be traveling. A gown so fine is far from befitting such use."

"'Tis better than sitting in the dark and collecting regrets."

Emma longed to touch the intricate weave, the beautiful workmanship. "If you are sure?"

The woman's smile widened. Marie held out the gown. "Try it on."

Moments later Emma ran her hand along the delicate embroidery, following the pattern of leaves.

"I was right, the gown is a fine color for you." Marie sighed. "To think I once fit into it, but I doubt I ever looked so well." She paused. "Would you mind if I fixed your hair?"

Emma hesitated. Never had a woman paid her any attention, unless as a child to be scolded.

"I have embarrassed you," Marie said. "'Twas not my intent."

Touched, Emma gave her a shy smile. "No, 'tis only that I am without words to repay your kindness."

The woman's smile widened. "There is no need for such. Take a seat and I will fix your hair for your husband."

Her husband? She believed Patrik her husband? Emma should correct the woman, but she allowed the claim to linger, to sift through her mind as if a wish as the woman deftly combed and braided her hair.

A short while later Marie stepped back, a satisfied expression on her face. "Your man will be pleased."

Heat stroked Emma's face. However wrong, for this night, she would live the dream that Patrik was hers. "My thanks."

A smile beamed on the woman's face. "My pleasure." She stowed the brush in a worn wooden box, then walked over and stirred the stew. "I have one more task before we eat. Would you like to accompany me?"

"Yes," Emma replied.

Golden rays wrapped by orange sank through a wash of purple as they stepped outside.

Marie sighed. "I so enjoy the long hours of the summer. There is something about the length of daylight that warms the soul."

Emma scanned the color-filled sky. Never had she considered the length of the hours of the day, much less how they affected her. Now, she took in the sweep of fields dotted with heather and a myriad of wildflowers she had paid little attention to before.

"'Tis beautiful here," Emma breathed.

"Aye, 'tis God's land."

The pad of running feet slapped behind them. "Mama, can I come?"

A warm, easy smile touched Marie's face. "Aye." She took her daughter's hand, cradling the small fingers within hers as she walked toward the west.

Emma followed. Upon a small rise, sheltered beneath the twisted limbs of a massive oak, she made out three small white crosses. Unsure, she halted at the outer edge.

The woman paused before the crosses. Sadness touched her face. "These are my children. One died during childbirth, the other two from fever. Gauwyn—" A smile touched her mouth. "He had the biggest smile. And his laugh could steal your heart." Her smile faltered.

Unsure what to say, to do, Emma walked to her side. "Do you come here often?"

"Aye. They are my children." Marie knelt beside the graves. One by one, she tugged the tiny weeds creeping from the soil, leaving the wildflowers blooming to sway before the carved crosses like a promise of hope.

Emotion stormed Emma as Marie tended to those she'd given birth to, only to watch them die.

As if sensing her grief, Joneta walked over, reached up.

Emma clasped the young girl's hand, her heart weeping inside. The image of holding Patrik's child flickered to mind. A child she'd cherish. But what if she lost their babe? If faced with such adversity, could she be as strong as Marie? Would she have chosen to go on? Though she lived a life filled with danger, the challenges she faced made no demands on her heart.

On shaky knees, she released the girl's hand, knelt beside the woman, pulled at a stubborn weed. "How can you come here and face such losses each day?"

"Losses? Aye, in a sense." Tenderness warmed Marie's face. "But for a time I was blessed with sharing their time on earth."

Emma focused on her task, humbled by this woman's faith. Memories of her youth in the orphanage tumbled past. Over the years, few workers had cared about the children within. Most often, those who ran the orphanage did so for the coin earned. In their eyes, the death of a child made one less mouth to feed, one less order given, one less child's cries to echo throughout the night.

"Here, Mommy."

Emma glanced over.

Joneta held out a sprig of heather to her mother.

She drew her daughter into her arms, gave her a huge hug. "And a gift you are as well."

The girl kissed her mother on her cheek, and then walked over to Emma. She brought her other hand from behind her back. A yellow flower lay within her palm. "For you."

Tears misted Emma's eyes as she stared at the delicate petals. To some it would seem a simple gift, but never had she received such a kind offering. "My thanks."

Ignorant of her emotional struggle, Joneta knelt before her, her wide green eyes filled with delight. "Hold it up to your neck."

Emma frowned. "Why?"

"It reflects yellow on your skin if you like the lads."

"And what if there is no reflection?" she asked, charmed.

A frown tied the girl's brow. "I am not sure, but I will ask my da. He is the one who told me about the flower."

Her father? Never had she believed a man would hold thoughts of such whimsy. Neither had she met such a caring family. Was this what a true marriage wrought?

"Do it," Joneta urged.

Her throat tight, Emma held up the flower to the curve of her throat.

"I knew it," the child squealed. "'Tis yellow I see."

Her mother shot Emma a wink. "I suppose she likes the man she came with."

Delight sparkled in the little girl's eyes. "Do you?"

"Yes," Emma said with a laugh. Emotion swamped her at thoughts of Patrik, at the enormity of what he made her feel. The lighthearted moment shattered.

Ignorant of Emma's panic, Marie chuckled. "As the lad is her husband, I would be agreeing."

"Here." The girl laid her doll within Emma's hands. Overwhelmed by thoughts of Patrik, of his growing importance in her life, she stared at the doll unseeing.

What exactly did she feel for Patrik? She could not feel love. She did not know how. Still, a hard pressure tightened in her chest, one she refused to study too deeply.

"You are not saying anything," the girl said.

Fingers trembling, Emma gripped the doll, focused on it. Carved wood made the sturdy body. A ball of undyed cloth made the face, the eyes two black stones, their centers carved and secured with a tiny piece of hemp. Long, brown hair lay secured to the head. Emma touched a length.

"'Tis from our horse," Joneta proclaimed.

Emma forced a smiled. "So it is. And a beautiful doll you have. Why did you share her with me?"

"You looked sad," the child replied. "I wanted to make you smile."

Her breath left her in a rush. She glanced at Marie, found the woman watching her with curiosity. "Here." Emma returned the doll. "She misses you."

A huge smile curved Joneta's mouth. "She does."

Somber, Emma watched as the girl skipped away, the child's mind already immersed in her next mind's inspiration.

"She is a thoughtful lass."

The mother's soft words had Emma glancing over. "Yes, as thoughtful as her mother. Your daughter is blessed to have you."

A blush touched Marie's weathered cheeks, but pride as well. "Come," she said, standing. "The stew should be about done. We need to set the table; the men will be hungry."

Joneta skipped at her side as Emma walked toward the solid cottage. What would it be like to live such a simple existence?

No, not simple, a life complicated by a man's desires and a country at war. But against the foils of life, they'd carved out a home, and against all odds, had found love.

Chapter 10

Patrik leaned back at the table, the easy conversation making him yearn for the times he'd supped with his brothers. A memory came of Duncan swapping Alexander's ale for wash water as they had broken their fast, and of how Alexander had spewed the lot. Without any hesitation as to who would pull such a prank, Alexander had rounded on Duncan, but the youngest brother had already bolted for the entry.

Alexander's bellows as he'd run after his brother still echoed in Patrik's mind. As did the howls of laughter of the knights within the great room, then Duncan's yell from outside as they'd heard a loud splash. Pride on his face, Alexander had hauled Duncan inside, the younger brother drenched from head to toe.

With his heart heavy, Patrik reached within his pocket, touched the tip of Duncan's arrow, which he'd kept from the campfire beneath the falls. They'd missed by hours.

Mayhap 'twas for the best. How would he have explained that he lived? And if he had, would Duncan have forgiven him for his attempted murder of his brother's wife? At the time, he'd allowed his actions to be ruled by hate, at the expense of those he loved. Too late he'd learned that life wasn't always so clear-cut, and even the noblest intentions could destroy.

"Would you like more to eat?" Marie asked as she held out a slice of bread.

"Nay," Patrik replied. "The fare was excellent. My thanks."

"I am full as well," Cristina added as the woman turned toward her.

"Never have I seen two people eat so little," Marie tsked.

Red brows rose in mirth as Fergus laughed. "See what the lass puts me through? Forever she is assuring me I should be eating more. The reason I spend so much time cutting logs."

A scowl carved Marie's expression, a soft censure filled with naught but love.

Cristina smiled, her face relaxed and golden within the hearth's glow, and Patrik savored her happiness. The color of the gown drew out the green in her eyes, and he appreciated the intricate braid woven in her hair.

"Will you go hunting on the morrow?" Marie asked her husband.

Shadows flickered across Fergus's face as his eyes met Patrik's. "Nae. Before dark, I caught sight of a band of English beyond the burn." He turned to his wife. "On the morrow, you and Joneta will stay near the house."

And he and Cristina would take heed in their travels as well, Patrik vowed.

The chair scraped as Fergus stood, then nodded to Patrik. "After your day of travel and with another ahead, you and your wife will be wanting sleep."

Wife? Patrik opened his mouth to correct the man, but the words fell away. Stunned by how right the crofter's words sounded, he stared at the woman who had made him feel more than any other lass.

Joneta snuggled her doll at her side, and Cristina smiled, her simple gesture stealing Patrik's breath. What would it be like to spend each evening with her, to share the strife of the day, or after finishing the chores, to take her to their bed?

The image of her round with his child whispered through his mind, the glow upon her face, the bond formed between them that none could break.

"The loft is where you will be sleeping," Fergus said, fracturing his thoughts.

Curious as to how Cristina would reply to the Scot's offer, Patrik ignored her flustered expression.

At Patrik's silence, heat burned Emma's cheeks. Why did he not decline the generous offer? They were not wed.

Uneasy, she arched a brow at Patrik, and he gave her a warm smile. The braggart. Fine then. Emma shook her head at the burly Scot. "We will not take your bed."

"You must," Fergus said. "We would be taking offence if you did not accept our offer."

Why did Patrik not say something? Emma sent him another panicked look. "We—"

"Would be thankful," Patrik finished.

Fergus nodded, then strode to the door and turned. "I will see to the sheep before I head myself to bed." The door settled behind him with a solid thunk.

Marie sent Emma a knowing smile. Humming, she rose and began clearing the table.

Emma leaned closer to Patrik. "What are you thinking?" she whispered. "We cannot take their bed."

Patrik stood. "I will be helping your husband." With a wink, he headed out the door.

God in heaven. Emma gathered the last trencher. With her hands as full as her thoughts of the oncoming night, she followed the woman outside.

Shame filled her. However wrong it might be, she would not admit the truth either. If she did, she would lose her one last precious night with Patrik.

Candlelight stroked Cristina's body, guided him as Patrik slowly took her over the edge. He covered her mouth and claimed her every moan, savoring her each shudder as she rode out her release. Then he drove hard and found his own. Bodies merged, he rolled over, drew her to his side and pressed a soft kiss upon her mouth.

"You are amazing," he whispered, then kissed along the curve of her jaw.

"And you," she whispered on a half groan, "are insatiable."

He nipped along the curve of her breast. "Only with you."

Beneath the flicker of flame, the shimmer of pleasure in her eyes faded to worry.

The playfulness of the moment fell away. Patrik pushed back the wisps of hair shielding her face. "What is wrong?"

"'Tis foolish."

"If it places sadness within your eyes, it is not."

Cristina's gaze softened, but she remained silent.

He stroked his thumb along her cheek. "Tell me."

"Did you see the three crosses upon the hill?"

"Aye."

"Each is for a babe lost."

He stroked her cheek. "'Tis tragic indeed, but sadly common, a reality of the life we live."

"But they have graves," she whispered, her words rough.

"They do," he agreed, confused by her words.

"And a mother, a mother who loved them very much." Tears misted in her eyes. "Do you not see? Never will they be forgotten. In an orphanage, there is no family." Her breath shuddered. "And within the cold walls, when children die they are forgotten, discarded as if trash."

And he understood. Given her youth, the idea of someone caring about a lost child was foreign, but the concept moved her. All her life, she'd been alone, her marriage but a farce, her husband a man who'd taken advantage of a desperate lass. Never had she truly been loved.

Patrik claimed her mouth in a soft kiss, aching, wishing he could give her more.

Cristina broke away, questions haunting her eyes. "Why did you not tell Fergus we are not wed?"

He stroked her silky skin. "'Tis selfish, but I wanted

to make love with you in a bed. On the morrow, we will reach my destination. There we will part." Silence stretched between them. He pulled the last length of hair from her braid, splayed it across the feather pillow. "Do you forgive me for allowing them to believe that lie?"

A slash of red touched her cheeks. "I should not."

Patrik arched a brow. "Neither did I hear you tell them the truth. Why is that?"

"It is unimportant."

He chuckled. "Lass, it would seem you are as guilty as I."

"It is not funny."

"Nae," he said, reaching down to slide his finger through her slick warmth. "It is far from a matter of jest." At her soft moan, he teased her, stroked her until her body shuddered. "I cannot again so soon," she gasped as he increased the pace. With pleasure, he proved her wrong.

Emma shifted, and bumped against Patrik. In the darkness, broken only by the near-gutted candle, she snuggled against his muscled warmth and embraced the memories of how they'd made love throughout the night. Too easily she'd grown used to his being at her side, to his protection, to the simple discussions that were anything but.

How easy would it be to give in, to ache each day for the night, to share with Patrik her every wish, her every dream, and her every desire? She stilled.

God in heaven, she loved him.

Her breath left her in a rush, the enormity of her realization stealing her every thought. Emma fought the panic, and more shocking, found need, a desperate ache that only Patrik could fill.

Tears welled up as she stared at a man who'd become too important, a man who should be her enemy, but against all odds had stolen her heart.

Except, he didn't love her. Regret scraped her throat. At least one of them had sense. But he cared for her, dangerously so. No, she wouldn't linger on his feelings for her, allow her mind to imagine a future between them, or the thought of children. But, for the first time in her life she wanted to.

Her heart aching with what never could be, Emma peered through a slit in the wall to the outside. Darkness clung to the sky, but hints of purple announced the oncoming day.

Regardless of what she wanted, this wasn't her life, 'twas naught but a temporary part played.

One now ended.

Sir Cressingham awaited her delivery of the writ along with the information she'd gathered. However much betraying Patrik hurt, if she did not bring the Scottish treasurer what she'd promised, he would brand her a criminal and she would live the rest of her life on the run.

Emma withdrew, embracing the numbness, doubting she would ever feel whole again. With care, she searched for the leather-bound document amongst the heap of clothes at his side.

"Mmmm."

She froze.

Patrik shifted, his arm reaching to where she'd lain moments before.

Her heart tore. Even in his sleep, he sought her.

Long seconds passed. A frown worked his face; then his body relaxed and he again began to snore.

With the oncoming dawn, his mind was beginning to wake. She must hurry. Pulse racing, Emma felt along the folds of his clothes.

A soft bump against Patrik's thigh had him frowning. The haze in his mind began to clear. Cristina. Images of her body as he'd claimed her poured through him like warmed oil, of her exploration, of how she'd blossomed beneath his touch. He smiled. Aye, soon they'd leave, but he'd make love with her one last time.

He shoved the remnants of sleep aside and opened his eyes. Outlined by the candle flame, Cristina knelt beside his hip. God's teeth, the lass would be the death of him, but aye, he'd die a happy man.

Her hand reached out.

His body hardened, ached for her touch, for the immense pleasure to come.

Instead, she reached past him and lifted his trews.

What in Hades? Patrik came fully alert.

With methodical thoroughness, she searched his garb. What was she looking for? He remembered her interest in the writ when it had fallen out of his pocket along the path.

Darkness edged his gut. "Cristina."

She jumped, her gasp that of the guilty caught. With a nervous laugh, she settled back upon her knees. "I did not know you were awake."

Cold silence settled between them, at odds with his

erotic thoughts of moments before. "What were you searching for?"

"A tie to secure my hair."

A lie, one betrayed by the nervousness in her voice. "I want the truth."

"The truth?" she repeated, hurt and surprise etched upon her face. "I told you." She hesitated. "Patrik, what is wrong? You are not making any sense."

"On that we agree," he replied, and prayed his suspicions were false.

"Mommy," Joneta's voice echoed from below, "I think they are awake."

"'Tis early and you will not be waking them," Marie said in a low voice.

"But the sun is coming up."

"Shhh," her mother replied.

"Get dressed," Patrik whispered to Cristina, his voice gruff. "We must leave."

"No, wait." She shuffled beneath his garb, then lifted a thin strip of leather from beneath a leg of his trews. "Here, I found it." In the meager light, wariness creased her face. "I am not sure what is going on, but I am innocent of whatever it is you think I have done."

He stared at the simple tie, grabbed his braies and dragged them on.

"Patrik? Please, you are scaring me."

Bedamned to this entire situation! Annoyed with himself, he grabbed his trews. Her claim rang true. After the incredible love they'd made through the night, why had he assumed the worst? And why did he still feel as if something was amiss? Nevertheless, the lass deserved an apology.

He reached out, thankful when she came into his arms. Her body trembled against his, and his guilt rose. He pressed a kiss upon her brow.

"Sorry I am, lass. I am on edge." He combed his fingers through her hair. "This day I will reach my destination."

She drew back. "That should please you, not cause you upset."

"If only it was that simple."

"I do not understand."

Neither could he explain. To tell her what she made him feel would only make the parting more difficult. "Once we arrive, I will ensure you are taken to wherever you wish." He paused, his heart heavy. "I doubt we will see each other after."

"I hear them talking again, Mommy."

"Outside with you," Marie whispered. "Pick me some fresh flowers."

After a dramatic sigh, the creek of the door echoed. Except for the soft steps of Marie, silence fell below.

Patrik stroked his fingers through Cristina's hair and gave her a tight smile. "If only we had such problems as the little lass."

She nodded, her gaze cautious.

He fisted his tunic in his hands. "As much as I long to stay, it is time we depart."

"You are not angry at me?" She hesitated. "I should have asked before I searched through your clothes."

"Nay, there is much on my mind." However much he wished to find peace, a niggling of doubt remained.

"I shall miss you," she said.

The anguish in her voice matched his own. He drew

her to him for a long kiss, savoring her softness, the taste uniquely hers. "I will miss you greatly as well." More than he could ever admit. He nuzzled her neck, drew the tip of her breast into his mouth and tasted her one last time. On a groan he set her aside. "Get dressed, lass."

Devilment glittered in her eyes as with seductive slowness, she lifted her gown, held it beneath her breasts, framing what he'd tasted, savored throughout the night.

He clenched his teeth. "Hurry, lass."

If possible, her movements slowed, the mischief in her eyes assuring him she was well aware of her effect upon him. She drew on the gown and left the ties hanging loose, her body half shielded, half exposed to his view.

Bedamned! Hard as a rock and aching with need, he caught her and tossed her beneath him.

As he pressed his body atop hers, a chuckle escaped her. "What are you doing?"

"You tease," he whispered.

"I tease you not," she whispered.

As if her claim or the yearning in her voice bloody helped? He gave her a solid kiss, wanting to rip away her gown and drive deep. Through sheer effort, he restrained himself.

"On with you," Patrik growled as he rolled free and tugged on his tunic, aware he'd be hard all day with thoughts of her.

With a wistful smile, she finished donning her gown. Moments later, his blood still pounding hot, Patrik descended the ladder. Cristina's every movement, her every shift above him drove him insane.

"You said last night you would leave at first light," Marie added after they'd reached the dirt floor and had exchanged good mornings. She set a bundle wrapped in cloth on the table. "It is dried meat and bread for your travel."

"My thanks," Patrik said.

"Will you be breaking your fast with us before you go?" Marie asked.

"Nae," Patrik replied. "But 'tis thankful we are for everything you and your husband have done."

Heart pounding, Emma placed her hand within Patrik's. "I add my thanks as well."

"If you both are ever this way again," Marie said, "our door is always open."

"Aye," Fergus added as he stepped to his wife's side.

"That is very kind of you," Emma said.

"If you would," Marie asked, "please tell Joneta good-bye. 'Twould break her heart if you left without seeing her."

Unbidden, tears burned Emma's eyes. "Of course."

Marie smiled. "The lass has a way about her that steals your heart."

"She does. I will miss her." Emma steadied herself, shaken to find her words true. Throughout her life she'd made sure she never cared, but since meeting Patrik, all her barriers lay crumbled. After she left, could she ever rebuild her emotional walls?

Overwhelmed by emotion, unsure of anything, Emma stepped outside and found the sun creeping over the horizon. A light coat of dew clung to the grass.

Purple light glinted off each blade, giving the field a magical glow, the air fresh and cool.

Against the wisps of sun peering through the leaves, she caught sight of Joneta sitting upon the hill, near the trees shielding the crosses.

Heart aching, she glanced at Patrik. "I will be but a moment."

"We must hurry."

"I know. I will not be long."

The rich scent of earth filled her each breath as she walked through the sway of moisture-laden grass, the lush blades streaking moist trails against the hem of her gown.

Emma cast a covert look at Patrik. Though he'd apologized to her, had responded to her teasing, she'd come to understand he thought things through long and hard. He'd mull over his suspicions, allow them to stew in his mind.

Thank God she'd hidden the leather tie within her hand, then had withdrawn it as if it was just found. She could not linger further. Somehow, in the next few hours she must take the writ and escape.

Guilt overwhelmed Emma. After making love to Patrik, could she steal it? Did she have any other choice? If she failed to secure the writ, she would be living on the run and in fear of her life.

The ground curved up. As Emma neared the trees, the soft hum of the child reached her, and a smile touched her mouth.

Her head bent in concentration, Joneta held several dandelions as she continued to pick more, their sturdy stems clasped within her hand, the doll dangling from beneath her other arm.

An image Emma would cherish forever. She halted several paces away. "Joneta."

The little girl turned. Happiness blanketed her face. She jumped up, the flowers flopping in her hand. "Look what I picked!"

"I see." She met the child halfway and knelt before her. "They are beautiful."

Her smile widened as she held them out. "They are a surprise for you!"

Emma struggled to keep from breaking down as she drew the girl into a hug. "My thanks. Never shall I forget you."

Joneta stiffened in her arms.

Confused, she leaned back, surprised by the girl's frown. "What is wrong?"

"What is that?"

She turned. A flash of light glinted across the field along the dark shadows of the trees. Emma stilled. God in heaven, they were not shadows, but knights. From the standard, English.

Heart pounding, she stood, glancing to where Patrik awaited her near the crofter's hut. The lower ground prevented him from seeing the threat. If she yelled, she would alert the knights they'd been seen.

"Do you know what that is?" Joneta asked naively.

Trembling, Emma took the girl's hand. "Let us show your mother the beautiful flowers," she said, keeping her voice steady. "She will love them. We must hurry before they wilt." She started forward at a brisk pace. Please God, let them reach the crofter's hut before the English attacked!

"Look over there," the little girl said as they started down the hill, "it looks like knights."

"So it does." She kept her voice calm, kept moving. "We must tell your father."

Joneta skipped at her side. "Do you think they are nice men?"

The thrum of hooves sounded from across the field.

The knights were heading for the crofter's hut! "Patrik!"

He spun toward her.

"English knights!" Emma pointed. "Across the field!"

Patrik withdrew his sword, waved her back. "Take Joneta and hide!" He sprinted toward the hut.

"Come." Fear whipping through her, Emma led Joneta back up the hill toward the wall of trees.

The pounding of hooves battering the earth grew.

The little girl began to cry. "I want to go home."

At this speed, they would never make it to the forest. Emma caught Joneta by the shoulders. "We must hide. Your parents would want that. Do you understand?"

Tears streaked the child's face, but she nodded.

"Good, now run!" The thunder of hooves increased, drowning out the slam of her heart against her chest. She glanced back. Flames shot from the thatched roof. The bastards had set the hut on fire! Why? Fergus and Marie had done nothing to them in the past but given them food and water.

She made out Patrik and Fergus taking cover behind a wagon. Where was Marie?

The flames on the roof grew, arching into the sky as more crawled down the home's sides.

Fury built atop fear as Emma pushed forward. The line of trees rose before them. If they made it to the woods, she could hide Joneta.

The contingent closed in on the hut. She scanned the knights. Twenty men. Patrik and Fergus were vastly outnumbered.

Wet blades of grass slapped against their feet. "Keep running," Emma urged.

"My legs hurt."

"I know."

The knights in the field below widened their line and guided their horses into a wide arc.

They were forming a maneuver to attack!

A shout echoed across the field. Two knights were pointing at her and Joneta.

God in heaven, they'd been seen!

The two men broke from the line and galloped toward them.

"Hang on!" Emma lifted the girl and ran.

Hooves pounded behind them. An arrow streaked by, drove into the soil a pace away.

Joneta screamed.

Another arrow flashed past, lodged in a nearby tree.

They weren't going to make it! Emma set the child down. "Run. Hide deep in the woods. Whatever happens, do not look back!"

Tears streaked the child's face. "I do not want to leave you."

"Go!" At her command, the girl stumbled back. "Hurry!"

Joneta turned and fled, the legs of her doll bouncing beneath her arm.

Furious, Emma reached for her knife as another arrow hissed by. She might die, but damn them, she would hold the knights off until Joneta hid.

Joneta's scream had her whirling.

As if in slow motion, the young girl slammed against the ground. Her gown flew into the air, then it crumpled upon the still form.

"Joneta!" Emma ran to her.

The child lay still.

A scream caught in her throat as Emma stumbled to a halt. God, no! From the folds of cloth covering the girl's body rose the shaft of an arrow.

Chapter 11

Cristina's scream ripped through the air.

Heart pounding, Patrik whirled. He searched the knoll where the two knights who had broken off from the contingent had ridden—straight toward Cristina and Joneta.

The knoll lay bare.

Were they dead? After witnessing Cristina's skill with a blade, he clung to the belief they lived. He glanced toward the tufts of sod that covered a hide-out belowground where Marie lay. If only time had allowed Cristina and the child to run back.

The rumble of hooves slammed against earth as the main contingent closed on them.

He peered through the weathered wood slats, cursed. The wagon he and Fergus hid behind would buy them seconds at best.

A flaming arrow shot past, sank into the crofter's hut. Dark smoke belched around them. The thatched roof, which had been set ablaze moments ago, now shuddered beneath the greedy flames. Sparks rained through the air, the stench of soot and growing heat suffocating.

Several more arrows whipped by.

Against the swell of smoke and the screams of the knights, Patrik readied his sword. "When they are within two lengths, I will take one with a dagger, then use my sword."

Fergus nodded. "As I."

That accounted for four of eighteen. Nae, he'd not think about the odds. If he died, 'twould be slaying the bastards.

Hooves pounded the turf like belches of thunder. The line of English knights neared.

"Ready?" Patrik called.

Fergus lifted his dagger. "Aye."

An arrow lodged a handsbreadth from Patrik. Another drove into the wagon. Shadows of the approaching men flickered across the slats.

"Now!" His weapons held tight, Patrik rolled away from the wagon. He sprang to his feet, aimed, then threw.

The closest knight tumbled from his horse.

With a war cry, Patrik angled his sword, charged.

Another knight, but paces away, whirled his mount.

Patrik lunged forward, swung. Steel echoed with a violent scrape. He angled his blade, drove it through the man's heart.

Shock rippled across the man's face. On a gasp, he tumbled from his mount.

Wild-eyed, the knight's horse reared.

Patrik caught the reins, swung onto its back, reined hard to face his next aggressor. Pain seared his back. He slammed against the mount's withers. Another blade from behind sliced into his left shoulder and his vision began to blur.

A knight rammed his horse, shoved his boot into Patrik's face.

Pain shattered Patrik as he tumbled off his mount, slammed against the ground. Body aching, he reached for his sword.

A harsh grin carved his latest enemy's face as he dismounted several paces away. The knight dropped his reins, raised a hand to the others who had approached.

"Finish off the other Scot," the knight ordered. "I will dispatch this wastrel."

The arrogant bastard! With a war cry, Patrik wiped away the blood smearing his vision and shoved to his feet. His body shuddered.

"Away with you, you dung-fouled cur," Fergus yelled at the knights attacking him. Steel scraped. A grunt sounded.

From the corner of his eye, Patrik caught a knight stumble back, drop. Another man less. He focused on his attacker.

The Englishman charged.

Patrik met his assailant's blade, twisted his sword. Before the man could break away, he shoved the knight back.

Fury darkened the warrior's expression as he regained his balance. The knight surged forward, his blows merciless.

Patrik met his swings, each impact taking its toll upon his already exhausted body. Heat from the burning building scorched his back, the smoke clogged his throat. At the next assault, he deflected the man's blow—barely.

Another drip of blood smeared his vision.

Bedamned, he'd not give in. Muscles screamed as he angled his blade toward the knight, swung. Honed steel wedged against bone.

The other man's face shifted from pain to fury. Nostrils flared as he again lifted his blade.

A horn sounded across the field.

The knight glanced to the west.

Patrik followed his gaze. Stilled. Saint's breath, another contingent rode across the field.

The English knight cursed.

Through his blurred vision, Patrik made out the Earl of Grey's standard. 'Twas Seathan, his brother!

"To arms!" the knight before him roared. The knight shot Patrik a furious look. "I will be back to finish your sorry arse." He bolted to his horse, swung up and kicked his mount to join his men, who were forming a line.

Patrik stumbled after him.

"Charge!" the English knight ordered. Dirt flew as he surged forward.

The thunder of hooves of the attacking rebels grew to an ear-thrumming barrage. At the first clash of steel, Patrik turned. He spotted Fergus lying on the ground and staggered over.

"'Tis rebels coming," Patrik said.

His body a mass of cuts and bruises, Fergus turned to where Marie hid. The turf lay untouched. "Thank God." Worry sagged his face as he scanned the knoll. "Joneta?"

"I will find her." Patrik prayed she, as well as Cristina, lived. He nodded. "Go to your wife."

The Scot started to stand, collapsed.

Patrik caught Fergus, his battered muscles rebelling at the extra weight.

On shaky legs, the Scot pushed himself free. He stood, barely. "Find Joneta. I—" Fergus muttered a curse, his haggard face roughened as if aged ten more summers. "—I must know."

"Aye," Patrik replied, understanding the other mans' fear. Even with Cristina's skill, well he knew the odds of finding either of them alive.

In the field echoed the familiar scream of horses, clash of blades and men's curses. The lust for battle sang on his tongue, the urge to run into the melee, to drive his blade into another English bastard's heart.

But if he tried, having lost too much blood and barely able to stand, he might well bleed to death before he ever reached the fighting. However much Patrik wanted to join the MacGruders, in his weakened state, he'd be more a hindrance to his brothers than a help.

And seeing a man alive they believed dead would give them pause. In the thick of battle, hesitation invited death. He blew out a breath. Seathan and his men outnumbered the English. His meeting with his brothers would come soon enough.

Patrik focused on the knoll. He must find Cristina and the girl.

Dizzy, exhausted, and his muscles rebelling with each step, he forced himself up the hill. Halfway up, the grass before him blurred. Gasping for breath he halted, his shoulder sticky with blood, the headstones in the distance a dark omen. He clenched his teeth and shoved forward.

Atop the hill, through the roll of grass, a flicker of clothing caught his attention. No, not clothing, but a body.

Cristina!

He ran, ignoring the pain, the jab of rock into his boots, how each uneven mound of dirt threatened to take him down. The clash of battle in his wake melded with the pounding of his blood, the scream of steel rang in cadence with his fears.

Several paces away, through the smear of blood and sweat, he made out English colors. Chest heaving, he stumbled to a halt. 'Twas one of the two knights that had ridden toward Cristina. The dagger she carried was embedded in his throat. He glanced down. The man's sword was gone!

Through hazed vision, he scanned the grass and brush lining the edge of the forest.

Nothing.

Bedamned. Where was the other knight? Had he rejoined the others, or, furious she'd taken his comrade's life, had he chased her down and killed her? Nae, she'd taken the dead knight's sword.

A chance they lived existed.

Heart pounding, Patrik pushed forward.

Near the edge of the trees, red stained a rock.

No! Patrik stumbled forward.

Over the top of a fallen tree lay another body.

Throat tight, he rounded the weathered stump. Saint's

breath, 'twas the second knight, the other man's sword embedded in his chest.

Tears of relief burned his eyes. His body shook, and he clasped a twisted root angling up, fought for balance as he absorbed the enormity of Cristina's single-handed act.

Distant screams merged with the clang of steel. A Scottish war cry tore the air.

Heart pounding, Patrik turned. Seathan's men were making quick work of the English. Thank God. Now to find Cristina and Joneta.

Body aching, he wove forward. How far had they gone? Was either injured? Please let the impossible have happened, that neither be harmed.

Despite the blur of pain, adrenaline kept him moving. The forest rose up before him. He stumbled into the shadows, fighting to stay conscious.

"Cristina!" His feeble call echoed into the woods as if a poor jest against the battle raging beyond. "Cristina!"

Shadows clung to him as he entered the forest, the sodden leaves smearing the drips of blood staining his tunic.

"Retreat!" someone shouted in the distance.

Patrik turned. Through the breaks in the trees, he caught flickers of the English knights fleeing toward the opposite side of the field.

A war cry rose as several of Seathan's knights gave chase, the rebels fading into the sea of green. The remainder of Seathan's contingent cantered toward the burning home where Patrik had left Fergus to aid his wife. His brother would ensure they were well tended.

Patrik turned, shoved away a limb.

A child's whimper echoed ahead.

He pushed forward. "Cristina?"

"Patrik?"

The relief in her voice soothed his ragged emotions. He stumbled forward.

From behind a thicket, she stood, Joneta in her arms, an arrow shaft extending from the folds of the child's clothing.

God no! "Joneta?"

"Is fine." With the child cradled against her, Cristina walked from the brush, tears streaking through the grime and smear of blood upon her cheeks. "When I first saw her, I-I thought the same. The arrow hit the doll's wooden chest." A weak smile wobbled on her lips. "Joneta would not let her go."

"Mama," the child whimpered.

Cristina pressed a kiss upon the girl's brow. "'Tis fine." She sent Patrik a questioning glance, her fear easy to read.

He nodded. "They are alive."

"Thank God. I—" Her face paled. "You are hurt."

"A wee bit."

She shot him a scowl. "'Tis more than a bit. I will tend to you once we return to the cottage."

"It is gone."

The stark emptiness of Patrik's words impaled Emma. Heartsick, she stared through the trees, where smoke swirled in heartless abandon as flames devoured this family's home. Despite war and tragedy, happiness had bloomed there.

Until now.

All her life she'd known emptiness and hurt; she'd

learned to bury her emotions deep, to forbid herself to feel or care. But Patrik had changed that. Now, 'twould seem the storm of emotions he'd unleashed would consume her, strip away her well-built defenses.

Emma clutched the child tight. The man she loved was wounded and bleeding, a family destroyed. Her anger grew. Fergus and Marie had given the English naught but water and food. Their payment, destruction of their home.

Tears burned her eyes, but she pushed them away. This was war. What the English delivered this day but a token of what her betrayal of Patrik would bring. At thoughts of her vow to Sir Cressingham, nausea swirled in her gut.

Joneta buried her face against Emma's neck, the child's tears hot against her skin. "I want Mama."

"I know." At least the girl's parents lived. Joneta didn't yet understand that family was the greatest gift, a treasure neither time nor money could buy. Emma knelt and set the girl before her on a moss-coated rock. In a deft move, she removed the arrow from the doll and handed it back to the child. "We will take you to—"

The thrum of hooves rumbled. Branches cracked.

Emma looked back. She swept Joneta into her arms. "More knights!"

Patrik took in the oncoming riders. His body relaxed. "'Tis the rebels. We are safe." But as the riders closed on them, his face paled.

If they were safe, then what was wrong? "Patrik?"

"Say naught," he whispered.

On edge, Emma set the child down. "Joneta, go behind the tree. Hide there until I tell you to come out."

"Nae," Patrik said, pain edging his voice, "she is—" He blanched, pressed his shoulder. "—in no danger."

From the conviction on his face, it was a fact he believed. So why did she detect a hint of dread? Uneasy, Emma lifted Joneta into her arms.

"Do you know them?" she asked, keeping her voice calm for the sake of the child.

A muscle worked in his jaw.

Hoofbeats grew closer.

Patrik wove, stumbled back into the shadows and caught himself on a branch.

"Patrik—"

"I am fine."

He wasn't, damn him. Emma turned.

Leaves scraped as a massive knight wove through the stand of trees upon a black steed. He drew to a halt. Piercing green eyes riveted upon the child in her arms, then shifted to Emma.

"We were told you would be here," the man stated, "with a girl."

The power of his gaze shook her; he possessed an aura of complete authority. Black hair framed the harsh lines of his face, tumbled over well-muscled shoulders. But the professional in her focused on his sword, exquisite in its simplicity, the understated design one crafted by a master.

Emma glanced toward his shield; its design was a blue canton, along with a sword bendways on its point and supporting an imperial crown proper. The coat of arms of the Earl of MacGruder. A shiver ran through her. Was this the noble Patrik had recognized? Did he know the MacGruders? Were they friends? Unsure of anything, she nodded.

Sticks cracked as another warrior, his hair as black as the first man's, rode up and halted to the left of the formidable knight. A menacing scar ran across his left cheek. Eyes as hard as they were fierce fell upon her, then shifted to the noble at his side.

"I see you have found the lass and child," the second man said.

"Did you find them?" another man called, his burr a touch lyrical. A third knight rode into view, his blond hair streaked with mud, and his face etched with sweat, blood, and confidence. His steed snorted as he drew to a halt on the right of the noble.

Eyes as dark as the devil's own watched her. "Aye," the noble replied.

Emma stepped forward. "The child is fine," she said, praying Patrik was indeed correct to give these men his trust. "But she is not the one needing your help."

The fierce knights glanced toward her side, frowned. "Whoever is hidden beyond, step forward."

Surprised by his request, she turned, then understood. Where Patrik stood, he was partially shielded by the trees.

"Lass, who hides beyond?" the blond-haired man asked, his deep burr firm but soothing.

She opened her mouth to speak, but Patrik shook his head. As he staggered forward, Emma's heart ached. The stubborn proud man, he had no business walking.

On shaky legs, Patrik strode into the clearing.

"By God's eyes," one of the knights gasped.

Confused, Emma turned.

The noble stared at him in disbelief. "Patrik?"

A combination of joy and disbelief swept the blond-haired man's face. "You are"—he shook his head—"you are alive."

Relief flickered upon the face of the knight with the scar, followed by anger. "By God's eyes!" He jumped from his mount.

Joneta screamed.

The rebel tackled Patrik.

"Stop it," Emma yelled.

The huge knight's fist connected with Patrik's already swollen face.

Patrik's head jerked back, his eyes dark with pain.

The warrior drove his fist again into Patrik's cheek.

Fear tore through Emma. "Stop it!"

As the fierce knight drew his fist back for yet another swing, Emma set Joneta on the ground.

Heedless of the man's size, of the two other knights who were dismounting, she dove onto the warrior's back, wrapped her arm around his neck. "Get off of him!" She tightened her grip and was rewarded by his gasp.

The black-haired man roared as he straightened. "Bedamned!" He tried to shake her off.

She held tight. "Leave Patrik be!"

"Get the cursed lass off of me!" the black-haired warrior boomed.

Hands, strong but gentle, clasped her arms.

Emma fought to break free. "He will kill Patrik!" she yelled as the two other men hauled her back.

The dark-haired man with the scar across his left cheek stood, cast a disgusted look at Patrik. "I did not kill him, I would not be so lucky. Vermin somehow manage to survive."

The fury of his words terrified Emma. She struggled against the men's hold. None of this was making any sense. "Patrik said you would help us."

"Aye," the black-haired man replied, his face raw with violence. "You. The lass." He glared at where Patrik lay. "Him, I have far from made a decision about."

"Why?" Emma asked, unsure of anything.

On a groan, Patrik arched a swollen brow. Pain-filled eyes watched her. "Because," he rasped, "they believed me dead."

Chapter 12

Emma stared in disbelief at Patrik, who lay sprawled on the ground. "They believed you dead?"

"Aye," Patrik rasped, "a fate I deserved."

Her entire body quivering, she glanced at the massive warrior looming over Patrik. A muscle jumped beneath the scar carved across the knight's left cheek. His mistaken belief that Patrik had died mattered not to her. He was severely injured and had lost too much blood. Whoever this knight was, he would not touch Patrik again.

Furious, she struggled to break free. "One would think men Patrik believed would help us would be pleased to find out that he lives."

Firm hands held her tight.

"Let me go!" she demanded.

The warrior above Patrik turned. Cobalt eyes held hers, narrowed with evaluation. He nodded.

Without hesitation, the men's strong grip loosened.

Free, she rushed to Patrik's side and knelt. Fresh bruises lay atop those darkening to an ugly purple. She glared at the fierce knight whose gaze held hers without apology. "Touch him again and I will kill you."

Surprise flickered upon the warrior's face; then shrewd eyes studied her, his mouth tightening another degree.

Patrik gave a rough cough, shoved himself up on his elbows, trembled. "Alexander, the lass who is threatening to kill you is Mistress Cristina."

The intimidating knight's eyes cut to Patrik. His nostrils flared. "How can you be alive? I saw you die!"

A shiver cut through Emma as she tended to Patrik's shoulder. "How could he have watched you die?"

Regret settled on Patrik's bloodied face. He scanned the men before him. "Th-The lass knows nothing."

Nothing? She tore a strip from her gown, secured it atop a deep wound. What in God's name was going on? "If you have not noticed," Emma said, amazed at the control of her voice, "Patrik is seriously injured. With so much blood lost, I am unsure how he still breathes."

The knight introduced as Alexander offered little compassion.

Anger flared within her at the knight's silence. "I know you not but—"

"Brothers," Patrik whispered. "They are my brothers."

"Brothers?" Her hands stilled upon another torn strip of her gown. His name was Patrik Cleary, not Mac-Gruder. Sir Cressingham had told her so, as had Patrik when they'd first met. How could they be brothers?

Fighting for calm, she noted a resemblance between the three newcomers, but little to Patrik. But, with no man disagreeing, it must be true.

God in heaven! The MacGruders were known, feared by the English. And Patrik was their brother?

"My full name," Patrik said, "is Patrik Cleary Mac-Gruder. After th-they believed me dead, I no longer used the surname MacGruder."

"The arrow you found in the cave?" she asked.

"'Tis Duncan's," Patrik replied.

The blond-headed man gave her a curt nod.

"Brothers?" The fierce knight grunted. "He deserves not the claim."

Emma narrowed her eyes at the fierce warrior, her shock smothered by anger, regardless of his name. "He should not talk."

"He is lucky talk is all he receives," the formidable knight stated.

"Cristina, me-meet Sir Alexander," Patrik whispered.

The black-haired man's hard eyes fixed on her. He nodded.

The noble strode forward, his green eyes clear, their intensity unnerving. "Seathan MacGruder, Earl of Grey." He nodded at Patrik. "Aye, you have the right of it; he should not be speaking."

Words failed her. God in heaven! This powerful Scottish lord and personal advisor to William Wallace, a man as well respected as feared, was Patrik's brother? Aside from those who led the rebellion, only two men had ever attained such a revered status, *Wulfe* and *Dubh Duer*.

Except *Wulfe* and *Dubh Duer* were men who shielded their identity behind the fable of a name. From Sir Cressingham she knew Patrik was *Dubh Duer*. Whispers claimed *Wulfe* was an English lord who had joined the Rebel cause.

Heart pounding, Emma fought for calm, focused her attention on cleaning, then covering yet another of Patrik's wounds. Had any of the men recognized her from one of her previous missions into Scotland? In her outrage, had her English accent slipped out? No, if his brothers had any suspicions, with their brutal frankness, they would have confronted her by now.

She took a calming breath, moved on to Patrik's next injury. They knew not that she worked for Sir Cressingham.

Sir Cressingham.

Her vow to the treasurer of the English administration seemed a blur. Her plan to gain Patrik's confidence, discover who within King Edward's circle betrayed him, take the writ, slip away, and erase Patrik from her mind had sorely gone awry.

Emotion swelled in her throat. But then, she'd not known love.

In love with a Scot. In love with the man she was paid to betray. Could she indeed follow through on her mission? If not, what of Sir Cressingham's fury? What of the men who he would pay to hunt her down? But, if she did, what of Patrik's outrage when he learned the truth?

Weariness poured through her. She needed to calm down, to think of a strategy, her strength in the past. After battling the two English knights to save Joneta, then finding Patrik seriously wounded, her thoughts were running wild.

"Lass," Lord Grey said, his deep burr ripe with concern. "Are you well?"

Heat stroked Emma's face. She knotted the last strip of cloth. "Well, but exhausted." Far from the truth, but tiredness indeed fed the nightmares strangling her mind. Her limbs shaking, she stood, gave a brief curtsy. "My lord." A tugging at her gown had her glancing down.

Arms raised, the child's terrified eyes met hers.

"Oh, Joneta." Emma lifted the girl into her arms. On a cry, the child pressed her head against the curve of her neck and hid her face. Heart aching, she stroked the girl's curly locks. Emma met the noble's gaze. "She is afraid and needs to be with her parents."

Lord Grey nodded. "Her mother is frantic to see the lass as well."

Sir Duncan stepped forward. "They can ride with me."

"Nae, you will be carrying Patrik," Sir Alexander stated. "They will ride with me."

Emma shot the arrogant Scot a cold look. "My thanks, Sir Alexander, but given a choice of riding with you, I would rather walk."

Amusement flickered on Sir Duncan's face, and Sir Alexander's expression darkened. The ominous Scot glared at where Patrik lay, then his gaze slid to her. "'Twould seem he has found a woman who deserves him."

"I am not *his woman*." She angled her jaw. "Patrik saved my life when several English knights were about to rape me."

Sir Alexander's face paled. "Forgive me. 'Twould seem I have allowed anger to guide my words."

Flustered by his apology, she shook her head, clung to her first coherent thought. "You did not know."

"Enough." Lord Grey walked over, knelt before his brother. "We will talk more once Patrik is cared for." He slung Patrik over his shoulder, stood, then strode to his steed.

Emma accompanied Sir Duncan to his mount with Joneta in her arms. At least she rode with the gentler man.

Gentle?

Far from it. Though his voice rumbled with mind-soothing ease, his body was honed for war. She scanned the three warriors. Each man alone was a threat, but together they were a force few could overcome.

And they were Patrik's brothers.

Each moment in these men's company invited danger. But she wished to remain at Patrik's side to ensure he lived.

Look at her acting like a love-struck fool. Where was the mercenary who had plotted to meet Patrik, who had set up a false rape with English knights to gain the rebel's trust? A shudder rippled through her. She existed, but the woman of before lay buried beneath emotions that had no place in her life.

Joneta's tiny body trembled in her arms. Emma held her close, understanding her grief, the wetness of her own tears staining her cheeks. She wiped them away. The inability to have Patrik's love was a penance paid, a penance that would forever haunt her.

Wind caressed the grass as Sir Duncan's mount broke from the trees, the scent of earth tainted by dregs of smoke.

Emma scanned the hill. Beyond the crosses, flames

licked the exposed timbers. No one attempted to put out the fire. Why would they? With the charred outline of the proud timbers but a skeleton, any chance of saving the home was long since lost.

As they neared the scorched remains, Marie came running toward them.

Sir Duncan drew to a halt.

Emma's chest tightened as she passed Joneta to the frantic woman.

Marie drew her daughter tight against her chest. Tear-filled eyes lifted to meet Emma's. "You saved my daughter's life." Distress creased her brow as she caught sight of Patrik. "Oh God!"

"He is alive," Lord Grey stated.

Relief swept Marie's face as she gestured to her side. "Bring him to the well. 'Tis where they are treating the other men who are wounded."

Lord Grey kicked his mount toward where his knights worked to tend their own. Patrik's body was limp against him.

Sir Duncan and Sir Alexander followed.

As they pulled up, two knights hurried to their lord's steed. Recognition dawned on both men's faces. "'Tis Sir Patrik," the closest man gasped.

"Aye," Lord Grey stated. "He needs to be tended immediately."

Both men bowed. "Yes, my lord."

"Nae." Sir Alexander dismounted, and stepped before the men. "I will care for him."

Stunned, Emma watched as the dangerous Scot took Patrik into his arms with infinite care, and then strode off with his brother.

Sir Duncan swung down.

"Are you not surprised Sir Alexander is caring for your brother?"

With a shrug, Sir Duncan reached up and lifted Emma to the ground. "Nae. Once Patrik is healed, they will be going at it again."

"Going at it?" she asked in disbelief. "You mean they will again fight?"

"Aye, but once healed, Patrik will give as good as he gets." Dimples flickered in his face. "'Tis what brothers do."

Her mind spun. "Sir Duncan?"

"Aye?"

"What did he do to make Sir Alexander so angry?"

Sir Duncan hesitated, then gazed at her thoughtfully. "He tried to kill Alexander's wife."

Several hours later, working alongside Sir Alexander as he tended Patrik, Emma had learned little more about why Patrik had tried to harm his brother's wife. However much Sir Alexander rubbed her raw, however tense their conversation, her respect for him as they worked soared.

Sir Alexander rubbed his face, tired eyes scanning Patrik. "There is little more we can do."

"His breathing is steady," Emma said.

"'Tis good he is settling down." Sir Alexander stretched his back.

"It is. He has lost much blood."

Sir Alexander met her gaze. "You care for him."

The confidence in his claim caught her off guard. She shrugged. "I told you, he saved my life."

Shrewd eyes studied her. "Mayhap, but your tenderness as you helped over the last few hours assures me your feelings for him run deep."

"How could they not after he risked his life to save mine?"

"'Tis interesting how defensive you become when I speak of your feelings toward Patrik."

He was right. Frazzled, she'd allowed her emotions to guide her, not a trait of one of England's top mercenaries. Or, did that woman any longer exist? Sir Alexander's intense gaze unnerved her further.

"I thought you hated him," Emma said, needing to change the topic.

Sir Alexander grunted. "Patrik has not seen the last of my fist, but my feelings are not what we speak of. 'Tis yours."

"Why would they matter to you?"

"Why do you ask?" Sir Alexander countered.

Flustered, she stood. "I answer to no one concerning my feelings, especially you."

"No one?" Sir Alexander said, his eyes assessing her as if he could see through her every lie.

Emma backed away. "I will fetch water."

"I took you not for a coward."

She glared at the dangerous rebel. "Tend to your brother, 'tis what you are good at." Emma turned on her heel and walked to the well, emotions churning, hating her weakness when it came to Patrik, and despising even more the treachery she had once planned.

Bedamned to the writ. She could return to Sir Cressingham, reveal the location of the rebel hideout, then claim they were attacked by thieves and she'd managed to slip free without time to steal the writ. But would he believe her? Never had she failed in a mission.

Before the neatly stacked stones housing the well, she hung her head at the thought of Patrik, at the anger and hurt he would feel once he learned the truth. It was unrealistic to suppose that somehow he would not learn she was a mercenary, or discover her role in his life. With his connections, he would find out.

Tears slipped down her cheeks. Bedamned!

"Lass."

Sir Alexander's deep burr had her stiffening. "Go away."

Muscled legs came into view. "I meant no harm in my questions."

She glared at him. "No? Did you not intend to pry? Are you not used to bruising your way through until you find what answers you seek?"

At her angry retort, admiration glittered in the rebel's eyes. "I have been accused of being a wee bit forceful."

Emma narrowed her gaze. "You are the most frustrating man. Your wife must be a saint."

"She is. And aye, he is a bloody pain in the arse," Sir Duncan agreed as he walked over and stood by her side. "But he loves Patrik as much as he wishes him dead."

Overwhelmed by these men, she stepped back. "I am going to stay beside Patrik." She started off.

"Lass."

At Sir Alexander's voice, she turned.

He nodded toward a full water pouch near the base of the well. "You came for water, did you not?"

At the touch of humor riding his voice, she scowled, swiped the pouch and strode toward where Patrik lay.

As she hurried off, Duncan crossed his arms. "What do you think of the lass?"

Alexander grunted. "She loves him."

"Aye, 'twas my thinking as well." Duncan rubbed his chin. "Did you see how she stitched up his cuts?"

"Her hand has done that work before."

"Neither did I miss how she has guided the conversation away from herself."

Unease crept through Alexander. "Something about the lass has me on edge."

His younger brother smiled, dropped his hand to his side. "I think 'tis your anger at Patrik spilling over."

Somber, Alexander shook his head. "When I was hitting Patrik, do you remember how she jumped on my back and tried to choke me?"

"Aye."

"Surrounded by three knights, most women would have screamed. Yet, the lass did not hesitate in her attack, her hold upon my neck true." Alexander grimaced. "An untrained lass knows not such defense."

Duncan stilled. "What are you saying?"

Alexander studied Cristina as she knelt beside Patrik. "I am unsure," he said at last, "but until I am confident she can be trusted, I am keeping an eye on the lass."

A tense silence settled between them. After a long

moment, Duncan laid a hand upon his brother's shoulder. "Patrik is back." He swallowed hard. "Can you believe it?"

Emotions squeezed as if a fist in Alexander's chest. "I am afraid to believe it. Almost as afraid as I am of my wife's reaction when she learns Patrik is alive."

Chapter 13

The stench of burning wood and death tainted the air as Emma worked alongside Marie, aiding the injured Scots. On edge, she glanced to where Sir Alexander helped Fergus reclaim any surviving goods from the charred home, their grim outlines framed in the afternoon light.

A shiver rippled through her. Since her confrontation with Sir Alexander this morning, she'd kept her distance. How had she ever believed Patrik unlike his brothers? In appearance mayhap, but his sharp mind and intelligence matched the other MacGruder brothers. Each was determined, fierce in his passion and utterly dangerous.

At the firm pad of boots upon earth, she glanced to her side.

Fatigue coated Lord Grey's strong face, along with concern. "How does Sir Eoin fare?" he asked Marie as she worked alongside Emma to bind his knight's wound.

"A deep gash or two," Marie replied. "'Twill heal within a sennight."

"Excellent."

Marie secured a final knot upon the bandage, stood, wrung her hands. "My lord, we have little food left to offer you and your men."

"'Tis unnecessary." Lord Grey scanned the field with a slow sweep. "You and your family will travel with us to my home. Go to your husband, gather what you wish to take."

Relief swept her face. "'Tis generous of you, my lord."

"Go. We will soon depart."

"Aye, my lord." She hesitated as if wanting to say more. Then, scooping up Joneta, Marie headed up the slope toward the crosses.

"God's teeth," the earl breathed, "I told the lass to go to her husband." He started after her.

"Do not," Emma said.

Lord Grey whirled. Piercing green eyes riveted on her. "Do not?"

The authority in his voice assured her few dared question him. Emma stood. "Her children are buried there. She is but going to say good-bye."

Shrewd eyes glanced at the woman's departing figure. "I see."

Did he? Could the earl truly understand Marie's need to say farewell to those she'd given life to, her children now entombed within the earth? A maternal need she would never before have considered. She remembered Lord Grey's interaction with his brothers, how without hesitation he'd helped Patrik, and his concern for each within his command. Yes, the earl was a man who understood family, a man who cared about his own, a trait infused in Patrik as well.

"You are a kind man." Emma stilled. She'd not meant to say the words aloud.

The earl lifted a dark brow, his intense gaze as potent as his brother's.

"How soon before we depart?" She prayed her question would guide his thoughts elsewhere, but as if sensing her intent, he studied her a moment longer.

At the echo of hooves, Emma turned to find Sir Alexander riding toward them. God in heaven. One brother to face at a time was enough.

"Stay," Lord Grey said as she started to step back.

A shiver slid through her. "I have tasks to complete."

"They can wait." It wasn't a request.

Sir Alexander reined his mount to a halt. "All of the men have been tended to."

"Excellent," Lord Grey replied. "Pass word we will depart for Lochshire Castle posthaste."

"Aye." Sir Alexander's shrewd gaze rested upon her, then flicked to his brother. With a curt nod, he kicked his mount away.

Thank God he'd left.

"Alexander's heart is in the right place, but at times emotions guide his actions." Lord Grey paused. "It does not make him harsh but caring."

Emma held his gaze. "A brother would see it as such."

A dry smile touched the harsh lines of his mouth.

"Mayhap Alexander was right—you are a perfect match for Patrik."

She remained silent. They knew not that she loved Patrik. But it would take little to expose a secret they must never learn.

"From where do you hail?" Lord Grey asked.

Though the question was easily asked, he sought information, a ploy she'd often used. "Why?"

"I am curious. I detected an accent and was but trying to place it."

Throat dry, Emma fought for calm. When she'd yelled at Sir Alexander earlier, her false burr must have slipped. "I have traveled much."

"Mayhap that is the reason I cannot determine from what region you come."

But he'd try. With his sharp mind, he'd mull over the fact until he unlocked the secret. By then, she would be far away.

"You will accompany us to my castle as well. This country is unsafe for a woman alone."

Unsafe? Remaining with the brothers presented a far greater threat. But she'd stirred the earl's interest and could not afford to draw his attention further. "You are generous, my lord."

"Am I?" Challenge lurked beneath his question.

Fine, let them not coat their words. She angled her chin. "I asked not for your protection."

"A fact I am well aware of."

"Yet you give it regardless. Your words held not an offer, but a command."

Respect glittered in Lord Grey's eyes. "Had I asked you to travel to my home, you would have refused."

"I find little use for men who wield their power to satisfy their curiosity."

"Patrik is my brother. You are important to him, which makes you important to me."

Important to Patrik? There she had her doubts. "I am but a woman he saved."

"And a woman he cares for as well."

She tamped down the surge of anger. It would earn her naught and but increase the earl's curiosity. Like Patrik, he was not a man to manipulate.

"When I first met you," Emma said. "I believed you little resembled Sir Patrik."

He arched a dark brow. "And now?"

"With the ample amount of arrogance you each display, you are indeed brothers."

"He is arrogant, a fact you would do well to remember." He swung upon his steed. "Prepare to leave." Lord Grey cantered off.

"The arrogant braggart," she muttered.

"And a man only a fool would dare to cross."

At Patrik's weak words, emotion swept her. She knelt by his side and brushed away strands of hair from his bruised face. "You are awake." And he looked pitiful, but thank God he was alive. "Here." She held the leather water pouch to his lips.

After several swallows, hand trembling, he pushed the pouch away. "I will take your words to Seathan as a compliment as well."

Heat suffused her face. "You would." Her heart squeezed at the weariness shrouding his features, the deep lines edged with pain.

"How . . . How long have I slept?"

"Most of the day," Emma replied, "not that your shifting about is what I would consider sleep."

Patrik eyed the ball of orange in the sky and grimaced. "Seathan must be worried to be departing so late."

A worry well placed. "The English will return."

"Aye, and this time with a larger contingent." Lines of strain carved his face as he sat. "When King Edward learns of this day's attack, 'twould not surprise me if the bastard follows Arnulf's twisted path and orders more Scots hanged."

Emma remained silent, well aware of the English judge Arnulf of Southhampton's recent despicable act. Panicked by the Scots uprising, the English judge had requested that all leading Scots attend an eyre-court in Ayre. As the Scots had entered the building they were seized, gagged, and strung from the rafters. To Southhampton's glee, over three hundred and sixty Scots had fallen prey to his ploy.

Yes, when King Edward learned of Lord Grey's men overpowering his meager English contingent, he would indeed give orders to slaughter more Scots, even if it means torching entire villages as he had in Berwick.

Sickened by the thought, she focused on Patrik, on a man determined to win his country's freedom, regardless of the cost. "You must remain still. You have lost too much blood to be moving about."

He settled into a more comfortable position. "And I will lose more with the travel ahead." He reached out, pushed a wisp of hair from her face. "I should have told you about my brothers before this day, that they believed me dead."

The regret in his voice moved her. "Why? We are but two people whose lives have crossed." She fought to smother her emotions. "Two people who in the end will go their own way."

"Will we?"

An ache built in Emma's chest. "Yes," she whispered. "It can be no other way."

He lifted her chin. "Can it not?"

Emotion storming her, she broke free.

Patrik caught her hand. "Cristina."

Guilt slid through her. "Leave it be."

"I cannot. Bedamned, do you think that I wished this? That I wanted to find you? It makes no sense; a relationship with anyone at this point in my life is nae a notion I can entertain."

His heartfelt words shook her further. Feeling too much, Emma tried to pull free.

He held tight.

"It will never work."

"Why, because you will not allow it?"

She welcomed the rush of anger. "Yes."

Silence fell between them.

Nerves trembled through Emma as she met his gaze. "Now what?"

As if he bloody knew? Patrik dropped his hand, unsure whether he was angry at himself for pushing her or frustrated that Cristina wouldn't even consider their future. God knew when they made love, the feelings she inspired matched none he'd ever experienced.

Why was he pressing her? Had he not warned

himself throughout their journey that a relationship between them was not possible? At least one of them had more brains than an ass.

Weariness settled over him. "Now what?" Patrik repeated, "I know not." Aye, he was wrong to push her, to voice his desires. "My brothers will want an explanation of why I am alive—it is the least they deserve."

Emerald eyes watched him. "Sir Alexander said you tried to kill his wife."

The pain of that day a year ago squeezed in his chest. Consumed by hatred, by a brutal past, he'd focused on Lady Nichola's nationality, had overlooked the genuine woman within. She was fair, honest, and loved his brother, Alexander.

Cristina shook her head. "No, you have already talked too much. You need to rest."

The excuse tempted him to remain silent, but he was not a coward. "It is true. I tried to kill Alexander's wife, Nichola, because I was trying to protect him."

"Protect Sir Alexander from a woman?" Disbelief and confusion cradled her words.

He nodded. "As odd as it seems, because the lass is English."

"English?" Her face paled. Frowning, she glanced toward where Alexander rode. "I-I cannot believe he would wed an Englishwoman."

Patrik grunted. "If asked prior to meeting the lass, my brother would have agreed. Alexander had traveled to England to abduct her brother, a wealthy lord. When he arrived at their home, her brother was away. With the rebels desperate for coin and believing the siblings close, Alexander abducted Lady Nichola instead."

"He married *his captive*?"

The shock on her face matched his own when he'd realized Alexander was falling in love with the lass.

"Aye."

"But why did you hate her? 'Twas not her fault she was English."

Patrik sighed. "Aye, a lesson I learned too late." He'd realized that truth during the months it had taken to recover from his near-fatal wound. He took Cristina's hand, drew it to his chest. "When I was eight summers, my family was attacked by the English. I managed to escape." And had damned himself for having survived ever since.

"You lost your entire family?"

He swallowed hard, still haunted by the spilling blood, the screams of his family as they lay dying. "Aye."

"Did you know the MacGruders before?"

"My father saved the life of the MacGruder brothers' mother in a raid," Patrik explained. "After my parents were killed, when the MacGruders learned of the murders, they adopted me as their own, gave me their last name. I included my own as well, Patrik Cleary MacGruder. Or, did until this year past."

Face pale, she shook her head. "Oh God, I am so sorry."

He curled his fingers over her hand. "Since then, many years have passed."

"But one does not forget."

Her somber words echoed between them. Aye, having grown up in an orphanage, then marrying a loveless bastard who'd taken advantage of her tattered emotions, she would understand the misery of loss.

"But," she said, "that does not explain why your brothers believed you dead."

"It does not." He swallowed hard, regretting his actions. "Caught up in his feelings for Lady Nichola, who was then Alexander's captive, my brother ignored my warning that because she was English, she was unworthy of his love. So, I arranged for Lady Nichola to believe she could escape. That night, when she slipped from Lochshire Castle, I followed with the intent of preventing Alexander from ever marrying the lass."

"You planned to kill her?"

"Aye, and almost succeeded," he admitted, needing to cleanse his soul of his sin. It was important that Cristina and his brothers understand the reason behind his actions. He shifted, gasped at the slap of pain. Sweat broke out on his brow, and he wiped his forehead. "I had but caught up to her when Alexander found us. When I threatened Lady Nichola with a knife, he dove on top of me."

Her eyes widened with shock. "Your brother tried to kill you?"

At the thrum of hooves, he glanced over to see Alexander drawing to a halt before them. Patrik nodded, faced Cristina. "Alexander was protecting Lady Nichola, a woman he loved. During the fight, my dagger fell to the ground, wedged against a rock. As we grappled, I rolled onto the blade."

"So that was the reason your brothers believed you

dead," she whispered. Cristina shook her head. "How is it you lived?"

"A fact I would be curious to know also," Alexander said as he dismounted.

Patrik met his brother's hard gaze. "The guard sent with my body to Lochshire Castle that day was loyal to me. I must have moved, groaned, something to alert him that I lived. Through the pain, I knew naught of where he rode, nor did I care. Thankfully, I fell into blackness. Later, when I awoke, I learned I was at his cousin's hut. The guard explained he'd dug and filled a grave, then informed everyone it was mine."

Alexander grunted. "And believing our man loyal, neither I nor Seathan nor Duncan, thought to question his words." His mouth tightened. "Where is he?"

"Riding beneath Sir Andrew de Moray's colors."

Alexander grunted. "And that is where he should stay."

Patrik said no more. To Alexander, the Scot had betrayed him, even though his act had saved Patrik's life. Well he knew Alexander's ability to carry a grudge. Would his brother ever truly forgive him? Did he even deserve such absolution? Unsure of anything, he shoved to his feet. Pain screamed through his body, and his legs threatened to give.

Cristina scrambled to his side, caught his arm in support. "What are you doing? You must rest until we depart."

"Which is why I am here." Alexander glanced at Cristina, his face hard. "You are to ride in the wagon with the woman and child."

Instead of backing down, she held her own. "With

the graveness of his injuries, Patrik should travel there as well. If space is short, I will ride."

Alexander scowled. "You will not be given your own horse."

The hardness within his brother's words set Patrik on edge. "Cristina, go help Marie and Joneta stow the last of their belongings."

She hesitated. "Patrik—"

"Go." Patrik nodded. "All will be well."

Doubt flickered on her face. With a final cool glance at Alexander, she headed to where Marie was packing her belongings into a wagon.

Several long seconds passed. Alexander crossed his arms. "An interesting lass. She claimed you saved her from English knights."

"Aye. I came across the bloody bastards about to rape her."

Blue eyes narrowed. "Did you kill them?"

"Aye."

"Good."

For a moment, a sense of camaraderie settled between them, a taste of the bond he wanted back.

"Cristina deserves not your anger," Patrik said. "She sought to protect me when she believed you a threat."

"She did." His brother's eyes hardened. "To let you know, had I wanted to kill you a year past, the deed would have long been done."

"Yet you allowed me to live."

"A decision I still question." Alexander hesitated. "I know not if I can find forgiveness for you."

Emotion scraped Patrik's throat. He nodded.

Silence stretched between them.

"Do you trust her?"

"Trust her?" Patrik frowned. "An odd question."

"Mayhap, but one you chose not to answer."

His lingering doubts tumbled through his mind: her skill with a blade, her calm during a fight, her search through his belongings. "'Tis not an answer simply given."

"You bed a lass about whom you hold doubts?"

"Bedamned!" Patrik stepped toward him, wove. He clenched his teeth as he fought to maintain consciousness. "Had I my full strength, I would knock you on your arse."

"You would try." Tiredness etched his brother's voice, at odds with the challenge. He rubbed his brow. "Once you had healed, why did you not return to Lochshire Castle?"

At the reminder of his home, guilt swept Patrik. How many times had he wondered the same? "And if I had, would you have forgiven me, accepted my apology?"

Alexander blew out a harsh breath. "Nay, I would have tried to kill you."

"And now?" Patrik asked. "Here I stand before you and admit I was wrong."

"I am thinking."

However much he admired Alexander's honesty, it pointed out the chasm between them. But he had to try to bridge it. "Your anger at me is no more than I feel for myself. The months of lying in pain allowed me time to think, to realize the grave wrong I had committed against Nichola, against you and my family." He swallowed hard. "I stayed away not out of fear, but because

I could nae understand how you would ever forgive me. I doubt I can ever forgive myself."

Alexander scanned the field where the men had begun to mount. "I find I need time to decide. As for Nichola"—he faced Patrik—"whether she forgives you is not for me to decide."

"Fair enough." And more than he could have ever hoped for. Patrik shifted, and his fingers bumped against seasoned leather. The writ! In the mayhem of the day, incredibly, he'd forgotten. "Alexander, I must reach Bishop Wishart immediately."

"Bishop Wishart, why?"

Patrik withdrew the leather-encased writ, stained by dirt, weathered by moisture. "I must warn him that de Warenne is preparing to rejoin forces with Cressingham before the end of July."

His brother's face blanched. "God's teeth, it cannot be."

"I was stunned by the news as well. I believed little could pry de Warenne back to Scotland."

"'Tis not what I meant."

"What?" Patrik asked, confused by the look of sheer disbelief on his brother's face.

"'Tis why we are here."

None of this was making any sense. "The bishop sent you to meet me?"

"Aye. Nay." Alexander shook his head. "By my sword! Before the bishop surrendered to the English, he deployed a runner to Seathan, saying that he'd sent you on a dangerous mission, and expected your arrival along with the fact that you would be carrying important news. The bishop instructed Seathan to intercept you before you reached Roxburgh Castle."

Terror sliced through him. "Wishart is in English hands?"

"Aye, he surrendered as well as Robert Bruce and William Douglas."

"God no," Patrik whispered. "What are we to do?"

Somber eyes held his. "Take this information to Wallace as the bishop instructed."

His mind spun a thousand thoughts. Then, an odd one fell to the fore. "Wait, you said you did not know I lived?" Patrik asked, even more confused. "Yet Bishop Wishart penned my name in the writ to Seathan?"

His brother grimaced. "Aye, a name he wrote, but 'twas not Sir Patrik Cleary."

Unease trickled through Patrik. He lifted his gaze to his brother's assessing one. "And what name did Bishop Wishart use?"

Cobalt eyes pierced him.

A long second passed.

"Dubh Duer."

Chapter 14

The creak of wood accompanied each rattle as the wheels of the wagon stumbled through another rut. Emma caught the side of the weathered wood, her other hand upon Patrik's shoulder to lessen his jolt. Fractured moonlight spilling through a thick layer of clouds exposed the whiteness of Patrik's face.

The pace Lord Grey had set was grueling despite the thick of the night. With English knights soon to return to where their troops lay slaughtered, the rebel lord's move was prudent. Emma certainly did not wish to remain and risk any of Sir Cressingham's returning knights recognizing her.

She laid her palm across Patrik's brow, frowned when heat met her touch.

"How does he fare?"

At Sir Duncan's voice, Emma turned. Carved within the swath of moonlight, the brother she'd learned was the youngest rode within a hand's pace of the wagon.

"He is finally asleep, but his skin grows warmer with each passing hour."

Duncan frowned as he scanned his brother sprawled atop the bundled clothes. "We are but a few hours from Lochshire Castle. Until we arrive, ensure he has plenty of water." He nudged his mount into a canter, headed toward where Lord Grey led his men.

She prayed they'd soon arrive. With Patrik's loss of blood, he'd continued to worsen throughout the night. Each passing hour nursed her fear, and his delay in responding to her questions stoked it further. Duncan's earlier announcement that they'd sent a man ahead to alert the healer to their arrival underscored his concern.

Gently, she angled Patrik's head up. Emma held the water pouch against his mouth, helped him take several sips. With care, she laid him back, then sagged against the slats. Each turn of the wheel, each creak of the wagon, fed her nerves.

In the distance, wisps of purple etched a subtle outline of the mountains around them as they continued to climb.

Dawn.

Please God, let them reach Lord Grey's home soon. Emma stilled. What was she thinking? She didn't have the luxury of remaining to tend to Patrik. She must escape before they entered the MacGruder fortress.

The writ!

Torn between duty, abandoning her mission and being on the run the rest of her life, she glanced around.

Marie slept near the front of the wagon, Joneta curled against her side with her thumb tucked into her mouth. Fergus rode ahead with Lord Grey's men.

Aside from the knight leading the horses that pulled the wagon, no one else rode nearby.

With ease, she could slip away with the writ before anyone noticed. Guilt swamped her at the thought of stealing the missive from Patrik's limp body. She should be relieved. Had she not worried about how she would retrieve the document?

But with her feelings for Patrik running so deep, the taking of the writ meant betrayal. As if revealing the rebel tunnel beneath the mountain to Sir Cressingham or the hideout behind the falls did not offer the same?

The wagon jerked, rumbled on. Clouds severed the shards of moonlight and the struggling dawn, casting the forest into an ominous abyss.

Queasy, shrouded in darkness, Emma pushed to her knees. Did she truly have any other choice? If she remained, once Patrik learned the truth, he would hate her.

Hand trembling, hating herself for this damning act, she reached toward Patrik's tunic to where she'd seen him slip the document beneath.

He groaned.

She pulled back. Another shaft of moonlight flickered through the forest, making his outline a shadow against blackness. God in heaven, why was she hesitating? He was unconscious; 'twas not as if he was going to catch her. She again reached out, again hesitated.

Emma fisted her hand. She hated this feeling of helplessness, of not wanting to hurt Patrik. But she must retrieve the writ now and escape. Once they were inside Lochshire Castle's gates, a healer would remain by Patrik's side and any opportunity to claim the missive would be lost.

Damn the entire situation! Refusing to think further, she lifted Patrik's tunic. Fingers trembling, Emma slid her hands beneath.

It wasn't there.

Impossible! She had seen the writ yesterday. With gentle fingers, she again probed the woven fabric.

Nothing.

Possibilities raced through her mind. In the heat of battle, the fight with his brother, Lord Grey carrying Patrik to the wagon, or any number of events after, the writ might have slipped free. If so, had someone found it? Mayhap, one of the brothers? Regardless, it wasn't here.

Now what? She glanced to where tender fingers of purple-edged light caressed the trees. No time remained. She must leave without the writ.

In silence she gathered the few items she would need. The dagger at her thigh weighed heavy, the water pouch secured around her waist more so. Emma wiped a tear from her eye. She was not abandoning Patrik. Sir Duncan had declared they would arrive soon, and a nurse waited to tend him.

Guilt had her glancing back. "I am sorry, Patrik. I can never be what you want." Heart aching, she leaned forward, pressed a kiss upon his mouth. "I love you." Before she changed her mind, she crept toward the rear of the wagon.

"Going somewhere, lass?"

At the gruff accusation in Sir Alexander's voice, Emma stilled. She'd been so caught up in her decision, she'd not heard him riding up. Pulse racing, she slowly turned.

Eyes, hard and accusing, watched her from beside the wagon.

"I . . ."

"Go on," he urged, his demand ripe with suspicion. "'Tis an explanation I find myself curious to hear."

Each clop of hooves upon earth echoed as if a sentence of doom. She fought for calm. "Sir Duncan informed me we would soon reach your home."

He arched a skeptical brow.

Think! "I was gathering my few belongings before we arrived."

He snorted in disbelief. Hints of dawn exposed the hard angles of his face, the shadows lending a ferocious appeal to an already intimidating warrior. A man who by his actions reminded her so much of Patrik.

However much Sir Alexander cursed Patrik, he loved him and would protect him with his life.

The ball of fear inside softened. "If possible," she said against the backdrop of jolts and bumps, "I wish to stay with Patrik as he recovers."

"Aye, you will stay with us, lass. As for exactly where, that is another matter."

Emma edged back to settle next to Patrik, refused to let Sir Alexander see her fear. "He is unconscious."

"He will be tended to." Shrewd eyes studied her. "I know not what game you play, but know this, 'tis dangerous."

"I play no game."

"That I believe. Whatever you are about," he said, his burr deep, "'tis very real."

She struggled for calm. He suspected that she'd tried to slip from the wagon.

Long moments passed. With the flare of his nostrils, Sir Alexander gave her a dismissive look, then continued to ride alongside the wagon, a harsh set to his jaw.

Emma glanced to the other side of the wagon where Joneta and her mother slept. A fool she'd been for allowing her heart to make her linger. No more. At the first opportunity, she would escape.

Once the Scots discovered her true identity, nothing would save her. Not even Patrik's self-professed feelings.

In the gray-smeared morning sky a soft mist began to fall. An air of expectancy built, a foreboding of something immense. The path before them narrowed, either side framed by dense, light-smothering pines. The clop of hooves echoed around her. The trail grew steeper, angling, carving its way up as if ascending to the heavens.

A gentle breeze whispered to life. The scent of wild herbs filled the air, a potent, clean aroma that rolled through her every breath. Through the gloom within the dense forest a break appeared.

The wagon creaked forward, hesitated as it moved over uneven ground. As they climbed higher, the dense swath of trees split like a door opening.

Her breath caught and Emma could only stare. Below, an immense lake curved within the time-worn land, its shores shrouded by lush green and the hills surrounding it clothed by the dense forest. At the southern tip jutted a peninsula. Forged upon its sturdy strip, a castle rose in proud defiance. A castle that could have been taken from the pages of King Arthur. A castle that could protect as well as imprison.

Drizzle saturated the air and clouds hung low, the dismal setting adding an ominous intensity to the landscape below.

Apprehension swept through her. It was easy to imagine Lord Grey ruling these unforgiving lands, a man backed by his brothers, rebels who cultivated their own brand of respect.

When she'd first met Patrik, she'd thought him intimidating, a man unlike most. Now, she realized his wit, strength, and intensity had been honed by his family. He belonged in this ruthless land, was hewn from its soil, its blood.

Whereas, she belonged nowhere.

Somber, she took in the single road. The only way in. Or out.

Movement upon the distant wall walk caught her attention. Guards making their rounds, guards who ensured the castle's protection, who would ensure she did not escape.

Coldness slipped through Emma, and she rubbed her hands upon her arms.

"'Tis Lochshire Castle," Sir Alexander stated.

Emma stiffened. "'Tis magnificent." And intimidating—a fact he well knew. She scanned the hewn walls, quarried stone that had taken enormous effort to haul to this strategic location. "It appears of Norman influence."

He grunted. "You have a good eye. Indeed, 'twas crafted by the Normans, and passed through the generations since." Pride etched his voice, that of a man backed by family, a man who knew his roots.

Roots at odds with the emptiness she called her life. She settled near Patrik, wished for a taste of such a bond. No, with the mire of her life, the deceit and the lies, such a dream was impossible.

"Are we almost there?" Joneta asked, the girl's voice groggy with sleep.

Marie sent a tired look toward Emma, then brushed her daughter's cheek with a tender hand. "Aye."

As if she were a colt trying out its newfound legs, Joneta shoved herself up and peered out. Eyes wide with excitement, she turned to Emma. "Look, a castle!"

Emma forced a smile.

"It is so huge!" The girl all but danced in the wagon. She scanned the thick woods. "Are there dragons?"

"No dragons, lass," Sir Alexander replied, the gentleness of his voice catching Emma by surprise. If asked, she would have doubted a gentler side to this fierce knight existed. 'Twould seem his terse manner was reserved for those he did not trust.

On edge, she laid her hand upon Patrik's brow. Sweat coated his face, pale with hints of a fever. Thank God they would soon reach a healer.

The crest of the hill grew smaller as they traveled down the steep slope, the trees of the forest giving way to fields. At the rough grate of wheels upon stone, she braced herself, aware they traversed the causeway to Lochshire Castle.

"Cristina?"

At Patrik's gravelly voice, Emma glanced down. Hazel eyes, drugged with pain and exhaustion, watched her.

Her chest constricted with the love this man inspired. She slid a stray lock from his brow. "How fare thee?"

"My th-throat," he whispered.

"Here." Water sloshed as she helped him take a sip.

With a cough, he pulled away, dropped his head against the cloth-tied bundle. "How far un-until we reach Lochshire Castle?"

"So you are awake then," Alexander said.

At his brother's voice, Patrik turned his head. He grimaced. "So it would seem."

Alexander grunted. "Sleep and a meal will serve you well."

They would, but at the moment, neither was his biggest concern. "Nichola will be there." The words stumbled out, but Patrik needed to say her name, prepare himself for the upcoming meeting, her justified anger.

Alexander's mouth tightened. "Aye. My wife will not be expecting you."

Nor any other within Lochshire Castle. Everyone believes me dead.

Alexander stroked his mount's neck, cast his brother a speculative look. "Duncan has married since you left."

Duncan was married? "Who?"

"Lady Isabel Adair."

"But she left him a week before they were to wed. Duncan swore . . ." Patrik closed his eyes, fought against the throbbing in his head, then opened them. "Makes no sense."

"It should not. But then, trust Duncan to step in the muck and come out as if a candlestick polished. A story I will let the lad tell you." Alexander hesitated. "You should know, Seathan has taken a wife as well, an English noble. She is a fine lass, one I would give my life to defend."

Beneath his calm delivery, Patrik heard the threat. His brothers would allow him within Lochshire Castle, but he had not yet earned their trust. Nor could he not blame them.

"Rest. I will tell Seathan you are awake." Alexander kicked his mount. Hooves clattered on stone as he rode ahead.

Patrik sighed. All of his brothers married. The news yet another harsh reminder of time passed, and of precious moments lost. Yet somehow within the mayhem of his life, he'd found Cristina. He sobered. Found her mayhap, but with his life given to reclaiming Scotland's freedom, he must let her go.

Needing to touch her, he clasped her hand, surprised to find it cold. Patrik glanced over.

Face pale, she stared at Lochshire Castle.

"What is wrong?"

"It is imposing," she whispered as if to speak the words out loud would unleash a spell.

Memories of the first time he'd beheld the Norman stronghold replayed in his mind. It was a home forged by unforgiving men, powerful lords who'd helped carve Scotland's destiny. Instead of nervousness, pride had filled him. But, he'd arrived at this formidable castle as a lad accepted, not a woman whose life at every turn lay shattered.

"You will be welcome," he said.

"Will I?" Nervous eyes remained unconvinced.

"Lord Grey returns," a sentry's voice boomed as they approached the drawbridge.

Pride as well as apprehension filled Patrik. His brothers knew he lived, but he'd yet to face Nichola.

Hooves echoed like thunder as Seathan's knights rode across the drawbridge. The forged walls closed, arched to the sky to scrape the rain-darkened clouds. A breeze swept past, rich with the scent of water.

Darkness encased them as the wagon rolled beneath the gatehouse. Then a dismal light exposed a crowd of men and women converging within the bailey to welcome their lord and his men.

But not a man who'd tried to kill his brother's wife.

Anxiety built, stealing his ability to move—he could only feel, regret the tragedy of that day a year past, regret the actions of a man driven by hate who'd understood his error too late.

Patrik swallowed hard. When the people of Lochshire Castle discovered he lived, please let them find it in their hearts to offer forgiveness. That his brothers allow him to return was the first step, but little more. Whatever transpired now would reveal whether Lochshire Castle would ever again be his home.

"Seathan!" a woman called.

The warm English accent had Patrik turning.

A slender woman, her amber-gold hair braided in a delicate plait, with a gold circlet framing her head, ran toward his eldest brother. In a deft move, Seathan dismounted, drew the woman in his arms and caught her in a fierce kiss.

Seathan's wife—the English noble Alexander had spoken of.

Patrik waited for the roll of anger, the bitterness he'd always felt when it came to the English. As he watched the Englishwoman in his brother's arms,

Patrik found naught but regret. Because he'd allowed bitterness to guide his actions, he'd missed coming to know the woman who had stolen Seathan's heart. If she had won his brother's respect, she must be an incredible woman indeed.

The wagon slowed to a halt. Several knights began unloading their meager belongings, while two others helped Marie and Joneta to the ground.

"Isabel!" Duncan jumped from his mount and sprinted toward a beautiful woman, her face framed by hair the color of aged whiskey. His youngest brother caught and whirled the woman around. With her face alight with laughter, he captured her mouth, the deep bond between them further evidence of the time Patrik had lost.

"Alexander!"

At the familiar, lyrical English accent, Patrik stilled. Nichola. While he'd lain in bed recovering, he'd replayed his poor decisions, how his hatred had prevented his mind from seeing the good within her.

Now, *his destiny* arrived.

Would she indeed be able to forgive him? With a prayer on his lips, Patrik turned.

Auburn hair slipped from Nichola's finely woven braid as she rushed toward Alexander, her smile full of love, the joy of a marriage strong.

Knights reunited with their families, squires led horses toward the stable, and children danced at their mothers' sides waiting to see their fathers.

Everything around Patrik faded. In gut-wrenching fascination, he watched for the moment Nichola noticed his existence, for the instant when the joy upon her face shattered.

The crowd parted as Nichola ran to her husband. As she neared, in a smooth move, Alexander leaned down and swept his wife up on his steed to claim her mouth.

"Patrik." Cristina's voice echoed as if a league away. She didn't understand the enormity of this moment. Couldn't.

"You are their family," Cristina said.

Throat dry, he shook his head. "After what I have done," he whispered, "I am nothing."

As if to back his words, Alexander broke the kiss, whispered in his wife's ear.

Nichola froze. Her fingers clasped his shoulders and a shudder rippled through her lithe form. Then, with time-wrenching slowness, her face lifted, turned toward Patrik, her amber eyes dark.

As if time had been erased, the past tumbled back.

The exact day.

The exact hour.

"No!" Nichola tried to jump to the ground.

Alexander held tight. "Steady, lass," he urged, shooting Patrik a warning glance.

"Get him out of here," Nichola demanded.

The surrounding crowd fell silent. Murmurs swept through the onlookers.

"He will harm no one," Alexander stated.

"He will!" Nichola struggled to jump to the ground.

Alexander held tight.

"He will try to kill me. What of our son? He cannot be trusted!"

Her angry words sliced Patrik's soul. A son? Alexander had not told him about a child. What else had he withheld? The last fragment of hope for Nichola's forgiveness blackened to wisps of ash.

She jerked, fought to pull away. "Release me!"

Alexander caught her face. "I am taking you inside. Trust me, wife, you are safe." Tenderness guided his movements as he dismounted.

No! Panic shot through Patrik as Alexander set his wife on the ground and started toward the keep. This was his only opportunity to plead for forgiveness. Once Nichola went inside, she would never allow him to see her again. Though she might never forgive him, he had to try.

"Nichola!" Patrik's raw voice cleaved the silence like an ill-honed sword.

Alexander's eyes cut to Patrik.

Pain screamed through Patrik's body as he shoved himself up. Battered wood gouged his knees, but he crawled to the wagon's end. In a mind-blurring move, he lowered himself to the ground, steadied himself upon the worn earth.

Cristina scrambled to the ground, caught his arm. "Patrik, what are you doing? You have lost too much blood. You—"

"Stay here," he said, keeping his gaze on Nichola. Cristina didn't understand the importance of this one moment. He broke free of her hold.

"I will go with you," Cristina said.

Eyes glazed with anger and a hint of fear, Nichola watched him.

"No. This I must do alone." On shaky legs, Patrik stepped forward, clenching his teeth against the pain. People swam into a blur before him. Through sheer determination, he took another step.

Alexander tensed, his body angled to protect as he held Nichola at his side.

A murmur wove through the crowd. One by one, those within the keep fell into a hush, focused on Patrik. Eyes, harsh and condemning, watched him. Whispers cursed his every step.

Patrik accepted their wariness, understood their anger. Had he stood in their place, he would have done the same. Sure of nothing, he pushed forward.

Chapter 15

Several steps away, vision blurring, Patrik halted, gasping for breath. "Ni-Nichola."

Nichola straightened, her eyes burning hot. "Stay away!"

Pain slammed Patrik's head. "I-I need to talk to you."

"By God's eyes!" Alexander stepped before his wife. "Enough!"

Seathan walked to Alexander, slanted a worried look at Nichola at her husband's side. "Now is not the time," he told Patrik.

Panic clawed through Patrik. "Nichola, pl-please, listen to me."

Face pale, Nichola shook her head. "Leave us." Roughness coated her words, betraying a loathing so great it would stain the pews of a church. Angry tears slid down her cheeks as she faced her husband. "Swear to me you will keep him away from our son!"

"Nichola," Alexander started.

"Swear it."

She believed he'd harm her or her child? Patrik's

heart broke, his guilt and regret for his actions twofold. "I wo-would not harm yo-your son nor you, ever."

Nichola turned. The contempt scarring her face tore Patrik's soul.

Seathan stepped between them. "Alexander, take Nichola inside."

"Aye." Alexander shot Patrik a hard look. Like a wolf guarding its mate, he drew her close, strode toward the keep.

Duncan moved to Seathan's side, his icy expression underscoring where his loyalty lay.

Loss smothered Patrik, a curtain so black he struggled to draw a breath. Had he not brought enough tragedy to those he loved? Though many despised him, none more than he himself. More fool was he for having entertained the notion of somehow finding forgiveness.

Blackness threatened. He fought for consciousness, braced his feet to remain standing. "I-I need but a horse and I wi-will go."

A horse? The stubborn, mule-headed oaf. Emma moved to Patrik's side and glared at Lord Grey. "Tell me, will you have your brother's death upon your conscience?"

Patrik caught her arm. "Cristina."

"He is barely standing." Emma tugged her arm free of Patrik's weak hold. "Tell me, will you allow your brother to leave?"

Piercing green eyes bored into her.

She held her ground. Patrik's life was at stake. Without a healer, he would die. Even with proper attention there were no guarantees.

Anger churned within Lord Grey's eyes, but surprisingly, respect as well. He nodded to the two nearest knights. "Take Sir Patrik to his chamber," he ordered, his gaze never leaving her.

"Blast it!" Patrik wove. "I need not—"

"Now!" Seathan's voice boomed.

"Aye, my lord," the closest man said. Two knights hurried to Patrik's side.

Weak, his wounds having begun to bleed, Patrik was half led, half carried to the keep.

Relief swept through Emma. Thank God. She started after him.

"Mistress Cristina." Lord Grey's voice wrapped around her with cold finality.

Heart pounding, she faced the powerful lord. Silence descended between them like a guillotine. "I wish to be with Sir Patrik."

The earl crossed his arms. "A healer awaits him."

And she understood. "You never were going to allow him to leave Lochshire Castle, were you? You just wanted him to suffer, wondering if he will ever again be accepted."

A muscle worked in Lord Grey's jaw. "He is my brother."

She hesitated. "And he is fortunate to have you."

"I doubt he would concur right now," Lord Grey replied, "nor will he for a long while. He has much to overcome."

True, but regardless of the challenges, Patrik's brothers would not dismiss him out of hand.

"Go," the earl called to those around him. "Welcome our knights home. Those without families, see to the wounded."

Whispers interwove the soft sound of footsteps as the people within the bailey dispersed.

"Duncan," Lord Grey said. "Oversee the wounded and ensure all are tended."

"Aye." With a wary glance at Emma, the youngest brother clasped his wife's hand and drew her with him.

In the distance laughter filled the air along with the excited yells of children. As if everything was normal.

Emma nodded to the earl. "I owe you an apology, my lord. 'Twas improper to challenge you. But, to protect Sir Patrik, I would do so again."

He arched a brow.

Emma pushed forward. "Though you are Patrik's brother, I thank you for caring for him when he himself does not expect it, or feel he deserves it."

"And do you feel he is deserving?" a woman at Lord Grey's side asked.

Caught up in the tension between Patrik and Lord Grey, she'd failed to notice this regal woman who stood beside the lord of the keep. Heat rose up Emma's cheeks.

"Mistress Cristina," the earl said, his voice somber, "my wife, the Countess of Grey."

Emma gave a brief curtsy. "My lady."

Lavender eyes studied her, the intelligence within potent. She was a match to her powerful mate, yet another daunting link within the MacGruders.

"Yes, I believe Sir Patrik is deserving of acceptance and more. Since he tried to kill Sir Alexander's wife, he has lived in shame." Emma paused. "He regrets his betrayal with his every breath."

"You seem sure," the noblewoman stated.

Emma lifted her jaw. "Never have I met a man more honorable."

"Patrik means much to you." Though softly spoken, conviction weighed heavy in the countess's words.

Feelings Emma could not deny, but her love for Patrik was private, a fact even he did not know. Tiredness slid through her, wiping away the sharp wit she desperately needed.

"Sir Patrik is a deeply caring man," Emma said. "A man who has made errors, mistakes he regrets and sincerely wishes to repair."

"Patrik saved Mistress Cristina from English knights several days back," the earl said.

Temper flared. "Do not attempt to explain away my feelings as gratitude. It takes little effort to see the incredible man Sir Patrik is. His loyalty, honesty, and integrity." Exhausted, Emma fought to rein in her anger. "Do you think 'twas easy for him to stay away, to be apart from the family, the people he loves? He has paid a great cost for his poor decisions."

Lord and Lady Grey absorbed her outburst with quiet interest.

"In the meager time you have known him," Lord Grey said, "you have learned a great deal about Patrik, more than most, a fact that intrigues me."

Emma bet it did. They were insights she'd not meant to give, but neither would she allow him to disparage Patrik.

The silence hummed with tension, a wordless challenge.

After a curious glance at her husband, the countess gave Emma a kind smile. "Mistress Cristina, you must be exhausted. My husband, I will take her to a chamber to rest."

Lord Grey's mouth tightened.

The earl wanted her nowhere near his wife, which suited Emma's plans fine. "It is unnecessary, my lady. I need but water, bread, and cheese and I will be on my way."

Surprise flashed across her face. "You are exhausted, your fine gown ruined, and neither can I allow you to travel into the dangers outside the castle walls alone."

If only Lady Grey understood the dangers she'd already faced, that she was one of England's top mercenaries, her kindness would bcome hatred.

Emma shook her head. "No, I—"

"You will remain," Lord Grey said. It wasn't a request. "We all wish to know you better."

Indeed.

"My husband," the countess said, "it has been a hectic morn for us all. Go and see your brother, and I will ensure Mistress Cristina is settled within a chamber."

The earl hesitated.

"Is there something wrong, my husband?"

"See me in private once you are through."

With a frown, the countess nodded.

The earl gave his wife a hard, brief kiss, whispered in her ear, then strode toward the keep.

Emma exhaled, feeling his departure like a storm evaded. But she had not escaped, merely gained a reprieve. "Sir Patrik's brothers do not like me, a fact you should know."

The countess turned. "My husband and his brothers

are formidable men, often hard to understand. But they care, love deeply, and would fight for one another to the end. Often, their gruff manner is but a shield."

"Traits Sir Patrik shares," Emma replied.

"He would," she said, glancing toward the keep where they'd carried Patrik, "if he is anything like his brothers."

The noblewoman's words held conviction, an unspoken understanding. "My lady, why are you telling me this?"

Her face softened. "Because you care for Patrik deeply, and he is my husband's brother."

Emma's throat tightened. "You know naught of me."

"Then it would seem we are even. Come. I will show you to a chamber, have a bath drawn, hot food delivered as well as a cup of wine to quench your thirst."

Emma fell into step beside the noble, feeling a fraud.

"I understand what it is like to be the outsider," the countess said.

"Because you are English?"

A smile touched her mouth. "One of many reasons. Mayhap in time I will explain. And please, call me Lady Linet."

"My lady—"

"In time," the countess interrupted, "I believe we will become friends."

Sadness weighed upon Emma. Time? However much she wished it, time here was not something she would ever have, nor the friendship offered.

Inside the keep, they passed through the great hall. Cooking meat and herbs simmered in pots hanging above the fires. At odds with that domestic setting, people hurried to tend the injured. A dais lay at the far end, topped by a huge table.

"This way." Lady Linet entered a turret and started up the spiral stairs. "The chamber you will stay in is on the second floor."

Torchlight illuminated the hewn stone. The pale gold light illuminated the tapestries hung along the walls.

Emma slowed. "These are beautiful."

"Gifts from my husband after we wed."

Within the flicker of light, she studied the intricate weave, the rich colors. "Fairies within a forest. Very unusual."

"They are. Or would be elsewhere." A smile edged Lady Linet's mouth as she pressed her fingers upon the halved stone around her neck.

A similar gemstone that Patrik wore came to mind. Were the pendants a family tradition?

"Come." The countess started up the steps, the rumble of men's voices below fading.

By the expression on Lady Linet's face as she'd stared at the tapestries, she loved Lord Grey. How had an English noble met and fallen for a high-ranking Scottish rebel?

She recalled Patrik's explanation of how the noblewoman Sir Alexander had abducted for ransom had become his wife. Did Lord Grey's relationship have a similar beginning? No, none would send a powerful lord upon a knight's mission. Still, something odd had occurred to allow such a union.

The love she felt for Patrik could never have such a chance.

Somberness settled over her, smothering her questions of how the powerful earl had met his wife. In silence, she followed the regal woman up the steps.

At the second floor, Lady Linet started down the hallway.

Emma paused, glancing to where the stairs wound up to another floor. Naught but an extension of the turret, yet an odd warmth beckoned her. Had they taken Patrik there? Did she somehow sense that was where he lay?

"Mistress Cristina?"

Heat streaked her cheeks. "Forgive me." Unsettled to have been caught staring, she followed the countess down the hall. En route, they passed a servant carrying water and lads bearing handfuls of wood.

Lady Linet halted a passing lad, gave him instructions to bring a tub and water, and then entered a nearby room. "This will be your chamber."

A bed was centered against the back chamber wall, a carved stand to one side with an unlit taper, and the wood in the hearth ablaze.

Fatigue washed over Emma. However simply adorned, the chamber looked like a piece of heaven. "Thank you, my lady."

"Once you have had your bath and have eaten, you will be left undisturbed." The countess paused. "This eve, if you have awoken, you are welcome to join our sup."

She doubted that the MacGruders would truly wish her in their presence. "My thanks," Emma replied, "but I will most likely sleep through the night."

"The rest will do you good."

Rest? However much she wished to sleep, using the

shield of night, she would make her escape. The food brought for her supper would come in handy as she traveled.

"Before I go to sleep, I would like to see Sir Patrik." To tell him good-bye.

Lady Linet hesitated. "He is with a healer. Once she leaves, 'tis best if he rests as well."

So that was what Lord Grey had whispered to his wife, to keep Emma away from Patrik. Fine then, she would not ask again, but she would see him one last time before she left.

Hands grasping the sturdy woolen coverlet upon his bed, Patrik clenched the aged wood between his teeth as the healer prodded. Yellow candlelight exposed several angry gashes across his shoulder and arm, wounds that had almost cost him his life.

"Bite harder," the old woman said, her eyes focused on the deepest gash across his left arm.

Patrik complied, trying to focus on anything but the pain as her hands quickly cleaned, then bound the severed flesh.

Her expression held grim satisfaction as she tied the last knot. She held up a ripe concoction. "Swallow this."

The pungent taste of herbs stung his tongue, and he gulped the water she handed him. "Tastes like mud."

"Aye," the healer agreed, "but 'twill lessen the worst of the pain. Rest now. You are not to be about for a sennight." The healer scowled. "A fortnight it should be, but I have known you too many years to believe you would ever be following that, if you even remain abed for a day." Though gently spoken, anger coated her words, caused by his attempt on Nichola's life.

Wood creaked as the chamber door opened. Seathan strode inside, followed by Duncan, then Alexander. The grim expressions upon their faces were far from welcoming.

The healer nodded at Seathan. "He should recover, my lord. With time. As yet, there is no sign of infection."

"Thank God," Seathan said.

In silence, the elderly woman secured the pouches of herbs, stowed them within her basket, and then closed the lid. "If he starts a fever, send for me."

"Aye," Seathan replied.

Soft footsteps echoed as the healer departed.

As the door closed in her wake, his brothers surrounded his bed. Tension throbbed in the chamber.

Patrik exhaled, taking in his brothers, the scowls on their faces. Nichola's outburst replayed in his mind. "No matter how many times I beg forgiveness for trying to kill Nichola, it will never be enough." He ached at the words, needing to say them.

Alexander crossed his arms. "She refuses to see you. A denial I will honor."

Patrik's throat tightened. "It is her right." While he'd lain healing within the crofter's bed, he'd had time, months to recount his actions, time in which he had found shame and self-recrimination in his attempt upon Nichola's life. Foolishly, he'd held hope that time could repair the severed ties with his family. But in his musings, Nichola had agreed to see him. Now, he didn't even have that hope.

Until she forgave him, though his brothers would allow him to remain at Lochshire Castle, their family bond would remain fractured, and this would never again be his home.

"By God's eyes, how do you live?" Alexander asked. "I saw you die, saw the light fade from your eyes."

"I . . ." Warmth pulsed within the stone at Patrik's neck. He frowned and touched the halved malachite, caught the exchange of curious glances between his brothers. "I remember pain, blackness, and then coming awake." He dropped his hand to his side. "I should have been dead."

The silence stretched.

Seathan cleared his throat. "There is a pressing issue that cannot wait."

At the seriousness of his tone, Patrik tensed. Then he knew. "The writ."

"Aye," Seathan replied. "Alexander gave it to me. I will send a runner to bring it to Wallace."

"My thanks," Patrik replied, still struggling to accept that the bishop had surrendered to the English. "Without the bishop's guidance, what will Wallace do?"

Seathan grimaced. "When Wallace learned of the bishop's surrender, he sent a missive to Andrew de Moray to bring his troops south. He was unaware John de Warenne was preparing to join forces with Cressingham, but it seems as though God guided his decision."

"Aye," Patrik agreed, his mind spinning with the

news. The addition of de Moray's forces would allow the rebels to deal a major blow.

At the continued silence, tension filled the room.

A muscle worked in Seathan's jaw. "Except, as Alexander told you, we were sent to intercept *Dubh Duer*."

Weariness settled over him. Aye, he had much to explain. In detail, Patrik revealed how after he'd recovered from near death, he had traveled to Bishop Wishart, begged for forgiveness of his sins, and pleaded to be allowed to continue to help the rebels. Then he spoke of the bishop's agreement as well as the new name he'd taken: *Dubh Duer*.

"So you hid behind an alias?" The rawness of Duncan's words echoed as if a slap.

"I could do no other," Patrik replied.

Alexander grunted. "You could have. Though I am proud of you for aiding the rebels, instead of daring to face us, tell us the truth, you shielded yourself behind a false name."

Anger erupted. Patrik shoved himself up; wove. "Bedamned!" he said as Seathan reached out, caught his good shoulder, steadied him. He faced Alexander, fought for consciousness, emotions slamming through him. "Tell me, Alexander, had you known that I lived, would you have found forgiveness after I had drawn blood from your wife, from you? Blast it, I tried to kill you both!" He glared at him. "I think not."

A flush stained Alexander's cheeks. "I—"

"What?" Patrik demanded, tired of the deceit, the lies that smothered him like a rag shoved over his mouth. "What would you have done? Do you not think while I lay within the crofter's bed, the days rolling into months, I had not the time to think out every possibility, time to wish to go back, time to erase the dishonor I took upon myself?"

The scar along Alexander's left cheek tightened. "And your suffering, reliving how you tried to kill my wife, is that supposed to rectify your actions?"

Sadness washed through Patrik. His legs shaking, he sank on the bed and steadied his hands upon his legs. "Nay. I have no ex-excuse but my loyalty to you."

"Loyalty?" Alexander grunted. "If trying to kill Nichola is an example of your loyalty—"

"Enough." Seathan glared from one man to the other. "Arguing will but deepen wounds already made."

The door opened.

Surprised someone dared interrupt their lord, Patrik glanced over.

A tall man entered, his stride confident, his build that of a warrior. Brown hair, secured by a leather thong, enhanced the hard angles of his face, his cloak of the finest wool, fitting his title—Baron of Monceaux, an affluent English lord, Advisor to the English king on Scottish affairs, and Nichola's brother Griffin.

The baron's eyes cut to Patrik, and he paled. Then anger brought crimson slashes to his cheeks. "You live?"

"Aye." How had they informed Nichola's brother so fast? Last Patrik knew, as King Edward's advisor to the Scots, Griffin was in England in discussion with John de Warenne on a pressing issue. He must have traveled north on business for the English crown, or, for the Rebels as *Wulfe*.

Seathan frowned. "Griffin, I thought you were meeting with Wallace?"

"I was, but our talk was interrupted by a missive from Wishart with his intent to surrender to the English." The baron stepped before Patrik, halted, his legs braced, his face carved with a fierce expression. "Needless to say, with that news our plans changed, and Wallace bade me here. Except," he drawled, fury slicing through his voice, "I had not expected to find the man who tried to kill my sister."

Chapter 16

"Saint's breath!" Patrik shoved to his feet again; once more, the room spun. He braced himself, held the Baron of Monceaux's damning gaze. "I was a bloody fool for trying to kill your sister, nay worse." His chest heaved as he struggled to breathe, to steady himself against the flood of emotions. "I regret everything about that day. More than you could ever know."

Griffin's eyes narrowed. "A mere apology and you expect me to forgive you?"

"Nay." Patrik cursed the entire situation, that he'd ever entertained the notion of returning to Lochshire Castle or reclaiming his family. "I expect nothing from you or anyone." Exhaustion weighed heavy upon his mind, he realized the herbs had begun to work. Aye, surrounded by four warriors, a fitting time for him to be slow of wit. "I was wrong to attack Nichola."

"Attack?" Alexander moved beside Griffin. "You shoved a knife to her neck and bloody tried to kill her!"

The image replayed like a nightmare in Patrik's hazy mind. "At the time I believed her unworthy of you and wanted her dead. But I was wrong." With heart-wrenching sadness, he took in each man, men whom he'd fought beside, men with whom he'd shared his dreams. Remorse balled in his throat. "Worry not, I shall not remain."

The scar on Alexander's cheek tightened. "Where will you go?"

Patrik gave a dry laugh. "As if where I am is of consequence? You will nae see me again, on that you have my word. But I will continue to serve Scotland's cause." He took a step toward the door; his body trembled from the effort.

"Sit, damn you," Seathan spat.

Feet braced, Patrik lifted his head as his soul crumbled. "An order, my lord?"

Seathan scowled. "Sit down before you fall."

"I—" The room blurred. Patrik struggled for words. "I will nae—" Blackness shrouded his mind.

Alexander caught Patrik as he collapsed. "Help me, damn you, Griffin."

"'Tis fine to see you as well," his brother-in-law said as he caught Patrik's other shoulder.

Alexander grunted. "Put the bloody fool back in his bed." Once they'd settled Patrik beneath the covers, Alexander stared down at the man who had tried to kill his wife, a man he still considered his brother. "The lad has the brains of an arse."

Duncan walked over, halted beside Alexander and shot his brother a grim smile. "Aye, but then, he always did."

On an exhale, Griffin stepped to Alexander's other side. "I would like to have wrung his bloody neck, but 'twas a waste to a man barely conscious." He cast Seathan a grim look. "Will you allow him to stay?"

"He is our brother." Seathan paused. "Why has Wallace sent you here?"

"He refuses to allow Wishart to remain in English hands," Griffin replied. "While he focuses his efforts on the English, we are to free the bishop."

Alexander nodded. "Wishart is too valuable for the Sassenach to keep, on that I agree."

"Where have they taken Bishop Wishart?" Seathan asked.

"He is incarcerated at Roxburgh Castle," Griffin replied.

Seathan grimaced. "What of the Earl of Carrick and Sir William Douglas? The missive Wishart sent stated they were to surrender as well."

"Robert Bruce has agreed to turn over his daughter as a hostage in his stead." Griffin paused. "As for Sir William Douglas, 'twould seem no quarter will be given. He was hauled to Berwick Castle."

"God's teeth." Seathan blew out a harsh breath. "We must free him as well. He cannot remain in English hands."

Darkness clouded Griffin's face. "I am not sure we have time. Douglas is to remain in Berwick Castle but a short while. During my brief meeting with Sir Henry de Percy, he explained King Edward demanded that once Sir William Douglas was caught, he was to be imprisoned within the Tower of London."

"To die there," Duncan growled.

Griffin nodded. "'Tis King Edward's wish."

"Bedamned to the English bastard," Alexander said, all too easily imagining the glee upon the king's face.

"Aye," Seathan agreed, "but for now, we must heed Wallace's orders and save Wishart. After, unless otherwise ordered, we will try to save Douglas as well."

Alexander grimaced, praying they'd have time to rescue Douglas before he was incarcerated within the Tower of London.

His brother-in-law turned toward where Patrik lay. "I am not sure whether to ask how Patrik is alive or how he came to be at Lochshire Castle?"

"He is the runner that Wishart asked us to intercept," Seathan replied.

Face pale, Griffin met Seathan's gaze. "Wishart told me the runner is *Dubh Duer*." He paused, stared in disbelief "*Dubh Duer* is Patrik?"

Seathan grimaced. "Aye."

"God's teeth," Griffin whispered, "King Edward would pay a hefty lot to display his head upon a pike."

Duncan arched an amused brow at Griffin. "A sum the English king would pay, if not more, for the spy they call *Wulfe*."

Brown eyes glittered with humor. "As for there being an English lord who shields his true name behind the title of *Wulfe*," Griffin drawled, "I often assure King Edward tales of this notorious noble are fables, stories crafted by the Scots to infuse doubt within the crown, that indeed, no such noble exists."

Alexander gave a rude laugh. "Aye, to save your bloody hide. Pray the bastard never learns that you, his Advisor to Scottish Affairs, are the man he seeks."

Silence descended in the chamber, laden with

knowledge of the dire consequences to those who rebelled against King Edward, and of the challenge in regaining Scotland's freedom.

Seathan withdrew the leather-bound missive, handed it to Griffin.

The Baron of Monceaux studied the blood red wax impression, flicked his eyes to Seathan. "'Tis indeed the royal seal."

"Aye," Seathan replied, "the informant's daring brand, which he uses beneath King Edward's nose, and proof we intercepted the runner Bishop Wishart awaited. It is also proof Patrik is *Dubh Duer*."

Griffin shook his head. "'Tis unbelievable. We thought Patrik dead, and he has fought alongside us throughout."

Somberness filled the room, the ache of old hurt joining the slash of new. Alexander stared at his brother sprawled upon the bed, his face pale. Time had hardened the broken lad who had come to them after his family was murdered. Time had tempered the pain, but not Patrik's anger toward the English. Over the years their adopted brother had learned to hide his outrage, to mask it with a quip.

Until he'd met Nichola.

Nay, until Alexander had fallen in love with an English lass, a woman who Patrik had stated at the time he'd found unworthy of his brother. By God's eyes 'twas a mess, but one they would muddle through. Patrik was family. A low pounding started in Alexander's temple. He rubbed his brow. How could he tell Nichola of Patrik's regret? Or, should he?

Seathan took the writ, distracting Alexander from his troubling thoughts.

His elder brother met Griffin's gaze. "Patrik said 'tis confirmation that John de Warenne is preparing to depart and rejoin forces with Hugh de Cressingham before the end of July."

"God's teeth, with the Earl of Surrey's dislike for Scotland," Griffin said, "King Edward must have ordered him poked with a hot iron to prod him from his estates in Surrey."

"Aye," Alexander agreed. "'Twould please me to see King Edward's minion be fool enough to ride into battle with the Earl of Surrey. I would savor the sight of his flesh upon my blade."

"With his lack of training with a sword," Duncan said, "he could spear naught but a morsel upon his trencher."

"Regardless, with his arrogance and believing that the battle is already won," Seathan said, "I would be more surprised if he did not ride alongside the Earl of Surrey."

Griffin nodded. "I agree. 'Tis folly to underestimate Cressingham. For a man of illegitimate birth, he has ascended far to become the treasurer of the English administration in Scotland."

"Mayhap, but the blood of the impoverished stains the bastard's steps. Nor does he care." Alexander shook his head. "Nothing will stop the king's minion from his selfish goals."

"Aye," Duncan agreed. "'Tis fitting that behind Cressingham's back the English label him the *Son of Death*."

"And," Alexander added, "the *treacherer* by the Scots."

"Both names testaments to the lengths Cressingham will go to achieve his goals," Griffin stated, "regardless of cost."

Silence hummed within the room, thick with tension. Alexander glanced at Patrik; his brother's face was ashen, his body wilted within his bed. "What of the lass?"

Confusion darkened Griffin's gaze. "What woman do you speak of?"

"When we found Patrik," Seathan explained, "a Scottish lass, Mistress Cristina Moffat, accompanied him. She told us Patrik saved her from being raped by English knights a few days past."

"The bloody miscreants." Griffin paused. "Where is she?"

"Asleep," Seathan replied. "And nearly as battered as Patrik. When English knights attacked a crofter's home, Cristina hid their little girl, then later fought off the English knights to save her."

Surprise shone in Griffin's eyes. "She killed two knights? Sounds like an amazing woman."

"She does." Alexander grimaced. "Mayhap too much."

His brother-in-law's gaze narrowed. "Explain."

"When we found the lass," Alexander replied, "she was in the forest with the crofter's child. Patrik was with her, but trees shielded him from our view. When I saw Patrik—" Memories stormed Alexander's mind. He clenched his fists, the taste of anger still fresh. "—I lost my head, jumped off my mount and began to beat him." He shook his head. "A fact I am not proud of, but all I could think was how he'd tried to kill Nichola."

Red slashed Griffin's cheeks. "Understandable."

"Nay, you do not understand," Alexander said, wanting him to comprehend the wrong he'd committed. "I cared not that Patrik's sparring with the English had left him seriously injured, or that he staggered before me, or that his body lay bruised and stained with his blood. I attacked. Brutally. At that moment, I wanted Patrik dead." He squeezed his eyes shut, opened them. "God's teeth. I tried to kill my own brother."

"You did," Griffin replied, his voice somber, "what any man in your position would have done. What I would have tried as well."

Alexander fisted his hands at his sides. "That does not make my actions right."

"No," Griffin agreed, "but it makes you a man, one who loves his wife, one who stops at nothing to protect what is his." He paused. "What about the woman?"

His body still trembling with emotion, Alexander unfurled his hands. "After I began hitting Patrik, instead of screaming as most lasses would, Mistress Cristina jumped upon my back and started to strangle me, her grip sure."

"After the years the English have ravaged Scotland, torched its towns and slaughtered its people," Griffin said, "why would you find a woman who knows how to protect herself odd?"

"I should agree," Alexander replied, "and I find myself trying to dismiss my worries. But en route to Lochshire Castle, I caught her trying to slip away."

Seathan's eyes narrowed. "Why did you not tell me this before?"

"What? That I saw the lass climbing toward the back of a wagon holding Patrik's water pouch? That at my words she jumped as if a thief caught?" Alexander grunted. "I should have allowed her to climb from the wagon and gained proof of my suspicions. Now, I have naught to base my claim upon but her reaction and the feeling that something about the lass is amiss."

"Mayhap," Seathan said. "But instinct often saves a warrior's life."

Alexander glanced at Patrik. "Curious I will be to hear his thoughts on the lass."

"As I." Duncan frowned. "Remember when Patrik stood within the bailey apologizing to Nichola, how he was barely able to stand? Remember how the lass defended him like a she-wolf would her cub?"

"She is knowledgeable as well," Alexander added, "and speaks as if schooled. She claims no lineage, but whatever she is, it is far from common."

Griffin arched a brow. "You believe she is of noble birth?"

"When we first found her," Seathan explained, "she wore a gown befitting gentry. She explained the dress was a gift and she but a commoner."

"I am confused," Griffin said. "Aside from Patrik saving her life, what significance does this woman hold?"

"The lass," Alexander grumbled as he eyed his brother-in-law, "is in love with Patrik."

* * *

Flames flickering within the hearth greeted Emma as she opened her eyes. On a yawn, she glanced out the window. Stars splashed the sky, shimmers of light as if a thousand wishes cast.

Stars?

The hand-spun blanket tumbled down the bed as she shot upright. She'd slept the entire day! By now she'd meant to be long gone.

And what of Patrik? Had he succumbed to fever? Was he recovering and lost deep within a healing sleep?

A plate of food sat upon a nearby table. Guilt crowded her as she stood, stowed the fare in a small sack and secured it beneath her gown. Before she departed, she must know how Patrik fared, see him one last time.

Heart aching, she walked toward the door.

Stopped.

Lady Linet's careful refusal to allow her to see Patrik echoed in her mind as did Lord Grey's whispered words to his wife. No, if she sought permission to see Patrik, she would not be welcome. So she would not ask.

After Patrik's previous attempt to kill Sir Alexander's wife, would his chamber be guarded? Or, had his apology this day swayed Lord Grey? If any, 'twas her chamber that should be guarded.

Emma walked to the entry. Hand trembling, she inched open the wood door.

Torchlight illuminated the corridor, the flicker of flames falling upon mounted tapestries along with ancient weapons of war. Not a guard in sight.

She blew out a relieved breath, then stilled. Why

was there no guard? The brothers did not trust her. Or did they believe she could not escape?

A claymore secured upon the wall directly across from her chamber caught her attention. A finely carved figure graced its leather-bound hilt. Intrigued, she stepped closer. Not a figure.

A fairy.

Delicate wings were spread open as if to take flight, the woman's face impish, her eyes captured in an expression of pure delight. The delicate carving should seem awkward atop the brutal weapon. But against all sense, the fairy's presence seemed right.

A shiver ran through her. Emma touched the hidden dagger secured against her thigh. Fortunately she did not need the claymore. Not that she would be foolish enough to try to procure this family heirloom. Though desperate, she was far from a fool.

The bells from the chapel pealed with a somber ring.

What was she doing wasting precious time? She needed to find Patrik, then slip away. The steps winding up the turret came to mind. Had they left no guards on this floor because he was installed above?

Unsure of anything, she glanced one last time toward the opposite end of the corridor. Not an echo or a whisper of movement anywhere. With quiet steps, she reached the turret and began her ascent.

A window above revealed the night sky, the shimmer of stars seeming brighter than usual. She blinked. They remained intense. Emma frowned, certain fatigue played with her mind.

Several steps up, a sturdy oak door came into view.

Fixed upon forged brackets, a bar straddled the wooden expanse.

Patrik! They'd locked him inside. At least they hadn't cast him in the dungeon.

Chest tight, she hurried up the steps. At the door, with a quick glance behind to ensure no one was coming, she quietly lifted the bar, then rushed inside.

She came to a standstill.

Moonbeams swirled within the single arched window, silvery strokes that sifted to illuminate the chamber as if at the wave of a hand. Near the back wall stood a bed graced with a hand-stitched coverlet, a unique blend of yellow and . . . With a frown she crossed the room, ran her hand over the finely spun fabric.

Silver.

No, silver embroidery would cost an enormous amount, possible only for kings. Or was it a gift from the crown? The sword below with the fairy on the leather-bound hilt came to mind. Odd, she sensed the two were related.

Unsettled, she took in the chamber. Nearby, an ivory-framed mirror lay upon a small table. A cross pendant sat askew upon the time-worn wood as if awaiting its owner, its chain trailing atop a simple gold ring. Upon the far wall, a finely crafted tapestry depicted a forest scene, one notably similar to the piece hanging in the turret below. Once again, fairies peeked through the breaks in the leaves.

Never would she have pictured Lord Grey allowing such a whimsical chamber in a fortress designed for war.

As she continued to scan the chamber, a sense of

peace swept over her, a contentment so complete she could have lain upon the bed, closed her eyes and slept. Odd, never in her life had she felt so accepted, so relaxed.

At an echo of laughter Emma glanced up. Caught within the strokes of a brush upon the ceiling, fairies played above her. They seemed vaguely familiar. She glanced at the tapestry, then back up.

Duplicates.

Upon the ceiling, the artist had recaptured the playful images woven within the tapestry. Except, whoever had crafted the imagery above had allowed their creativity free rein. Instead of mere eyes, or a hint of wings, entire fairies appeared.

Understanding dawned. Of course, this room belonged to a woman, someone important to the brothers. It explained the unexpected whimsical feel. This was a place where dreams abounded. And more important than the wealth within was the feeling of love.

Love.

Emptiness filled her, an ache for what she would never have. Emma rubbed her arms. However much she yearned to stay, to lie upon the bed and wish her troubles away, she must leave. The morrow would bring but more complications, more questions that she could never answer. First, she must find Patrik.

"He is two doors down from the chamber given you."

At the woman's lyrical voice, Emma whirled.

Within a chair near the hearth sat an elderly woman regarding her with wizened eyes. Flames danced within the fireplace, and she held a half-completed embroidery within her hand.

"I-I did not see you when I entered." Nor the fire. Wouldn't she have noticed the flicker of flames upon her arrival?

"Your mind is troubled." A smile warmed the old woman's face. "Worry not, Patrik is out of danger."

Whoever she was, the brothers must have informed this woman of her and Patrik's arrival, his wounds, as well as any changes in his condition.

"My thanks." Emma worried her thumb over the tip of her fingers. "My apologies, I wished to see him and thought he was here."

Warmth caressed the woman's smile. "Patrik sleeps. On the morrow, he will fare better, but this night he should rest." The matronly woman set aside her delicate handiwork. "And what of you?"

Nervousness slid through Emma. "What of me?"

"'Tis late to be about, especially for a lass in an unfamiliar castle." She arched a brow. "Will you return to your chamber this night and find your bed?"

"As you said, it is late. Where else would I go?" But her words fell out too fast, and the food stowed beneath her gown gave evidence of her guilt. Emma caught a glimpse of sadness in the woman's eyes, as if she knew her thoughts. Impossible.

"Indeed, where else would you go," the elderly woman agreed. "But beware, secrets are spun in the dark of the night, secrets crafted with innocent intent, but in the end, secrets that could destroy."

"Sir Alexander has little liking for me," she said,

aware this woman's beliefs could only have come from him.

Sadness settled upon the elder's face, aged lines that hinted she'd braved many challenges throughout the years. "Alexander is a lad who bears the hard weight of youth as guilt." She paused. "As do you."

Shaken, Emma stepped back. What was going on? This woman could know nothing about her. "It is late."

"For some the hour grows long," the woman said, "but the gift of time remains if you so choose."

If only the choice was so simple. Her time for truths had long since passed. "I am indeed tired," Emma said. "I am sorry to disturb you."

"You did not disturb me." She picked up the embroidery, and Emma caught the outline of wings upon the delicate cloth. The woman smiled. "This was but a task to entertain me until your arrival."

Shaken, Emma took another step back. "How did you know I would—"

"God's teeth, what are you doing here?"

At Sir Alexander's furious voice, Emma spun. Heart pounding, she faced the warrior. "I was looking for Patrik."

The scar across his left cheek jumped. "Were you?" He scanned the chamber and his scowl deepened.

"I was speaking with . . ." Heat stung her cheeks. She'd forgotten to ask the elderly woman her name. Emma turned. Stilled.

"Who?" Suspicion carved Alexander's voice.

"An elderly woman. She was sitting before the fire

with her embroidery when you arrived." Emma stared at the empty chamber, her panic growing. Where was she?

Anger tightened his face. "There is not a stick of wood within the hearth."

As if she could not see that? God in heaven, where had the woman gone? "There was a fire. I swear it."

Sir Alexander snorted in disbelief. "Truth, you were outside your room. When you heard me coming up the turret, you ran and hid in this chamber believing you were safe."

"No."

"Why do I find myself not believing you?" His gaze cut past her, widened. "By my sword!" He strode past her.

Emma turned.

Near the bed, Sir Alexander stared at a bowl. Inside, sat two halved gemstones. Framed within the rough exterior of one half, she recognized the pale green sweep of color, a shade that darkened to a deep, tumultuous olive hue at its center. A gemstone identical to the one Patrik wore around his neck; a gemstone that had warmed within her hand when she'd touched it. The stone was a potent reminder of the love she and Patrik had made.

On unsteady legs, she moved closer, studied the other halved gem at its side. Though similar in size, this gemstone held a mixture of gray and stark yellow. Never had she seen such an unusual mix.

Sir Alexander whirled, his face pale. "I will take you to your chamber."

With cold silence he guided her from the chamber, but his emotional turmoil was clear. Before she stepped from the room, a flicker of light from the ceiling had her glancing up. Sadness creased the fairies' faces that had shimmered with happiness moments before.

Sir Alexander wanted her away from this chamber, and she was not about to object. As she started to walk through the entry, Emma glanced at where the mate to Patrik's halved gem lay. She stumbled. It was glowing!

As if the hounds of hell chased her, she hurried through the door. Sir Alexander need not escort her out of this room. Never had she been so afraid in all of her life.

His mind still racing from finding Cristina in his grandmother's chamber, Alexander strode along the wall walk, too upset to go to his bed. As he passed a crenellation he paused, staring past the granite that framed the moonlit view beyond.

The image of the second halved stone within the bowl scraped through his mind as well as Cristina's claim to have seen an elderly woman. The lass knew not who had lived there, but he did—his grandmother. By God's eyes, it could not be.

"Alexander?"

At his wife's concerned voice, he turned. Nichola walked toward him, their son cradled in her arms, his eyes wide and wondrous. A sense of completeness infused him. He walked over, laid his hand upon his son.

Soft, tiny fingers clasped his thumb. A smile wobbled upon chubby cheeks along with a bright-eyed smile.

"A fine son you have given me."

Love caressed her face. "A son who now has cousins to play with."

Alexander shrugged. "With twin daughters, 'tis a good thing Duncan was always won over by the lasses."

She chuckled. "And they have stolen your heart as well."

Alexander shrugged. "Mayhap."

The smile in Nichola's eyes faded. "What is wrong, my husband?"

He withdrew his hand from his son's hold, turned to stare across the moonlit loch. Alexander was struck by the memory of he and his brothers lying upon the distant shores after Duncan and Patrik had stolen his garb. The chase, Duncan's cries as he'd fetched Alexander's clothes from the brush, and then the wine they'd drunk as they lay upon the bank.

"Alexander?"

"There is another halved stone in my grandmother's bowl."

"What? Why would you go up to your grandmother's chamber?"

He turned. "As I was heading to bed, I saw a light in the turret."

"No one has been in the chamber?"

The nerves in her voice left him further on edge. "Aye, after Linet's foray into the room a few months ago, the chamber was left with the door shut and barred."

"But you said you entered the tower chamber?"

He blew out a deep breath. "Aye, the door was open. When I entered, I found Mistress Cristina standing before an empty chair, talking."

"Talking? To whom?"

Alexander gave a gruff laugh. "No one."

"My husband, you are making little sense."

"A fact I well realize. When I asked the lass who she was speaking with, she said to an elderly woman."

Nichola stilled. "Your grandmother appeared?"

"I did not see her."

"Do you believe Mistress Cristina did?"

"I believe the lass was outside her chamber, heard me coming and when confronted, crafted a tale."

"But you are not sure."

He muttered a curse. "Nae, which helps naught. Mistress Cristina's surprise at seeing me seemed real; she seemed startled when she turned and found no woman sitting before the hearth."

Nichola laid her son upon her shoulder, rubbed the middle of his back in a slow sweep, but Alexander saw a slight nervous tremble.

"What do you think your grandmother appearing before Mistress Cristina means?"

"It means the lass was where she shouldna be."

Silence.

"Alexander?"

"Aye?"

"When the malachite appeared before . . . It was your grandmother's way of letting us know Patrik lived." Their son burped, and with shaky movements, Nichola tucked him within the swaddling cloth, then laid him against her chest. "Was Patrik's halved stone still within the bowl?"

"Aye," he said, irritated he'd mentioned his brother's name.

She inhaled, released a shaky breath. "Do you think . . ."

"That the lass is the woman meant for Patrik?" He shrugged. "She did not take the stone."

"But?"

"Blast it. I do not wish to speak of this. 'Tis foolery. The story of the stones is a myth, a fable crafted by my brothers to tease me when I abducted you."

"Mayhap." A smile wobbled on her mouth. "But do you not find it odd that every woman who has married a MacGruder brother has taken the halved stone of her mate?"

He scowled. "Patrik's stone remains."

"But, you said Mistress Cristina saw your grandmother?"

"The lass stated that she spoke with an elderly woman, if I am to believe that." Alexander drew his wife and child within his arms.

She laid her cheek against his shoulder. "What will you tell your brothers?"

"I know not. 'Tis a bloody mess."

"Alexander?"

He met her gaze. "Aye?"

"You said there was another stone?"

"Aye. Never have I seen it before."

"What do you think it means?"

"I do not know, but I assure you, I will speak with my brothers at first light. Exactly what I will tell them is another matter."

Anger sparked in Seathan's eyes as he stood in Patrik's chamber by the window. "What was Mistress Cristina doing in our grandmother's chamber?"

In complete detail, Alexander explained to his brothers and Griffin last night's events.

"And when you arrived within your grandmother's chamber, no one else was within the room?" Griffin asked, clearly intrigued by the new twist in the Mac-Gruder family mystery.

"Nay." Alexander thrummed his fingers upon the hilt of his dagger. "But from the shock on Mistress Cristina's face as she turned and found no one there, 'tis hard to discount her claim as a lie."

Duncan shook his head. "It had to be our grandmother."

Alexander eyed his younger brother. "I do not want to believe it. I fought throughout the night to find another reason, yet nothing else makes sense." He muttered a curse. "The lass knows not 'twas our grandmother's chamber, nor has she ever met her. Yet, she described her in exact detail."

"So, it seems our grandmother's spirit indeed visits the chamber," Seathan said, his voice raw with wonder. "And it would explain the reappearance of Patrik's stone months ago."

"It was your grandmother's way of revealing Patrik lived," Griffin said. "But why would his gemstone have disappeared to begin with?"

"At this moment," Seathan replied, "the only one who knows that is our grandmother."

Silence filled the chamber as the brothers shared a look of agreement as to what their grandmother's appearance to Mistress Cristina meant.

Alexander frowned, not liking the mystery. Was Cristina indeed meant for Patrik? Nay, had she taken the stone, then he would be convinced.

"But," Alexander said, "it does nae explain the appearance of the other halved stone within the bowl, a gem I have never seen before."

Duncan frowned. "A second stone? Sword's wrath, 'tis a muddle."

"Think you I do not know that?" Alexander said. "I had barred the bloody chamber myself."

"It would seem barriers matter not when our grandmother is involved," Seathan said.

"Do you think there are more halved stones to appear?" At Alexander's scowl, Duncan raised his hands. "Do nae give me that look."

"At this moment," Seathan broke in, "our most pressing need is to figure out how to free Bishop Wishart, not the stones or their importance."

Griffin rubbed the back of his neck.

His brother-in-law's nervous action caught Alexander's attention. "What is wrong?"

A hesitant look crossed Griffin's face. "What did the stone look like?"

Alexander crossed his arms. "Why?"

"On my many trips to Lochshire Castle over the years," Griffin replied, "I had the pleasure of meeting your grandmother."

Seathan's gaze narrowed. "You would."

"On one such visit, she requested my presence in private. And," Griffin said as he withdrew the chain from around his neck, "gave me this halved magnesite."

Alexander gasped, his gut dropping to his toes, "'Tis a bloody perfect match!"

Chapter 17

Patrik's body ached and his head pounded as if a mace had struck it. He blinked against the morning sun filtering into his chamber.

Though furnished with little more than a bed, a wooden nightstand and a chest for his garb, this represented his home, a place where, when but a broken lad, he'd come and rebuilt his shattered life.

He noticed his brothers and Griffin standing within the chamber. For the past year their absence had left an aching void within him. Now, desperately, he wanted them back.

Seathan muttered a curse at Alexander's comment about the English, dragging Patrik's thoughts to the discussion at hand. "Aye." He shifted and pain shot through his arm, sending his shoulder muscles into spasms. With a muttered curse at his weakness, he cleared his throat. "With Wishart in English hands, Wallace's leadership is essential if we are to stop the English."

Seathan nodded. "Wallace is gathering forces in

Selkirk Forest. Andrew de Moray and his forces should join Wallace before the end of August. Whatever it takes, the English must not reach Stirling Castle."

"Aye," Patrik agreed. "We must stop them before they cross the Forth."

"Wallace plans to set up the combined armies north of the bridge that crosses the Forth," Griffin explained.

"'Twill be dangerous," Duncan said.

"More so if the Earl of Surrey sends troops upstream to cross the river where sixty men can ride abreast." Alexander met each man's gaze. "If they choose such a tactic, I am unsure whether Wallace's and de Moray's troops can hold them."

"What other choice is there?" Patrik asked.

Duncan exhaled. "Bloody none. Regardless, we will fight."

Somberness smothered the chamber, thick with unspoken fears, raw with determination to free their country. Too well Patrik understood. If the English claimed Stirling Castle, the bloodied ground so far won by the rebels could be lost.

Patrik met his oldest brother's gaze. "Have you begun plans to free Wishart?"

"A foundation," Seathan replied. "I have sent runners to those familiar with the keep where the bishop is held to be sure the plan is solid."

"I wish to help." Patrik held his brother's gaze. "And when you prepare to leave I will go with you."

"You are too weak," Seathan replied.

"And with your wounds raw, you hurt like a bastard," Alexander added.

"There is that," Patrik agreed, "but in a few days I will be able to ride and carry a sword as well as any man."

"When the time comes to depart," Seathan said, his eyes hard, "I will judge if you are strong enough."

As much as Patrik wished to push for Seathan to agree, his brother's decision was fair. Neither could he forget he stayed within Lochshire Castle by Seathan's grace.

"How fares Mistress Cristina?" At Alexander's covert glance at Seathan, Patrik tensed. "Is she well?"

"Aye." Seathan hesitated. "She sleeps but a few chambers away."

"But there is more?" Patrik asked, reading his brothers too well despite his year away.

Duncan cleared his throat, and Griffin shot Seathan an uneasy look.

Patrik's nervousness built. "What?"

Alexander thrummed his fingers upon his dagger. "Last night I discovered Mistress Cristina within our grandmother's chamber."

"If her room is but a few doors away," Patrik said, "what reason would bring her to the third floor?"

"A question I asked her," Alexander replied. "The lass said she was searching for you."

She'd tried to find him? Warmth touched Patrik's heart, then he frowned. "Why would the lass have to search?"

"We thought it best for you to rest," Seathan stated.

Rest bedamned. "She was not told where I was. Why?"

A muscle worked in Alexander's jaw. "There is something about the lass that sits not right."

Patrik eyed him. "Explain."

In detail, Alexander recounted her skilled attack upon him during his fight with Patrik, then later, how he had found her creeping toward the back of the wagon in the dark as they'd neared Lochshire Castle.

"After my rescuing her," Patrik said, "it makes sense she would try to protect me."

Alexander grunted. "Mayhap, but when the lass wrapped her arms about my neck, she knew what she was about."

Images of her killing the English knight flashed through Patrik's mind. When he'd witnessed her skill with the blade, had he not wondered the same? But 'twas different. Now, they'd made love, shared a bond of trust.

Patrik shook his head. "Cristina was terrified for my life. Had Nichola seen you attacked, she would have done the same."

"What of slipping toward the back of the wagon?" Seathan asked. "Do you think she was trying to leave?"

"There could be many reasons for her quietly moving about the wagon, including consideration," Patrik stated, recalling his own unjust accusations within the loft when he'd believed she was searching for the writ. "I was injured and asleep. Marie and her daughter slept nearby." He glanced toward Alexander. "You saw her moving about, not trying to leave the wagon."

Alexander muttered a curse. "I know what I saw, but aye, as you said, I do not have proof." He slanted his brothers a look, then faced Patrik. "We know you care for the lass. Your feelings may sway your thoughts."

"My thoughts are nae swayed," Patrik stated, his voice cool.

"Mayhap," Duncan said, "but is she a woman you can trust?"

Pride filled him. "I have placed my life within Cristina's hands throughout our journey."

"But do you trust her?" Seathan asked with no accusation.

Patrik's doubts again came to mind, and one by one each fell away. An ache built in his heart, like an arrow to his soul.

"Aye." That, and more. The realization shook Patrik to the very core. Images of their bodies entwined as they'd made love filled his mind, and he recalled their talks as he'd held her after. "I love her," he whispered, shocked by the words as much as that he'd spoken them.

"By my sword," Alexander muttered. "You did not even know your feelings for the lass?"

"No." Patrik gave a rough laugh, his mind floundering with the revelation. "Saint's breath, until this moment, I was focused only on the mission."

"Her actions show that she cares for you," Seathan said, "but does she love you as well?"

"I do not know." Sadness wove through Patrik. "It matters not. However much I care for the lass, until Scotland is free, I can offer her no guarantees."

Duncan grunted. "As if any of us can offer our wives the same? I have twin daughters now, yet I go on. We cannot wait for sure things before we continue with our lives."

Frustration surged through Patrik. "Easily said when you have a family to shelter you."

"A family your actions sought to destroy," Alexander charged.

Patrik shook his head. "Nae, a family I sought to protect. I have explained my reasons." Patrik paused. "And I understand you can never find forgiveness." Somber, he shook his head. "As I said before, once I am well enough, I will leave. Before I go, I ask to be allowed to ride with you to free Bishop Wishart."

"You will leave after we have found you?" Duncan asked.

"Found me?" Patrik gave a cold laugh. "Nae, I chose to reveal myself."

"And now?" Seathan asked.

"Now?" Patrik stared at the men within the chamber, brothers of his heart. "Have I a choice?"

Tense silence filled the room.

Seathan cast a glance at Alexander.

"Aye," Alexander said. "'Tis up to you to choose if you remain. We are family. Wrongs were committed, but they are past."

"You forgive me?" Patrik asked, stunned, afraid to repeat the words as if they would be swept away.

Alexander grimaced. "I am working on it. It is not something I can rush nor lie about. As for Nichola, 'twill be her decision to make."

Nichola. The woman who was the gateway to his true acceptance within their family. "Do you think she will ever forgive me?"

Alexander shrugged. "I do not know."

Tension vibrated within the chamber. Patrik swallowed hard, prayed he would find a way to overcome the wrongs he'd done her. He touched the halved malachite around his neck, caught his brothers stealing glances at the other. "What?"

Seathan grimaced. "Your malachite."

"What about it?" Patrik asked.

"When we thought you had died," his oldest brother said, "your halved stone disappeared from our grandmother's chamber."

"It disappeared?" Patrik asked.

"Aye," Alexander replied. "A few months ago, it returned."

Patrik frowned. "How?"

"It would seem," Duncan said, "'tis a question for our grandmother to answer."

"Your grandmother is dead," Patrik said. None of this made sense.

Duncan nodded. "Aye."

Hope ignited within Patrik. Was the return of his stone a sign he would reclaim his family?

"You should also know," Alexander hesitated, "when each of us met the woman who eventually became our wife, each one left Lochshire Castle, taking with her the respective half of our halved gemstones."

This was becoming more confusing. "Are you telling me Cristina took my stone?"

"Nae," Alexander replied. "The lass recognized your stone within the bowl, but not the other." He gestured to Griffin. "One that belongs to him."

"Griffin?" Patrik glanced toward the baron. "I never knew he was gifted with a halved gemstone."

Seathan shook his head. "Nor did any of us. Now, tell us everything about the lass that concerns you."

"'Tis not so much concern as surprise." Patrik

recounted her killing of the knight during their confrontation on the path, then about finding the English bodies after Cristina had taken Joneta to safety; her quick actions had protected both her and the child.

"Her killing one knight might be feasible," Griffin said, "but to take on two?"

Patrik nodded, pride for her filling his heart. "The first man she felled with her dagger, the second she used the other knight's sword. But then, a woman protecting a child is one to be wary of." An image flickered in his mind. He frowned.

"What is it?" Seathan asked.

He wanted to dismiss the thought, but his brother had asked, and he had nothing to hide. "While we stayed overnight within the crofter's hut, when she believed me asleep, I caught her searching through my garb."

"What?" the men in the room said in unison.

Alexander's face tightened. "Was she searching for the writ?"

"Nae," he said, irritated they'd believe the worst, and that he had, too. "When I asked, she claimed she was looking for a tie to bind her hair, one she found a moment later."

"And you believed her?" Seathan asked.

"Aye, 'twas my own fear for the writ that invited doubts." Doubts he no longer held for the woman he loved. Saint's breath, how could he have failed to recognize his feelings before? Because, for too long he hadn't considered love possible for him.

Alexander grunted. "Believe what you will, but I know what I saw. Had I not spoken, the lass would have slipped from the wagon. I say she cannot be trusted."

Irritation slid through Patrik. "'Tis your anger that a slip of a woman jumped you."

"Mayhap," Griffin agreed, "but Mistress Cristina has seen the writ, the English seal upon it."

Seathan nodded. "Before she is allowed to go free, we must know her loyalties."

Unease crept through Patrik that his brothers could not see the sincere, loving woman he'd come to know. "She would not betray us."

"Can you swear that upon your life?" Alexander demanded. "Those of your fellow Scots?"

"Patrik," Seathan said. "Let not your feelings for the lass blind you to the risks."

A muscle worked in Patrik's jaw. "They do not."

"Aye, they do," Seathan replied. "If you love someone, regardless of what you wish, the heart interferes."

Patrik wanted to argue, but found wisdom in his brother's words. "So, what do we do?"

"Allow her to find the writ," Seathan replied, "and see if indeed she takes it."

Nausea swept Patrik. "Set her up?"

"The stakes are too high to take any risks," Griffin stated, somber.

"I will post extra guards at the castle exits in the event she takes it," Seathan said, "to ensure she does not escape."

"And if she does?" Patrik asked, hating the question.

"Without a horse she will be easy to track down," Seathan replied. "Regardless of your belief about the lass, we must know."

Patrik despised what they proposed. They didn't
know Cristina, or understand the horrors she'd overcome. That against the odds, she'd grown into an
amazing, caring woman, one whom he'd grown to
love. To even consider agreeing to their plot reeked of
betrayal. Still, he understood their concern, respected
their caution. He blew out a harsh breath. Nodded. Let
them set up a ploy to test her, but he well knew the
result—she would leave the writ untouched.

Seated at the dais within the great hall, Emma
sipped the last of her wine. The rumble of people filling the room as they ate was far from calming, and
she found their curious stares disturbing. She damned
her failed attempt to see Patrik before she left, but at
his door this morn she'd heard male voices from
within. One, she'd recognized as Alexander, the others
those of his brothers. No, she was not foolish enough
to enter the lion's den.

"You are full?" Lady Linet asked from her side.

"Yes." Guilt edged through Emma that Lady Linet
had honored her with such status as to sit upon the
dais while she broke her fast. If they knew Sir Cressingham had hired her, they'd offer her little but the
coldness of the dungeon, if not death.

Lady Linet set her goblet upon the table and smiled.
"You are free to move about the keep."

Stunned by her offer, Emma hesitated. "Including
seeing Patrik?"

"If you wish."

Unease crept through Emma. "Why am I now allowed to see Patrik?"

A touch of color rose in the other woman's cheeks. "My husband but wanted Patrik to have a night's rest."

It was the same reason given before, yet she had her doubts. Had Lord Grey's decision to do with his meeting this morning in Patrik's chamber? Mayhap she was imagining danger where none lurked. Regardless of the earl's reason, she could see Patrik one last time.

A whirl of blond curls rushed toward her.

Delight infused Emma. "Joneta."

"My mum told me to leave you be as you are busy eating, but I stole away when she was not looking," Joneta whooshed out, her eyes shining with excitement, "You are not upset, are you?"

"Of course not." Emotion swamped Emma as she smiled at Marie, who stood a few paces away. After giving the child a warm hug, she leaned back and caught Lady Linet watching her with interest. After a brief introduction, she turned to the girl. "And what have you been doing since your arrival?"

"Yesterday afternoon, a woman took my mum and I around. And my father has been given a task. We will live here!" Joneta's voice squealed with excitement. "Is not this castle wondrous?"

"It is," Emma agreed. Lord Grey was truly a kind man. She smiled at Marie. "And 'twould seem you have found a new home."

"We have." Marie nodded to the countess. "Our thanks, my lady, to you and your husband."

Lady Linet smiled. "I hope you will enjoy living at

Lochshire Castle." She stood, motioned to Emma. "If you are ready, I will show you to Patrik's chamber."

Excitement filled Emma as she rose. "I must go." She gave Joneta one last hug. "And, your mother is waiting."

Blond locks bounced as the child hurried back to her mother. Once there, she turned and waved.

"She is adorable," Lady Linet said.

"She is." And Emma would miss her when she left. Somber, she turned, followed the countess up the turret steps. With each one her sense of regret deepened. This would be the last time she saw Patrik.

A tall, muscled man descended the stairs above. Brown hair secured at the nape of his neck framed a hard face and brown eyes that sparked with intelligence. Why did he seem familiar? Her blood turned to ice.

God in heaven, the Baron of Monceaux!

Cristina stumbled.

Lord Monceaux caught her. "Be careful, my lady."

Panic stormed her. *Please God, do not recognize me.* "My regrets, I was clumsy."

He frowned, his eyes studying her curiously.

"Griffin," Lady Linet said. "You have not yet met Mistress Cristina. She arrived with Patrik. Mistress Cristina, it is my pleasure to introduce you to the Baron of Monceaux. He is Lady Nichola's brother."

He gave her a half bow. "'Tis my pleasure to meet you."

"As mine, my lord." What was King Edward's advisor to Scotland doing within a rebel stronghold? More important, did King Edward realize one of his most trusted advisors held rebel ties? Was he the man who sent the writs? No, it made little sense as he often traveled to Scotland himself.

The baron frowned. "Have we met?"

"Not that I can recall." Not formally, Emma silently amended. But she'd seen him from a distance, admired his ability to calm heated tempers. With his sharp mind, he would soon place her.

"We are on our way to see Patrik," Lady Linet said.

"Be warned," the baron said, "he is ornery as a bear, proof he is indeed healing."

Lady Linet's face softened. "Glad I am to hear it." She glanced at Emma. "Let us go."

"A pleasure to meet you," Lord Monceaux said.

"As you, my lord." With a curtsy, Emma hurried after Lady Linet, grateful for a catastrophe avoided.

At the second floor, she peered up the stairs. "Whose chamber sits at the top of the turret?"

Curiosity flickered upon Lady Linet's face. "The brothers' grandmother. The room is amazing, is it not?"

So her husband had informed her of Emma's visit. "It is, but . . ."

"What?"

Emma shrugged. "It matters not."

"Please, I would be interested to hear."

Unsure why, Emma found herself wanting to share her experience with Lady Linet. "Never have I felt such acceptance, a sense of peace, but it is unnerving as well."

Warmth touched Lady Linet's face. "The chamber made me feel the same."

Images flickered through Emma's mind. "The fairies upon the ceiling, they are wondrous, a match to those upon the tapestry. Were they made at the same time as the tapestries hanging in the turret?"

Lady Linet's brows lifted with surprise. "They were. I am surprised you noticed." She turned toward the corridor. "Come, I am sure Patrik wishes to see you."

Emma followed, mulling over what they'd discussed. Somehow, her experience within their grandmother's chamber had changed Lady Linet's feelings toward her, which made little sense. 'Twould seem the more she learned about the MacGruders, the more perplexed she became.

They walked down the corridor. Two doors past where Emma had slept, Lady Linet halted, opened the door.

A young man inside the entry bowed. "My lady."

The countess nodded. "Master William, please leave us. After a short while you may return."

"Yes, my lady." The young man hurried out.

"He serves the healer and remains to ensure Patrik's fever does not return," Lady Linet explained. "I hope you think me not rude, but there are duties I must see to."

"I understand," Emma said, thankful to see Patrik, more so to have time with him alone.

"Do not stay too long. Patrik needs to rest."

"I will not, my lady."

With a smile, the countess turned and walked down the corridor.

On edge, Emma slipped inside and closed the door. When she caught sight of Patrik asleep in his bed, she stilled. Bruises marred his handsome face, his paleness told her the fever had indeed taken its toll. But he lived, and for that she was grateful. Aching to speak with him, she remained silent. After all he had endured, she could not wake him.

With quiet steps, she walked to the bed and sat in a chair at its side. Hand trembling, she laid her palm against his cheek. Cool. Thank God. She stroked his stubbled skin.

If only she did not have to leave him. Her hand stilled. What if she told Patrik the truth? She removed her hand. No, he would never forgive her intended betrayal. It was best if she left.

"I will miss you," she whispered, her voice breaking. "But you would never understand." She swallowed hard. "I cannot stay." Heart aching, Emma leaned forward, pressed her mouth gently upon his lips. "I love you."

Her entire body trembled as she stood. Emma stared down one last time at the man she loved, at the man who would forever hold her heart. Mayhap it was best if he slept.

Cristina's emotion-torn words echoed in Patrik's mind like a gift. She loved him. He ached to tell her that he loved her as well, to draw her to him and make love, except her softly whispered intent to leave severed his reply. And after agreeing to his brothers' plan to discover Cristina's loyalties, he had no choice.

The soft sound of steps alerted him she was leaving. "Cristina?"

She turned, her face pale, her eyes still bright with unshed tears.

"I did not hear you." The lie sat upon his tongue like curdled milk.

"You were asleep when I entered. I did not want to disturb you."

He held out his hand; she walked over and laid her trembling fingers within his. "What is wrong?" But he knew, damn her—she was going to leave.

"I was worried about you," she said.

"Sit beside me."

Cristina glanced at the door. "I should not."

"We will not be bothered."

"You look better."

"Clean, you mean. The bruises will fade." Her eyes were brimming with tears. "You are crying?"

"I-I have been worried about you."

"There is no need now, is there, lass?"

She sniffed. "No. Forgive me, I am being foolish."

If only it was so simple. "Are you sure there is nothing more upsetting you?"

For a split second panic flashed in her eyes. Then a brittle smile wobbled on her face. "No, I am just tired."

No? For the first time since he'd met her, he realized she never said nae as most Scots did. There you go, convict her, lad, without knowing the full truth. The reasons could be many, including her time spent along the border.

She'd never mentioned the location of the orphanage or where she had lived with her husband.

"Lie with me."

She cast a nervous glance at the entry. "Patrik, 'tis indecent."

"Aye." Desire filled his voice. He did not have to

feign that. "It is." And, might very well be the last time they spent together.

She hesitated. "But you are hurt and—"

He tugged her hand. "Come, I will do naught but hold you."

She eyed him, far from convinced.

"Well, mayhap a wee bit more." Instead of a smile, sadness touched her gaze, and his heart squeezed tight.

Cristina again glanced toward the door, then with care, lay by his side. "I feel foolish."

He ran his hand over her face, down the curve of her neck wanting more, wanting it all. "You feel bonny to me."

She shivered beneath his touch as desire darkened her gaze. "You are healing."

"I am a better man already." He claimed her mouth, took it with intensity. As her body relaxed against his, he softened the kiss. On a groan, he pulled back, smiled. "Look at this, I have you in my bed."

"'Tis not a joke."

A chill swept through him. "Nay, 'tis anything but." He searched her face as his mind clamored in turmoil. At least for this moment, regardless of where this day should end, she was here with him. And loving her, aware she was in love with him, he wanted her in every way. Patrik leaned forward and nuzzled her neck.

She sighed. "You will open your wounds."

He pushed away her gown, drew her breast into his mouth. "Tell me you do not want this."

Cristina held his gaze, the desire within her eyes tempered with regret. "I cannot."

He ignored the latter and sat up. "Wait here."

"Why? Patrik, you should not be about."

He shot her a wink. "I will be doing more than that in a moment. Stay."

Wincing at the pull of skin, slightly dizzy from moving, he walked with care to the entry and barred the door. Though he knew no one would enter, he would take no chance. And 'twould ease her mind. He walked to the window, pushed the shudders wide.

Sunlight poured into the chamber, a warm silk that flooded the room within its golden glow.

He turned, stunned at how she lay upon his bed, her chestnut hair disheveled, half exposed. She had never looked so amazing. "I want you."

Cristina sat, her gown still splayed open from his touch, looking like every man's dream. "I will be yours, always."

His body hardened to a ferocious ache. With slow steps, he walked over, knelt before her. "I have dreamt of seeing you in the light, of having time to make love to you, of lying beside you after you fall apart." He pressed a finger over her lips as she made to speak. "Nae words." He caught her hand, pressed it over his heart. "This moment it is only you, only I, and what we have together."

Tears again filled her eyes.

His heart trembled. "Are you happy here with me?"

A tear rolled down her cheek. Cristina nodded.

Patrik leaned forward, caught her mouth, tasted her essence, a sweetness uniquely hers. On a moan, he took the kiss deeper as he slowly peeled away her gown, inched off each wisp until she sat before him with her clothes rumpled around her in a delicate puddle.

Appreciation filled him as he leaned back. "Much better."

"Better? I am naked."

"You are."

"But you are fully clothed."

"A matter I will be fixing." With movements as quick as his injuries would allow, he disrobed.

"Wait," she said as she moved closer. "I want to see you as well."

"Be on with it, lass," he said through gritted teeth.

With an impish look, emerald eyes scanned him with sensual delight. Her gaze roved, paused, widened as she slowly took him in.

Worried eyes lifted.

"Remember before," he said, his words tender, filled with the memory that although once married, in many ways she was a virgin. "Our joining will only bring you pleasure."

"I knew not you were so big."

He chuckled. "Flatter me, will you?"

A blush stroked her face.

"Do you want me as much as I do you?"

"Yes."

"Come here."

She walked over.

On a sigh, he gently lifted her into his arms.

"Patrik, you are not strong enough!"

"Shhh, if I cannot carry you, I should not be making love to you."

"Will I ever know you?"

He sobered at her words. "I pray so." Desperation slid over her face, shaking him to the core.

"Make love with me, Patrik."

Afraid to look deeper, wanting this moment to be all that he'd dreamed, he laid her upon his bed and claimed her. He took his time, allowed his hands, his body to show her his love, wishing desperately he could use words as well.

As she found her release, Patrik let go, exploding within her tightness. He had never felt so complete. For long moments he lay within her, their bodies claimed within the golden heat, spirals of dust shimmering above them as if a magical mist.

Cristina's eyes widened. "Patrik."

"What is it?"

"Your pendant, 'tis glowing."

He lifted the pendant. As she'd claimed, it pulsed with a soft light.

Nervous eyes lifted to his. "What does it mean?"

"I am unsure." He remembered his brothers' talk of the halved gemstone and the woman each had married. Nay, he'd tell her naught. It mattered little as Cristina had left his halved gemstone in their grandmother's room untouched.

"There is a match to it in the chamber above," she said.

Alexander's tale of finding her in the tower chamber echoed through Patrik's mind as well as his brother's suspicions. "Aye, the room belongs to our grandmother. When each of us was knighted, she gifted us a halved gemstone. This is malachite. It is said to nourish inner peace." He remembered his turbulent childhood, his struggles since then. Aye, their grandmother had been wise in her choosing. Even his meeting of Cristina had been filled with strife.

The bells of Terce echoed outside.

Her face paled.

"What is wrong?"

"It is growing late."

"'Tis but midmorning." At the flicker of panic on her face, he understood. Even after they'd made love, it had changed naught. She intended to leave. Grief tore through him, shattered the fragments of his hopes, dreams he'd dared.

Dreams of a fool.

Anger trampled upon the hurt. His brothers' suspicions again rose to mind. Nay, he still believed them wrong, believed she would never share rebel secrets with their enemy.

Patrik damned his last role in this heart-wrenching act. On with it, lad. She loves you. After she leaves, you can find her again and help with whatever struggles she is battling. Now 'tis important to prove to your brothers she is a woman they can trust.

On a sigh Patrik shifted, allowed the covers to roll aside, and bumped the rolled leather. The writ fell off the bed and dropped to the floor.

Cristina's eyes riveted upon the stained bound leather.

With a groan, he picked up the missive, set it upon the edge of the table. He didn't miss how her gaze lingered upon the writ a moment too long.

Nae, please let me prove them wrong. "Stay with me," he whispered. At the hesitation in her eyes, hope ignited. She would remain, the writ and whatever its importance discarded.

A long second passed.

Sadness shadowed the warmth within her eyes. "I cannot. Besides," she said with false brightness ringing in her voice, "the lad sent to sit with you will return any moment." Cristina pulled the covers away, her naked body gleaming.

Heart aching, he prayed that when she left, it was with an empty hand. But, indeed the time for truth had come. "I am tired."

"You did over much."

"Mayhap." He forced a smile. "But it was well worth any damage caused." Patrik drew her against him. Angst swirled in his throat. Let him be wrong. He prayed she was just a lass struggling to feel again, not a spy after the writ. On a sigh, he closed his eyes, feigned sleep.

Long moments passed. The clash of knights in practice outside echoed in the distance. A summer breeze kicked up, its silken flow sifting into the chamber to sweep across his flesh.

He didn't move.

"Patrik?" Cristina whispered.

He remained silent, made not a movement, nothing to betray that he was alert.

"Patrik, are you awake?"

Do not touch the writ, he silently willed. In this let my brothers be proven wrong.

The bed shifted. Coldness brushed his skin where she'd lain. The soft pad of her steps grew distant, then paused. A scrape, then a soft creek. The door closed with a gentle thud.

With a prayer the writ remained, Patrik slowly

opened his eyes. Pulse racing, he glanced toward the table, and his heart broke.

The writ was gone.

Outrage mixed with pain. Bedamned, he would catch her. Patrik shoved himself up. Dizziness swamped him. Gritting his teeth, he fought the wave of blackness.

And failed.

Chapter 18

At the entry to the turret, Emma halted and turned back toward Patrik's door. Guilt swept her. When she'd accepted this mission from Sir Cressingham, 'twas but a mission like so many others in her past. Once completed, she'd walk away, focus on the next without another thought.

Except from the first Patrik had broken down her defenses. He wasn't the cold, heartless man she'd expected. With each passing day her resistance toward him had crumbled. Then foolishly, she'd fallen in love.

Images of him asleep moments ago swept through her mind. He believed her a woman he could trust, a lie she'd nurtured to achieve a goal. No, worse than a lie, she'd used his outrage of the English to craft a woman he could not deny.

The writ within her hand burned as if afire.

Emma closed her eyes. The bound parchment represented naught but shame, the emptiness of her life. A life she'd worked hard to build. A life she now detested with her every breath. She fought the surge of panic sweeping her at leaving the man she loved, at her ultimate betrayal.

Tears burned her throat as she turned and started down the turret steps. At the tapestry, she paused. A sad smile touched her mouth. Odd, before she'd found the intricate weave out of place within this formidable stronghold. Now, the fairies made perfect sense to her.

Nor would she have guessed such a formidable man as Lord Grey would soften toward a woman who should be his enemy. Yet somehow he had fallen in love with Lady Linet and claimed her as his wife.

It seemed Sir Alexander, too, had overcome incredible odds to make *his captive* his wife. Though she had not yet heard Sir Duncan's story of how he'd met and married his wife, she guessed it would match his brothers' unexpected journeys.

Melancholy swept her. Who would have believed that Lochshire Castle, a rebel fortress that should instill fear, instead inspired hope? But however much she wished to be with Patrik, naught could repair her deception.

She glanced up the spiral steps. Or, could she make amends, at least in part?

If she returned the writ before she departed Lochshire Castle, Patrik would not suspect her treachery. Then she could vanish from his life, and leave at least part of her wrongdoing repaired. When he searched for Cristina Moffat, he would find no one.

As for Sir Cressingham, when she didn't return, he would label her a traitor and put a price on her head. A risk she was willing to take.

After years of playing different roles, she would craft yet another character, invent a new name, and sail to France. Or, mayhap slip away to Spain. Regardless, she could never return to England or Scotland.

She started toward Patrik's chamber. Though he could never be hers, she prayed that one day Patrik would find a woman who loved him as he deserved.

Echoes of Sir Alexander's and Sir Duncan's voices rose up the turret.

God in heaven, she would never reach Patrik's chamber in time! Neither could she allow them to find her with the writ. Heart pounding, she ran up the tower steps.

The door to the tower chamber stood open and sunlight flooded the room. Emma halted, a chill sweeping her skin. 'Twas as if their grandmother's room welcomed her.

"I am far from convinced," Sir Alexander growled.

"Nor I," Sir Duncan agreed.

They were coming up! She bolted into the chamber and flattened herself against the wall behind the door. Cool stone pressed against her back as she awaited discovery.

Long seconds passed.

The brothers' voices faded.

Emma sagged back. They'd entered the corridor on the second floor.

A door creaked. Silence.

Were they with Patrik? No, if they checked on him, they would find him asleep and allow him to rest. Regardless, they were too close to try to return the writ. Now what? She must find a way before she left.

On a shaky exhale, Emma stepped from behind the door. The chamber stood empty, with no sign of the old woman who'd spoken with her the night before. As well, the hearth lay black. Neither ash nor a cold ember sat within.

Had she imagined the woman as well? No, she'd seen the elder, had spoken with her. From Sir Alexander's stunned expression when she'd described the woman, he'd thought her mad.

Fatigue spilled through Emma and she rubbed her brow. Mayhap she was. At this point she was unsure of anything except the fact that she must go, leave Cristina Moffat behind without a trace.

"Emma Astyn," she whispered, testing her name against her tongue. It sounded odd. She gave a rough laugh. So long had she played different roles for her missions, even her real name sounded foreign. Without intending to, she'd severed the ties of her past. No longer did Emma Astyn exist. Did her true identity really matter?

She stilled.

Yes.

Because Patrik had taught her to love, to want a man at her side, and most of all, to wish for the impossible.

Emotion tightened her chest as she scanned the fairies woven within the tapestry and those upon the ceiling. Their faces remained empty, devoid of expression as if the other night her mind had indeed played tricks.

"Riders coming!" a man's voice boomed from outside.

Emma hurried to the arched window.

A small contingent rode two abreast upon the narrow road leading to the castle. Across the broken sweep of water, knights were setting up camp upon the hillside as more men continued to pour from the dense forest.

Was Lord Grey planning another assault upon English troops? She studied the confident man leading the small group.

God in heaven, Sir David de Moravia!

Her blood chilled. She would never forget her meeting with the Parson of Bothwell, uncle to Sir Andrew de Moray. At the time, she'd played yet another character, but if she met up with Sir David, a man of sharp wit, he would recognize her.

Hooves clattered upon timber as the rebels rode beneath the gatehouse. The bailey flooded with the echo of horses and men as squires ran to take the knights' horses while those within Lochshire Castle gathered to meet the small party.

The Earl of Grey strode to Sir David de Moravia, his face hard. The leaders clasped hands, and then the earl motioned Sir David toward the keep.

Shaken, Emma stepped back. A glow from the corner caught her attention. The other half of Patrik's gemstone.

"'Tis yours."

On a gasp, Emma whirled. The chamber stood empty. No one was here. Her mind was playing tricks. She was tired, overwrought, terrified.

Unsure of anything, she glanced at the bowl. The other half of Patrik's gemstone pulsed. As if guided by a force, she crossed the chamber. Sadness filled her as she lifted the malachite. Its warmth pulsed against her skin, offering strange comfort.

An ache built in her heart. This was a part of Patrik, a reminder of the love she'd found. Though she would never have him, she could have this. Before she could change her mind, she slipped the gemstone into her pocket and hurried from the chamber.

At the second-floor entry, she peered down the corridor. It lay empty. She held her breath and slipped past.

"Cristina!" a child's excited voice called as she paused at the opening to the great room.

"Joneta," Emma said, fighting for a smile. Mouth dry, she scanned the enormous chamber, thankful for the mill of people. "Where is your mother?"

A smile curved the cherub cheeks as she cradled her doll against her chest. "She is outside helping with the wash. Would you like to see her?"

A commotion at the entry caught Emma's attention.

Lord Grey and Sir David de Moravia strode into the great room.

She couldn't let Sir David see her! Emma nodded to the girl. "Yes, I would."

Ignorant of her panic, Joneta smiled. "This way." The child skipped down a side hallway, then out a back door.

The smell of bread wafted in the air along with herbs and other savory scents as they exited the keep. Beyond the buildings knights clogged her view, their faces weary with travel. Claymores clung to their backs; daggers were secured to their waists. Men prepared for war. Men who would give their lives to win. Men like Patrik.

Joneta turned. "Cristina, are you coming?"

If only she could linger, if only her days could be filled with mundane chores and each of her nights spent in Patrik's arms.

On an unsteady breath, Emma knelt before the child. "I must go, but I need you to do me a great favor." She forced a smile. "Will you do that for me?"

Joneta nodded, her curls bouncing with delighted innocence.

Hand trembling, Emma withdrew the writ. She pressed the bound leather within the child's hand, and then curled her fingers over the top. "Hide this. For now, tell no one. After the bells of Vespers, bring this to Sir Patrik."

Excitement shone in the girl's eyes. "'Tis a gift?"

Emotion swamped her. "Yes." But in his anger at finding the writ gone, Patrik would only see that she'd betrayed him. A situation too late to repair. Mayhap it was for the best.

"I know," Joneta exclaimed, "it is like the story of the fairies!"

Her mind a muddle, needing only to escape, Emma nodded, far from understanding the child's ramblings. "Promise me. Swear you will show no one and not deliver it to Sir Patrik until after the bells of Vespers."

"I swear." Green eyes swirled with excitement as Joneta slipped the writ beneath the folds of the blanket covering her doll. The girl hesitated. Delight crumbled to sadness upon her face. "Why are you leaving?"

"'Tis complicated." An understatement.

"Will you return?"

She shook her head. "I do not believe so." Emma embraced the child in a fierce hug, wishing times were different, that she could share her life with Patrik. "Never will I forget you."

A tear rolled down Joneta's cheek. "I do not want you to go."

"I would like to stay as well." Emma wiped away the child's tear. "But we cannot always have what we wish."

She sniffed. "Like when my mother buried my brother?"

Emma's heart broke. "Yes." On shaky legs she stood. "I must leave, but know that I will miss you terribly. And, after you give Sir Patrik the writ, tell . . ." She fought for control. "Te-Tell him that I love him."

Somber, Joneta nodded.

Before she broke down, Emma went to where a line of clothes dried, removed an old cape, donned the garb. With the unhurried steps of one who worked within the castle, she walked to the bailey. It was crowded with people, some loading supplies for the rebels camped outside while others secured ropes over loads already piled. Near the gatehouse, men and women were walking alongside wagons topped with bags of food. Keeping her head bowed, Emma fell in amongst the group.

As they moved past the drawbridge, plumes of dust spewed from the wheels, shrouding her and the others in a haze. Emma wiped her eyes, thankful for the concealing haze. Each step was laden with fear, each step one closer to escape.

Once the party reached the shore, amidst the roll

of wagons, snorts of horses and the wave of knights continuing to arrive, Emma quickly slipped away. At the edge of the forest, within a dense copse of trees, she came upon a squire tying a mare to the bough of a small tree.

With practiced ease, she knocked out the squire, hid his body within a dense thicket and covered him with the stolen cape. With the number of knights nearby, the squire would be safe until he came to.

With quiet, hurried steps, she led the horse farther into the dense tangle. At the top of the steep slope, through the swath of fir trees, she took in Lochshire Castle, where Patrik still slept, where but a short while before they had made love, and where, if only for a little while, she had found love.

The horse shifted, and she released the bough. Thick needles of pine swung back and severed her view. A fitting reminder that her time here was past.

Now, to reach a port.

With ease she swung up on the mare. The fragrant bed of needles and earth absorbed the clomp of hooves as she wove through the forest. When she reached a clearing, she urged her mount into a canter without looking back.

"Patrik."

At Seathan's gruff voice, Patrik forced his lids open. Orange-red rays of the fading sunset tumbled into his chamber, the scent of the summer evening and roasting venison a wonderful mix. A memory gnawed at his mind, something important he must remember. He searched, but it fell away.

"Patrik," Seathan repeated.

"I am awake," Patrik grumbled as he waded through his mind's haze, clawing for the thought. He glanced over at the table, froze.

The writ was gone.

Memories poured through him of trying to go after Cristina, then blackness. He'd passed out. Patrik glanced over, found his brothers and Griffin in ominous silence at his side. No words were necessary; the upset on the men's faces matched his own.

"She took it," Patrik whispered.

Seathan nodded. "Aye."

An ache built inside, stripped any warmth within until Patrik was left empty. Cold. "Where is she?"

Anger flashed in Alexander's eyes. "We are not sure."

"What?" Patrik sat up. Dizziness assailed him. He ignored the aches that came with healing, and focused on his outrage.

"Sir David de Moravia arrived with a large contingent shortly after we left you this morn." Seathan cast a glance at Griffin, frowned. "During the commotion, she disappeared."

"Do you think she has left?" Patrik asked.

"I have guards scouring the entire castle," Seathan replied, "but with each entry well guarded, I believe she is still within."

Patrik glanced at the empty table. However much he wanted to agree, a part of him sensed otherwise.

"Aye, we will find her," Patrik agreed, with more

confidence than he felt. Saint's breath, the English could not learn of their informant!

He hadn't wanted to believe Cristina would take the writ, hadn't wanted to believe his brothers' doubts. Be-damned, they'd made love, she'd given herself to him in the most intimate of ways. Yet, 'twould seem with the first opportunity, as Alexander had suspected, she'd taken the writ.

Who was this woman he loved?

She'd whispered that she loved him. Was that a lie as well?

Furious, Patrik sat, swung his feet on the floor and stood. Another wave of dizziness assailed him, threatened to take him under. He focused on his anger, determined to find her, to learn the truth.

"Christ's blade," Seathan said. "What do you think you are doing?"

"Looking for her."

"Like bloody hell," Alexander spat. "Do nae worry, we will catch the lass. On that I swear my life."

Griffin crossed his arms over his chest. "With darkness coming and the drawbridge up, she is locked within."

"Besides," Seathan said, "Sir David has asked to meet with you."

Patrik met his eldest brother's gaze.

"As I, Sir David was shocked to learn *Dubh Duer* is my brother." Seathan grimaced. "Since you find it necessary to move, come down once you are dressed."

His mind a haze, Patrik nodded.

"I will stay and help you," Duncan said.

Patrik shook his head. "Nae."

Duncan hesitated. With a frown, he followed his brothers out.

Alone and on unsteady legs, Patrik walked to the window. Clouds skimmed the sky in delicate wisps. The sun, an angry blaze of orange, lowered upon the horizon. What else had Cristina lied about?

The bells of Vespers echoed.

Against the darkening skies, fires upon the shore sprouted.

"Blast it, where are you?"

A soft knock sounded upon his door.

"Enter," he called, supposing a servant brought fresh water or food.

The door inched open and wide green eyes peered inside.

Surprised to see the wee lass, Patrik stepped forward. "Joneta?"

"Can you come here, Sir Patrik?"

Confused, he walked to the door, opened it wide. "Methinks it is late for you to be about." He peered down the corridor, surprised to find it empty. "Where is your mother, lass?"

The child shifted before him. "She thinks I am abed."

"As you should be. The hour grows late."

"But I promised," she rushed out.

Coldness sifted through him. "What did you promise, lass?"

Small hands lifted her blanketed doll. Joneta unwrapped the woven fabric, exposing the leather-bound writ.

Cristina had taken, then returned, the writ. What did

that mean? A better question: Why had she wanted it at all? "Where did you get that?" He kept his voice light, free of anger.

"Mistress Cristina." With a tug, the child pulled the rolled leather, held it out to him. "She said to give it to you after the bells of Vespers."

He took the bound leather, checked. The seal upon the writ remained unbroken. Relief swept him. At least their informant within King Edward's castle was safe, as was the news he passed. His brothers and Griffin would be relieved.

"And a fine task you have done," Patrik said.

The girl fidgeted. "There is more."

"More?" Hope ignited. Did Cristina await him below?

"Aye. She said to tell you that she loved you." She leaned toward him conspiratorially. "'Tis silly as you already knew such."

He swallowed hard. "Where is she?"

Sadness tugged the corners of her mouth. "She left."

"The keep?"

Joneta shook her head. "Nae. This morn I watched her don a cape and go through the gatehouse with the men and women who walked alongside the wagons filled with supplies."

"My thanks."

The girl turned to leave. Hesitated. "Sir Patrik?"

"Aye, lass?"

"Mistress Cristina said she did not think she was coming back."

Unable to speak, he nodded.

After a curtsy, Joneta hurried down the hall.

Heart breaking, Patrik closed the door. He dragged on his garb, ignoring the aches, the pain of moving his sore limbs. Aye, he would meet with Sir David de Moravia and give Seathan the writ, but he would not tell his brother she'd left the castle. After, he would leave to find Cristina—alone.

However much he wanted his brothers' aid, the burden of finding her, and gaining answers concerning her interest in the writ, lay upon him.

The slap threw Emma back. The knights holding her arms prevented her from slamming to the floor. The coppery taste of blood filled her mouth as she pushed past the pain.

"Sir Patrik Cleary and I were caught in an English raid." She shook her head to clear her mind, exhaustion skewing her thoughts. That same exhaustion had caused her to miss the English knights hidden within the brush. They'd easily captured her and hauled her before Sir Hugh de Cressingham. "Sir Patrik was killed." A lie, but she hoped to be long gone before the treasurer of the English administration in Scotland discovered the truth.

Face red, Sir Cressingham shoved himself up from his oversized gilded seat and waddled toward where the guards held her tight. Lids puffed, jowls drawn down by fat, he halted a pace away. "Where is the writ?"

"I found none."

"You lie," Sir Cressingham boomed.

Through the roar of pain she shook her head. "'Tis the truth. I swear it."

Malice flared within his puffy eyes. "Emma Astyn, you are acclaimed as one of England's top mercenaries, a woman who has never failed in a mission, a woman I paid a king's ransom to befriend *Dubh Duer*. Now, after a setup to meet with Sir Patrik Cleary that left four of my knights dead, you dare tell me you have failed?" His hand shot out.

Pain exploded in her skull.

"Where is he!"

"De-Dead," she replied, sinking into the welcome blackness. Cold water splashed her face. She gasped, fought the flood of pain.

Sir Cressingham hauled her to him. "You will find no reprieve."

A commotion outside had her turning. Vision blurring, she fought to focus.

Chubby hands shoved Emma toward the guards.

A knight shoved open the door. "Sir Cressingham, we have caught *Dubh Duer*."

No! She'd left him asleep in Lochshire Castle. Horror flooded her as they hauled Patrik inside, his body slumped against the guards who carried him, his face a mass of purple where their fists had pummeled his flesh.

"Patrik!" She'd not meant to talk, to expose that she cared.

Sir Cressingham's eyes narrowed on her. "He seems not dead to me. What other lies have you told me?"

"Cristina, wh-what is going on?" Patrik rasped.

"It seems," Sir Cressingham said, "Emma has played us both."

Patrik frowned. "Emma?"

Sir Cressingham grunted. "For a man known for his wit, 'twould seem you are a fool."

Confusion marred Patrik's face, his eyes a haze of pain.

"Emma, dear," Sir Cressingham drawled, "tell him."

The words curdled in her throat. Please, let Patrik not learn the truth this way.

Silence.

"Then allow me to introduce you," Sir Cressingham said, venom dripping from his every word. "Meet Emma Astyn—"

Patrik's face paled. "A woman acclaimed as one of England's top mercenaries."

Chapter 19

God in heaven no! Emma ached at Patrik's stricken expression, struggled to somehow try to explain. She had never meant for him to learn the truth. "I am so sorry! Patrik—"

"Silence her!" Sir Cressingham ordered.

A guard cupped her mouth, another held her secure.

Disbelief carved every line of Patrik's face. "Na-Nae Scottish?"

"Emma is English." Satisfaction rolled through the treasurer's words. Sir Cressingham shot her a caustic glance. "'Twould seem she achieved a bit of her task for the coin paid."

Fury swept Patrik's face, anger so hard, so deep, Emma wished to shrivel up and die.

"Emma was paid to meet you," Sir Cressingham continued, the cold enjoyment of his words heightening her remorse. "To retrieve the writ you carried and unveil the one who betrays us within King Edward's trusted circle. But as we have you, she is no longer necessary—for now." He nodded to the guards. "Use her as you will, but leave her alive. I will deal with her once I am through with the rebel."

"No!" Emma screamed. Fury spewed from Patrik's eyes. Anger she deserved, but he should not pay for her treachery. "Do not kill him. Please."

Sir Cressingham's face darkened. "Remove her!"

Lust gleamed in the guards' eyes.

She struggled against their hold; they pulled her back. "I am sorry, Patrik. You were never supposed to follow me."

Two guards hauled her out, shoved the door shut. Torchlight cut through the blackness, ominous flickers battering the night.

Her heart slammed in her chest. Think. She could not allow Patrik to die.

Night-chilled grass gave beneath her steps as the guards half led, half dragged her.

With hard laughter, they hauled her inside a room barren except for a half-made bed and a near-gutted candle. Rough hands shoved her back. In the murky torchlight, she caught the predatory gleam of their eyes.

A brutal hand caught her gown, tore.

Coolness swept her naked breasts.

Laughter echoed within the chamber. Then silence descended, a silence so cold and deadly, she struggled to breathe.

"Take off your garb," the closest knight ordered. "Let me see what you gave the Scottish bastard."

"Please, no," she whispered, allowing the fear of her youth to fill her voice, shrinking back as if terrified. She crouched amidst their vicious leers, slid her hand beneath the folds of her gown and clasped her dagger.

The closest man shot the other a warning glare. "I will have the wench first. Hold her for me."

Revulsion filled her as the other man nodded, then strode forward. *Step closer, you tail of a dog.*

His booted foot strode across the floor, each echo harsh with his intent.

A handsbreadth away, Emma unsheathed her blade, slashed the man's neck. As he gasped, she spun and drove the dagger into the other man's heart.

Shock scraped her assailant's face. "Bitch."

"No, a woman."

On a pained moan, he crumpled to the floor.

Emma jerked the blade free, rushed to the door and peered into the blackness.

No guards.

As she tied her torn gown, she glanced toward the building where Sir Cressingham held Patrik. She must save him. But how? Alone and with but a blade against a roomful of knights, she posed little threat to them. Her mind rumbled with thoughts, ideas she cast aside as quick as they came.

Emma stilled, knew what she must do, a choice that might cost her life. For Patrik it was a risk she would take.

With a prayer for his safety, she bolted into the night.

Hours later, exhaustion shrouded Emma as she stood within the bailey of Lochshire Castle. A ring encircled the full moon low in the sky, at odds with the rising sun as it struggled against the angry cast of gray.

Torches severed the eroding darkness, the battle of flame against night naught compared to the furious glares of the MacGruder brothers and the Baron of Monceaux as they bore down upon her.

The guard on her right, his hold upon her arm firm, nodded. "Lord Grey. Mistress Cristina was caught trying to slip along the shore past the knights camped there."

The earl and his brothers halted before her, the four massive men forming an intimidating wall. "Where is Patrik?"

Emma held his angry gaze. "Sir Hugh de Cressingham has him." She fought to control her emotions. "When I left, he was alive. Please, you must save him."

Sir Alexander stepped forward. "Save him?" He glared at his eldest brother. "'Tis a bloody trap."

Sir Duncan's eyes narrowed. "Is he dead?"

She shook her head, ashamed, deserving their wrath and so much more. "When I escaped he was alive."

"Escaped?" Sir Alexander snorted.

"If we find Patrik dead," Lord Monceaux said, "none will save you."

"Who are you?" Though softly spoken, cold fury rolled through Lord Grey's voice.

She steadied herself. "Emma Astyn."

Sir Alexander cursed, Sir Duncan stared stunned, and the Earl of Grey's eyes narrowed dangerously.

"One of England's top mercenaries," the Baron of Monceaux said, fury etched within each word.

The pride she'd held at her hard-earned title, wilted beneath the reality of the harm she'd done. "Yes, but no longer."

Lord Grey arched a skeptical brow. "And we are to believe you?"

"By God, lass," Alexander growled, "Patrik lies dead and you think to spew words we will be foolish enough to swallow? Or to follow you to where Patrik is supposedly *held*?" His jaw tightened. "For what, the bastard Cressingham's men to kill?"

Panic stole through her. "'Tis the truth. I swear it. If you do not save Patrik, he will die!"

"That I believe," the earl said. "If the deed is not already done." Lord Grey stepped closer. "You will regret your part in this. Guards," he called without taking his eyes from her, "take her to the dungeon."

"No!" Emma struggled against his knights' hold. "You must believe me!"

The earl motioned his men to take her away.

The knights started forward, their grasp firm.

Tears streamed down her face as she dug her heels into the dirt. Damn them! "You need me to show you where Patrik is."

Silence.

The guards continued.

"Without my help, you cannot save him!" Frantic, she twisted in their hold, and caught sight of Lady Nichola near the keep holding her son, her face pale. Alexander's wife had heard everything. As if it mattered. Or, maybe it did.

"Nichola," Sir Alexander called, "go inside."

"No." Hysteria washed over Emma. To think, her only chance to save Patrik was to gain the help of the woman he'd tried to kill. A vague hope, but at this moment, all she had. "My lady, if help does not arrive, Patrik will die."

Remoteness shrouded Lady Nichola's eyes. "The choice to save him is not mine."

"But your opinion matters," Emma pleaded as the guards wrestled her forward. "You know the terror of being a captive, of believing your life is forfeit."

Nichola swept a protective hand around her son, stepped back. "It is not the same."

"No? Like Patrik, were you not betrayed?" Tears burned Emma's throat as the guards continued to lead her away. "Patrik regrets his deed, damns his attempt on your life. In penance, he kept away from his brothers, away from a family he loves. My lady, a year has passed. Tell me, has he not sacrificed enough? Has he not grieved his mistakes long enough? Or will you never forgive him?"

"Enough!" Lord Grey said.

Emma struggled against the guards. "No—"

"Wait," Lady Nichola interrupted.

"Bedamned!" Sir Alexander stormed over to his wife. "You will not be badgered about by Cressingham's hireling, a woman who lured my brother to his death!"

If possible, Lady Nichola's face paled further. The child in her arms shifted, struggling.

"Take our son inside," Sir Alexander said. It wasn't a request.

Lady Nichola's somber eyes held Emma's. "She is right. You have reclaimed a brother believed dead. Instead of accepting his heartfelt apology, acknowledged his sacrifices made, I clung to anger."

"Patrik tried to kill you," Alexander spat.

"Mayhap," Lady Nichola replied, "but 'twas not out of malice. He loved you, tried to protect you, believed me unworthy of your love. His past guided his actions; actions he now understands were wrong, actions he now regrets."

The scar on Sir Alexander's face jumped. "'Tis not the time to discuss this now."

Lady Nichola's expression softened. "It is. Long past time." Taking an unsteady breath, she turned toward Lord Grey. "I believe her."

"Guards, halt," Lord Grey ordered.

Sir Alexander spun to face his brother. "Bloody hell."

Humbled by Nichola's faith, Emma shook her head. "How, my lady, when I have but lied to you from the start, entered your home with naught but deceptive intent."

"I thought you were trying to sway me to convince the men to help?" Lady Nichola asked.

Emotions swamped Emma. "I am. Thank you, my lady. Never will I forget your generosity."

"'Tis a lard-bloated lie," Alexander grumbled.

Lady Nichola gave her husband a quelling glance, then turned to the earl. "As I said, the choice is not mine to make, but if I was asked, I would take Mistress Emma's word, allow her to ride along with you to save your brother."

Anger sparked in Lord Grey's gaze.

Emma trembled, prayed Lady Nichola's belief was enough. "I will lead you to Patrik. No tricks, no deception, to that I swear."

The earl's nostrils flared; then he nodded.

The Baron of Monceaux studied her a long moment, then crossed his arms. "'Twould please me to take down any bastard who would bring a woman harm."

A hard smile kicked up Sir Duncan's mouth. "Likewise."

Heart pounding, Emma turned to Sir Alexander, his glare raw with displeasure.

"I will ride," Sir Alexander said between clenched teeth, "but expect naught of my trust."

As if she cared. All she wanted was Patrik alive. Tears filled Emma's eyes. "My thanks."

Alexander shook his head. "Do nae thank me. I go for my brother."

Sprawled upon the damp earthen floor, Patrik opened his eyes. Through swollen lids, he stared at the seep of afternoon light beneath the entry as the guards' steps faded.

On a muttered curse, he dropped his head and gasped for breath, each draw shoving pain through his chest. Saint's breath, somehow he still lived. With a grimace, he tested his arms, surprised that either worked. He lifted a leg, ignored the burst of pain, and then raised the other. Neither broken.

For now.

Cressingham's knights took but a respite. They wanted him to think, to fear their return and the next round of abuse. A wry smile edged his mouth. 'Twas the third time since last night that they'd hauled him back from another beating. He sobered. The next time they came, he doubted he'd see these walls again.

Regardless, they'd nae drag a secret from his lips. The rebel contact within King Edward's court would remain safe.

Images of Cristina's face . . . nay, of Emma's, rolled through his mind. Hurt beyond what the English could ever deliver battered him. She'd lied, slept with him to gain information for that bastard Cressingham. Like the stories of her past. Lies, the lot of them. Had anything that'd spilled from her mouth held truth?

A fool.

She'd played him, was quick to use his weaknesses to ensnare him in her trap. And he'd fallen, given her his trust, and worse, his love.

He remembered her destroyed look when Cressingham had announced her scheme along with her real name. Nae, 'twas but another act well played. He'd heard of the mercenary Emma Astyn. Her abilities to pull off the most dangerous mission were legendary, and the reason Cressingham had chosen her for this task.

Memories flashed by, the days of her travels with Patrik, the deceit she'd crafted with a woman's smile, the love they'd made. Aye, 'twas no doubt why she was one of England's top mercenaries, she would do anything, hurt anyone for a bloody farthing, including profess her love.

Where was she now, congratulating herself after a fine meal and counting the coin made? A part of him wished to accept that she indeed regretted her act, that Emma's pleas had been real when Cressingham had ordered her hauled away. He swallowed hard, damned himself. When it came to her, he no longer knew what to believe.

Sickened by the swill of lies, he braced himself against the waves of pain. What had she told Cressingham about the rebels? Saint's breath, she'd seen Griffin at Lochshire Castle. As well, she knew of the rebels' pathway beneath the ben, and the hideout behind the falls. If he did not warn Seathan, hundreds of Scots could die. And with Griffin's position exposed . . .

God help them all.

Body shaking, Patrik pushed himself up. His legs gave way, and he crumpled to the floor. Through sheer determination, he pushed to his knees. Sweat streamed down his face, mingled with blood as he crawled to the door. Panting, he clawed to reach the handle. His hand closed upon the rough wood. He held tight.

Tugged. "Open, you bastard!" He again pulled.

It held firm.

Dizziness swamped him and Patrik slid to the floor. Hopelessness descended. "Nae, damn you. I will not give up!" Teeth clenched, he grabbed the door, jerked.

Nothing.

"Nae!"

Head pounding, Patrik lay back. He'd ignored his instincts about Emma, the subtle hints that something was amiss. Blast it, how many times during their days together had he allowed his need for her to trample common sense? Now, due to his neglect, many Scots would die.

Tree limbs scraped the building like clawing fingers. Another soft scratch echoed near the entry. A moment later, the soft brush of branches was repeated.

Numb, he stared at the sturdy wood. The wind was kicking up. A storm must be moving in. A weak, pain-roughened laugh battered his throat. What did that matter? Here he would die, but his death mattered not. It was the loss of the people who had given him their trust that he could not accept.

Patrik again glanced at the door. Mayhap a chance still existed. After the hours of beatings, the guards would expect him to be subdued. When they again entered, they would nae expect an attack.

With his legs screaming, Patrik shoved himself to his feet. Head spinning, he pressed himself back against the wall. *Enter, you bastards.*

If a chance existed to warn his fellow Scots, he would take it. He knew it would be his last.

A slight thump echoed from outside.

Patrik frowned. That did not sound like a tree. Guards? Why did they not bloody barge inside as the arrogant bastards had three times before?

The door gave a subtle creak, edged open.

He readied himself to attack.

"Patrik?"

At his eldest brother's whisper, Patrik almost dropped to his knees. "Seathan?"

"Aye." The door was shoved open wider. Weak afternoon sun outlined his eldest brother as he hurried inside, with Alexander on his heels.

"Wh-Where are the guards?" Patrik stumbled out.

Alexander's nostrils flared. "Dead."

Seathan peered out the door, and then glared at Patrik. "I told you not to go after the lass."

"Th-This was personal," Patrik replied.

"If it involves one of us, it involves the family," Seathan stated. "Come. We must hurry."

On shaky legs, Patrik stepped forward, crumpled. His brothers caught him.

"Aye," Alexander muttered, "'tis a threat you are."

Patrik stayed his tongue. He would nae take his anger at himself out upon his brothers. Despite the pain, he staggered out with their aid.

At the side of the building, they pressed against the rough wood, hiding in the shadows.

A short distance away, within a small clearing at the edge of the woods, fractured rays of light exposed Emma.

"What in Hades!" Patrik hissed.

"Say naught," Alexander warned as he glared in her direction.

Say naught? What in God's name was going on? Sickened, he knew. Emma had lured his brothers to their death. "Nae. 'Tis a trap," Patrik forced through the pain. "The la-lass is not Scottish, but an English mercenary!"

"She is." Anger edged Alexander's voice.

"Bloody hell! Do-Do you not hear what I am saying?" At Alexander's nod, Patrik shot the middle brother an incredulous look. "Then why are—"

"Quiet, both of you," Seathan warned. "'Twill be time enough to discuss this once we are safely away." He scanned their surroundings. "Go."

With his brothers half carrying him, they hurried across the open field. At a cluster of brush, they halted; Patrik worked to catch his breath.

"Christ's blade," Seathan hissed.

Alexander edged closer. "What is it?"

"Look toward the other end of the field," Seathan said.

"Bedamned," Alexander cursed, "Knights are headed to their quarters and will pass close by."

"Aye." Seathan glanced at Patrik. "We have but a short distance. Can you make it?"

Patrik nodded. If necessary he would crawl.

Seathan and Alexander caught his shoulders, helped him up, and then bolted toward safety.

An English knight appeared from a tent a short distance away, shielded his eyes against the slant of the sun. "The rebel escapes!"

"Run!" Seathan ordered.

Pain roared through Patrik; he willed his body forward.

As Patrik and his brothers reached the edge of the woods, Emma withdrew her bow, as did several rebels hidden nearby. Arrows whizzed over their heads, followed by the cries of the wounded English.

A limb slapped Patrik; he pushed it aside, kept moving.

"To your mounts," Seathan ordered as they moved past.

Emma and the other rebels loosed another slew of arrows toward those giving chase.

Screams and outraged yells echoed in their wake.

Fragmented sunlight spun around them as they ran through the forest. Amidst his painful haze, Patrik's fury grew. He wanted her nowhere near his brothers. What lies had she told them to make them believe her, to lead them to their deaths? Bedamned, well he knew her expertise when it came to twisting truths.

The crash of brush in their wake alerted them the English had reached the forest.

An arrow hissed past. Another whipped by a handsbreadth away and lodged in a nearby tree.

Patrik forced himself forward, his side aching, his entire body threatening to collapse.

They forged through a dense thicket, and Duncan came into view at the head of a small contingent.

"Mount," Seathan ordered.

Duncan swung up, reached down for Patrik.

A yell had Patrik glancing back.

Several paces away, an English knight trained his arrow on Alexander.

Fear tore through Patrik. "Nae!"

At Patrik's shout, Emma turned. As if in slow motion, she watched Patrik dive against Alexander a second before an arrow sank deep within Patrik's chest.

"Patrik!" Fury tore through her. Emma drew her bow, released; the knight who'd shot Patrik collapsed.

"Help me put Patrik on the horse," Lord Grey ordered.

Sir Alexander caught Patrik's other shoulder, lifted him to Sir Duncan.

The English broke through the trees.

"Go!" Lord Grey called as he swung up on his steed.

Sir Alexander mounted, caught Emma's waist, hauled her before him and dug his heels into his mount. Clods of dirt flew as his bay surged ahead.

She clung tight as flashes of trees whipped by. A league away, they galloped toward a ridge thick with fir. As if a door opened, they rode through. Immense rock jutted up before them, and within a crevice lay a large gap.

Without hesitation, the earl and his men cantered inside. The last of their party halted, then hurriedly covered the entry.

As his men worked, Lord Grey turned his mount,

pinning Emma with his ominous gaze, his threat clear. Never would he allow her the freedom to reveal this rebel hideout. It was an unfounded worry. With deception a foul taste upon her tongue, she would never reveal this secret.

Through the shards of waning light, Emma glanced at Patrik, found him slumped in Sir Duncan's arms. Fear tore through her. "Is he . . ."

"He is alive." Angst darkened Sir Duncan's gaze. "Barely. If he does not see a healer soon, he will die."

Chapter 20

The fading glimmer of stars etched the sky as Emma, positioned behind Lord Monceaux, rode toward Lochshire Castle. Sir Alexander had not grumbled at the move. With his brother rescued, he wanted naught more to do with her. A matter upon which they both agreed.

She glanced over at Patrik's slumped form. The long hours of riding throughout the night had taken their toll. In the gray dawn light she could see the paleness of his face.

We are almost there, hang on please.

"Lord Grey arrives," a guard called from the wall walk.

The steady thrum of hooves upon wood echoed as they crossed the drawbridge, then cantered beneath the gatehouse and into the bailey. Amidst the flicker of flames inside, knights awaited them. Unlike before, they now eyed her with distrust.

The earl drew his destrier to a halt, nodded to his

brothers. "Take Patrik to his chamber." He glanced toward one of his men. "Sir Malcolm, fetch the healer."

"Aye, my lord." Sir Malcolm hurried off.

Exhausted, Emma remained quiet as Patrik's brothers carried him to the keep. She wanted desperately to be at his side.

"If he lives, 'tis because of you."

At Lord Monceaux's solemn comment, she turned. "If he dies, 'tis because I betrayed him."

The baron nodded, his face grim. "A fact neither Patrik's brothers nor I will forget."

"Or should." Emotions threatened Emma as she scanned Lochshire Castle. A Scottish stronghold held by men bound together by the strength of family, by the fight to reclaim their country, and by love.

It was Patrik's home.

Though division existed between Patrik and his family, in time wounds would heal and he could rebuild the foundations of a life in which he could again find happiness. For that, Emma would give thanks.

Lord Monceaux dismounted, lifted her to the ground.

She turned toward the keep, the image of Patrik's battered body all too clear.

"Mistress Emma."

At Lady Nichola's voice, she turned. Beneath the torchlight, Alexander's wife stood upon the steps of the keep, the strain on her face telling Emma the woman had not slept this night. Her worry was yet another sin to add to Emma's enormous list.

Heart pounding, Emma curtsied. "My lady."

Her body trembling, Lady Nichola stepped closer. "You saved my husband's brother."

"No," Emma said. "My deception did naught but place Sir Patrik, your husband, and your family in danger."

"It did," Lady Nichola agreed, "but you chose to return to Lochshire Castle, to expose the truth at the risk of your life. As for my family facing the English, 'tis not the first nor the last time for such."

Guilt clung to Emma. "My deed is far from heroic, my lady. I returned because I love Patrik."

"Regardless, he is safe." Lady Nichola nodded. "Let us go inside. It has been a long night and you are tired."

As was Lady Nichola. She'd earned none of this woman's kind words.

Lord Monceaux drew his sister into a fierce hug. Then, in silence they walked to the keep. After entering the great room, Alexander's wife headed for the turret.

Stunned, Emma glanced at Lady Nichola.

"You believed we would cast you within the dungeon?" she asked.

"I have earned such grim quarters, my lady." No, in truth, her betrayal could win her death.

"I will not lie, 'twas considered," Lord Monceaux stated. "Neither will you be allowed to roam free. Too many questions remain to be asked."

"Questions, my lord, I will answer," Emma said.

The baron nodded.

In silence, Emma followed them up the spiral steps.

Outside the chamber where she'd slept before, they halted.

The baron spoke in private with his sister, and then stepped back. "It has been a long night for you, Nichola. Go and rest. I will ensure Mistress Emma is cared for."

Face pale, Lady Nichola glanced to where Sir Alexander's voice echoed from inside Patrik's chamber. "For all of us." She nodded to her brother. "My thanks, Griffin." She walked down the corridor.

Unease crept through Emma as the powerful lord followed her inside her chamber.

He closed the door, barred any path to escape. "This is my family. I will protect them by whatever means necessary." He leaned forward until he was a handsbreadth away, his words laden with threat, his hazel eyes fierce with intent. "I would kill for them without hesitation."

She angled her jaw. "As I."

"And I am to believe you?"

"I have given you little reason to," Emma agreed. "But I swear to you, I offer no threat."

Lord Monceaux crossed his arms, his expression grim. "Words easily given, but do they hold truth?"

She remained silent. What could she say? In his place she would feel the same anger, hold as much doubt. Emotion scraped her soul. His family was all she had dreamed of: people who cared, people who would lay down their lives to protect each other.

For a long moment, he studied her. "For the first time since Patrik's supposed death, my sister has begun to heal." He paused. "Because of you. Because you spoke to her of what none of us dared."

"What, that Patrik desperately regrets his attempt on your sister's life? Do you not see, he cares, would do anything to regain his family?"

He exhaled and his warrior's frame eased. "If asked before Patrik reappeared, I would have disagreed. Now, having watched him, witnessed the sincerity of his actions and his words, I agree. Regardless of my feelings, 'tis what my sister believes that is important." Lord Monceaux paused. "Had you not confronted Nichola, she would have clung to her belief of Patrik's intent, her hurt and fear blinding her to the truth or the ability to ever fully recover."

"Do not paint my actions as valor," Emma said. "My words to Lady Nichola were for Patrik. The horrors of witnessing the English slay his family stole his childhood. That same loathing guided his decisions toward your sister. His actions were wrong, an error he admits. I believe he should be given a chance to reclaim his family."

The baron arched a curious brow. "And what of you?"

Caught off guard by his question, by her need for Patrik, and her longing for a chance at happiness she could never have, she shook her head. "I will find my own way."

"In England?"

The coolness of his question left little doubt of his suspicions. "No, never will I return."

"Where will you go?"

She arched a brow. "If I am allowed to leave Lochshire Castle?"

Shrewd eyes studied her. "You know who I am. Considering your past actions, how can either the MacGruders or I believe you?"

A fate she'd earned. "How long will I be kept here?"

"I do not know. For now, too much lies at stake to allow you freedom." The baron stepped back. "A guard will remain at the bottom of the turret. Do not try to leave."

As if she could slip away without learning Patrik's condition?

"Go to sleep." The baron strode out and closed the door.

Alone, Emma's legs threatened to give way. Exhaustion and guilt weighed heavy upon her as she stumbled to the bed. She yearned to go to Patrik, to remain by his side, but the brothers refused to allow it. Heart aching, she knelt before the bed and folded her hands in prayer.

A tear wobbled down her cheek, dripped upon the bed. She sniffed. "Please, let Patrik live."

Warmth pulsed in her pocket.

Shaken, she withdrew the halved stone. It glowed within her palm as if a gift.

A gift?

No, she'd stolen what was not hers to take. Another wrong she must right. On shaky legs she pushed to her feet, crossed to the door and inched it open.

The corridor stood empty.

If she tried to leave, a guard blocked the entry to the turret below, but she had access to the upper chamber.

Fatigue weighted her steps as she made her way up the turret.

The first light of dawn welcomed her to the chamber.

On wobbly legs, she entered and walked to the bowl. Her fingers trembled as she laid the halved stone near the other.

"I return you to your home," Emma whispered. Another tear slid down her cheek. Foolish. 'Twas but a gemstone, an inanimate object hewn from the earth. Though it didn't make sense, it felt as if a part of her was torn away.

"That is because it is yours."

At the older woman's whisper, Emma whirled.

The elder stood before her, sadness woven upon her face, a woman Sir Alexander claimed no longer existed.

"Sir Alexander believes my spirit lives," the woman explained. "He but fights the fact you see me and why."

Emma closed her eyes. "No, you are not here." Exhaustion had brought on this illusion.

"Nae, lass, 'tis no illusion."

With her body trembling, Emma peered through her lashes.

The elder remained.

She gathered her courage. This woman, real or delusional, needed to understand. "Patrik and his gemstone belong here. This is his home, not mine. That he has made great steps in reclaiming his family is a blessing. If he lives—"

A sob escaped her, then another, the storm of emotions she'd held so long within spilling out. As she fought for control, the room spun around her. Emma put her hand to her head, fighting to focus. Staggering, she made it to the bed, barely.

A sad smile touched the weathered face as she looked down. "Sleep, my child. It has been too long since you have truly found rest."

The soft voice curled around Emma like a tender hand. "No," she whispered, "I must return to my chamber. I cannot stay here." Heaviness weighed upon her. Unable to form coherent thought, she curled upon the bed. A sense of peace filled her. From above the fairies stared down. And she swore she saw one smile.

The healer stowed her herbs, a grimace weighing upon her wizened face. She nodded to Lord Grey. "Sir Patrik is gravely ill. Worse, he shows signs of a fever."

"Will he live?" Seathan asked.

Alexander's gut tightened at the question.

"I do not know," she replied. "Only time will tell."

The creak of the door had Alexander glancing toward the entry. Nichola stood at the doorway. "Go to our chamber. I will be there when I can."

Face pale, his wife stepped inside. "I wish to see Patrik."

Seathan nodded to the healer. "Leave us."

The healer cast an unsure glance between them, secured the last bag of herbs, then hurried out.

Tense silence filled the chamber.

"Patrik is gravely ill. We do not know if he will . . ." Alexander muttered a curse.

Anguish darkened Nichola's eyes. "God no."

Alexander took his wife's hand, cupped it in his own. "Go, please."

"I would like to stay," Nichola said, "if only for a while."

At the rumble of voices, Patrik forced his eyes open. A pounding in his skull rewarded his efforts. His vision was blurred. Through sheer will, he focused. Stilled. "Nichola?"

At Patrik's rough whisper, she whirled. With hesitant steps, she crossed the room. "I am here."

Through the blur of pain, emotion swept Patrik as he stared at the woman he'd tried to kill.

She drew a slow breath, the turmoil in her eyes battling with anxiety.

"I am sorry," Patrik forced out, doubting anything could ever cleanse his soul. "Never will I try to harm you again. That I swear."

"When I believed you dead, I was relieved." Nichola's voice trembled; Alexander walked to her side, clasped her shoulder. Nichola shot him a thankful glance, and then faced Patrik. "When you first rode through the gates, I was as angry as I was afraid. The terror of your attempt upon my life left me feeling weak. For that, I hated you. For that, I wanted you dead."

"And now?" Patrik asked, his question but a rough gasp.

Nichola shook her head. "As Mistress Emma pointed out, your actions were guided by the tragedies of your past."

"Emma?" Patrik hesitated. "What do-does she have to do with this?"

"She is an interesting woman," Nichola replied, "and loves you very much."

"Lo-Loves me?" He grunted with disgust. "She betrayed me."

"She did," Nichola agreed. "But she also faced your brothers, admitted everything, her real name, and that she was hired by Cressingham. She risked her life to save yours."

Head pounding, Patrik turned away. "I-I do not wish to speak of her."

"Why?" Nichola demanded. "Because someone you trusted did naught but use you, gave but false words to achieve her goal?"

"Aye," he hissed, his anger finding a foothold. "Nothing she said was the truth." Including her feelings for him, and that hurt the worst.

"Think you, you are innocent?"

At the bite in Nichola's words, he met her gaze. Shame washed through him as he recalled his own deception when Alexander had first brought Nichola before them as *his captive*. Patrik had spoken to her with respect disguising his outrage; he'd plotted to keep her and Alexander apart. When that had failed, he'd abducted Nichola with the intent to take her life.

Humbled, Patrik shook his head. "Nae. Emma's path is one I, too, have trod."

Thick silence filled the chamber as his brothers witnessed his shame.

"Will you forgive her?" Nichola asked.

The oddity of her question struck Patrik, but he would offer her truth. "Forgive her? How, when I know not if I can ever trust her again?"

"And that," Nichola said, her voice breaking, "is exactly how I feel."

Alexander drew his wife against him, stroked her hair as her quiet sobs filled the chamber. "Go," he murmured. "You have said enough."

She broke free of his hold, faced Patrik, her gaze fierce. "No, I must know why you took an arrow aimed for Alexander, why you saved his life?"

Emotion clogged his throat. "Be-Because Alexander is my brother, the father of a beautiful son, husband to an incredible woman whom I wronged."

A tear rolled down her cheek. She wiped it away. "Patrik?"

At Nichola's nervous whisper, he tried to speak, but heaviness weighed upon him as if a hand pressed against his chest, and his entire body seemed as if on fire.

"Patrik?"

Through the haze of pain, Nichola's voice seemed more frantic. Patrik tried to speak, to make his mouth work, but naught would come. A sense of doom filled him, a heartache that swamped his every thought. Tired, he was so tired. Thankful, he gave in to the sheer exhaustion, closed his eyes and succumbed to the blackness.

Alexander cursed. "He has passed out."

Nichola laid her hand upon Patrik's brow. "He has a fever."

The healer's words rumbled through Alexander's mind. He met his brothers' worried gazes, turned to his wife. "Nichola, await me in our chamber. Please."

She hesitated. Then, as if understanding that he needed to speak with his brothers in private, she left.

As the door closed, Seathan stepped to Alexander's side. "Patrik's fate is not your burden to bear."

"By my sword, he took the bloody arrow meant for me." Guilt seared him as he faced his brothers. "As did our father in my youth, and he died to protect me. Now, we know not if Patrik will live." He closed his eyes, opened them. "By my sword, twice it should have been me lying upon my deathbed."

Anger flared in Duncan's eyes. "Patrik has not died."

"Nae," Alexander rasped. "We have that."

Patrik shifted, sweat lining his brow. He tossed his head back and forth. "Cristina."

Alexander knelt at the bedside, placed his palm against Patrik's brow. Fiery heat met him. "Patrik."

His brother's words were garbled.

"I will send for the healer," Seathan said.

"What will she do?" Alexander stood, furious he could do naught but let his brother burn up with fever, let him die. "She has given him herbs to ease the pain. 'Twill take time and a miracle to heal his wounds." Silence descended upon the chamber.

"Cristina?" Patrik whispered.

Alexander muttered a curse as he strode to the door.

"It will be good for you to be with Nichola," Seathan said.

At the door, Alexander turned. "'Tis not who I am going to see."

"Who then?" Seathan asked.

"Emma." Alexander slammed the door in his wake and strode to her chamber, unsure whether he was angrier at Patrik for taking the bloody arrow for him or at Emma for being in league with his enemy. At Emma's chamber, he shoved open the door, strode inside.

Empty.

He scanned the corridor. With a guard at the bottom of the turret, she could not have escaped. Blast it, where was she? An outrageous thought came to mind. Anger stewed. Nae, she would not dare!

Alexander bolted down the hallway, then took the stairs to the tower chamber two at a time. God help her if he found her within.

Above, the door stood open.

He stormed through the entry, his mind blazing hot.

Framed within the sheen of sun, the lass lay upon his grandmother's bed asleep. Curled within her hand lay Patrik's halved stone.

Bedamned! He stalked over. He should rip the gemstone from her hand. She was English and had no place in their home!

"A belief Patrik once held about Nichola as well."

At the whisper of his grandmother's voice, Alexander whirled. Heart slamming against his chest, he scoured the chamber. It stood empty, but a fire blazed within the hearth that had lain empty moments ago. He'd heard her voice, as if the words were spoken to him with a smile.

Shame filled him. Aye, when Patrik had first met Nichola, he'd believed she had no place within their home or Alexander's life. Had not Emma risked her life to save Patrik by returning to Lochshire Castle? He swallowed hard. Like Patrik, he was wrong.

"I understand," Alexander said to the fairies on the ceiling. "But that does not mean I like it."

A sparkle flickered within the eyes of the fairy wearing the dark green gown, and then faded.

The flames within the hearth disappeared.

He muttered a curse. "Mistress Emma."

She shifted.

Blast it. However tempted he was to haul her up, Alexander gently touched her shoulder.

Emma's eyes flew open. Confusion, then recognition flared. "Sir Alexander!" She shot from the bed, her eyes wide with panic. "I did not mean to stay here. I but came to return Patrik's halved stone."

He scowled. "The one in your hand?"

Mistress Emma looked down and red slashed her cheeks. "I will return it now."

By the sword, he was making a mess of it. "The stone does not matter. Patrik has a fever. We know not whether he will live."

Her face paled. "God in heaven, I must see him."

The desperation of her words did not move him. But if her presence helped Patrik, so be it.

"Please, I beg of you—"

"You do nae have to ask." Alexander grimaced. "'Tis why I came."

Chapter 21

Fear slid through Emma as Sir Alexander escorted her down the turret, erasing the last wisps of sleep. No, Sir Alexander was wrong. Patrik would live. Though well she knew life offered no guarantees.

Grim-faced, the fierce Scot strode down the corridor.

Outside the chamber, he stepped aside, motioned her forward.

Emma entered. The cloying scent of blood filled the air, accompanied by the stench of illness.

Lord Grey stood beside his brother's bed along with Sir Duncan, desperation ravaging their faces.

Shaken, her gaze riveted on Patrik; sweat slicked his face as he shifted within his bed and began to ramble. "My lord?" Her voice trembled.

"Patrik has been asking for you. We hoped—" Lord Grey shot Sir Alexander a grim look. "We hoped your presence would calm him."

A futile hope indeed. "No, my lord. After the lies I have told him, I am the last person he would wish to see."

Sir Alexander grunted. "My belief as well, but in his delirium he asks for you."

"For me?" The displeasure on the men's faces assured her the fierce knight's claim was true. On unsteady legs, she crossed the chamber.

"A guard will remain outside if you have need of anything," Lord Grey said. "If Patrik's condition changes, we are to be informed."

God in heaven. "After all I have done, you would entrust me with Patrik?"

"We do this for our brother." With a grim look, the earl and his brothers strode out. The soft thud of the door echoed in their wake.

Struggling to keep hold of her emotions, Emma sank onto the chair. "Patrik?"

He tossed his head back and forth, and garbled words fell from his lips.

"Patrik, 'tis Emma." Fingers trembling, she laid her hand atop his. Warmth invaded her palm, a wash of unhealthy heat. Terror slid through her. "Patrik." Please God, let him hear her. "Patrik, I am here."

A frown creased his brow. "Cristina?"

"Yes," she replied, her heart breaking. He wanted Cristina, a woman he believed was honest, a woman with whom he'd found peace. Not Emma. Not the traitor. Fine then, if 'twas Cristina he wanted, that she would give him.

Ignoring the call of sleep, Emma spoke of their journey, of the laughs they'd shared. After the first few moments, he calmed. As he lay there, the rightness of this moment filled her. How easy it was to envision sharing the months, the years ahead. Time she had lost because of her betrayal.

A cloud slid over the sun and cast the room into dismal shadows. The church bells began to toll.

She counted each ring. Sext, time for the prayers at midday. Prayers? How dare she think of God after the numerous lies she'd told Patrik. But if she asked Patrik for forgiveness, would he give it?

A tear slid down her cheek.

No, she'd earned nothing but Patrik's hatred. Long moments passed. Though it would change naught, she found it important to offer Patrik her confession.

Golden rays filled the room as she took his hand, clasping it within her own. "I know not how to begin. Many a lie I have told you since our first meeting." She blew out a breath. "A meeting I planned."

Her heart ached as she told how she'd plotted with the English knights, how she'd used Patrik's hatred of the English. She had realized that, caught up in his outrage at a Scottish woman being raped, he would save her without question, his protectiveness wiping away his normal wariness of a stranger.

"Except, I was not supposed to fall in love with you." Warmth slid through her at the memories of his touch. And, shame. "Patrik, I was never married. Gyles never existed. Nor was I a virgin, because in my youth, I was raped." She steadied herself, pushed on. "The man whom I cherished was Father Lawrenz, a priest I met while living in the orphanage. He was a beacon of light and for the first time in my life, I had begun to believe good existed, and from the lessons he taught, believed that I could build a life, mayhap even find love." She swallowed hard. "One day as I had hurried to meet Father Lawrenz, I cut through an alley. I found him dead. Murdered for a pence."

Dark memories assailed her, but she shoved them away. She fought not to drown in the horrors of her past.

"At that moment, as he lay before me within a puddle of his own blood, hope fled. I realized that no one would protect me but myself. And I vowed never to care for anyone again, ever. A vow I kept—until you." She wiped away a tear. "And though you may not believe it, I have dreams. Dreams that before I met you I would not have dared."

A smile wavered upon her mouth as images shimmered in her mind. "I wish to help orphans, to show them that good exists, to teach them as Father Lawrenz did me, as well as give them hope." Her smile fell. "I understand dreams of our life together, of our children, never will be." She fought for composure. "But for a moment, however fragile, I held them. For that I thank you."

Her entire body trembling, Emma leaned forward, pressed a soft kiss upon Patrik's mouth. "I love you, Patrik Cleary MacGruder. Though you will not remember my words, I give them to you." Exhausted, she leaned back, sniffed. "Look at me. I am supposed to be sharing stories to make you sleep, yet I ramble as if an old woman lost."

She was hungry for sleep, but for Patrik's sake, she forced herself to stay awake. For the remainder of the day, she shared tales she'd heard from bards as well as those of intriguing sights seen in her travels.

Beneath the orange-red rays of sunset, Patrik's pallor remained the same, but that he continued to sleep, to give his body much-needed rest, bolstered her hope.

A scrape of the door had Emma turning.

Lord Grey entered, gestured for her to remain seated. "How does he fare?"

"He still sleeps, my lord."

The earl scanned his brother's face, nodded. "You are exhausted. My family will take turns sitting with Patrik throughout the night. You are free to return to your bed."

Emma's throat tightened. Once Patrik regained his health, if that miracle occurred, he would demand that she leave. "If possible, my lord, I would like to remain."

The powerful noble studied her a long moment, glanced at Patrik, who quietly slept. "Though I hesitate to allow you such favor, for this night, if your presence allows him to rest, mayhap 'tis for the best." With a solemn nod, he departed.

Humbled, she swallowed hard. She would savor this time, for there would come no other.

Hours passed. With the night seeping into the sky, Patrik began to shift about.

Emma lifted the blanket from where he'd cast it off, tucked it around him with a gentle hand. "Rest now."

"I . . ." Eyes closed, Patrik began to shift, his words undecipherable.

"Lie still," she urged.

His body jerked; his eyes moved quickly beneath his lids.

"Patrik, please remain still. You will loosen your bandages."

He twisted on the bed.

Emma glanced at the door. Should she send for his brothers? If she did, she would never see Patrik again. Desperate, praying it helped, she sat upon the bed, then lay beside him.

A muttered curse stumbled from his lips; he turned his head, then slowly, he began to settle.

She snuggled closer, his warmth enveloping her. When he remained sleeping, Emma closed her eyes with a thankful sigh and succumbed to the exhaustion weighing upon her mind.

Sunlight flooded her lids and Emma winced. With a start she opened her eyes. Morning sun filled the room. She sat up. God in heaven, she'd slept beside Patrik the entire night! She glanced toward the door. What had his brothers or their wives thought? Or, had they seen her?

Emma laid her hand upon Patrik's brow. It was still too warm, but dry. The fever had subsided, and his face held a tinge of color. Thank God. At the slide of the door, she scrambled from the bed.

A slender woman with whiskey-colored hair stepped inside, followed by Lady Nichola.

"My lady." Emma tugged to straighten her rumpled gown, gave up. "I . . ." How did one explain the obvious? Warmth slid up her cheeks. "I fell asleep."

Tenderness touched Lady Nichola's face. "That my husband and I saw last night when we came to check upon Patrik. You appeared so exhausted, I had not the heart to disturb you." Nichola nodded to the woman at her side. "Lady Isabel, this is Mistress Emma Astyn."

Curious amber eyes studied her. "I have heard much of you and regret we have not been introduced until now. Sir Duncan is my husband."

Emma recalled seeing the woman within the court-yard when she'd first arrived.

"The healer will be here shortly," Lady Nichola said.

The reason she'd come was to wake Emma and spare her the further embarrassment of being found in Patrik's bed. "My thanks." The last haze of sleep faded, and with that clarity and the unspoken deter-mination upon their faces, she understood. "But you have come to ask questions?"

"I have," Lady Nichola said. "We know you returned for Patrik, but why did you leave behind the writ?"

Regret swept Emma as she glanced from one woman to the other. "Because I am no longer the person Sir Cressingham hired. Had you of known me over the years, you would not have believed me capable of change. Then I met Patrik." Tears formed in her eyes; she damned them, fought to push them back. "Lady Nichola, I understand your distrust and dislike for Patrik, but I also understand his reasons. He is a good man. Though battered, his heart is enormous. He does nothing by halves, loves with a fierceness I have never seen."

Lady Isabel took Lady Nichola's hand in support.

Alexander's wife gave her sister-in-law a thankful smile, and then turned to Emma. "I admit having Patrik at Lochshire Castle is difficult, but yester eve he took an arrow meant for Alexander. He saved my husband's life." Gray eyes narrowed with conviction. "Do you know why? Because Patrik wanted me to be happy, for Alexander to have his family." Tears blurred her eyes. "I am not proud of my fear, or of wishing him again dead, but though anger and hurt still well inside me, Patrik has proven that he is sincere."

Emma stilled. "You will give him another chance?"

"Yes," Nichola whispered.

The door slipped open. The earl's wife entered.

Emma curtsied. "Lady Linet."

"Mistress Emma." Lord Grey's wife nodded to the two other women, then glanced at the bed. "How fares Patrik?"

"His fever has broken," Emma replied.

Relief swept Lady Linet's face. "Thank God. How do you fare, Mistress Emma?"

"Fine, my lady."

The scrape of steps had them all looking back. The healer, carrying a basket of herbs, stepped inside. Wizened eyes opened with surprise, then landed on Patrik as he lay sound asleep.

"His fever has broken," Emma said.

Relief swept the aged lines of the healer's face. "A good sign. It appears as if he will live."

Sun streamed across the morning sky like a wash of promises made, of hope given. Emma clutched the hewn stone beneath her hand at Patrik's window. Hope that Lord Grey had given her. An unlikely source, considering only days before he'd viewed her as his enemy.

But, last eve he, his brothers, and Lord Monceaux had questioned her extensively about the English. After she'd replied to everything they'd asked, and then had informed them of more, the earl had dismissed all within the chamber but her.

Alone, Lord Grey had warned her that after the English secrets she'd exposed, Sir Cressingham would pay handsomely to see her dead. A warning she'd acknowledged. Then he'd surprised her by asking what she wanted to do. Caught off guard, she'd blurted her wish to help orphans. Surprise had flickered in his gaze, but he'd agreed to help.

Sadness sifted through her as she withdrew her hand from the stone. However much she wanted to remain at Lochshire Castle, to be with Patrik, her lies had severed such a choice. Neither could she keep Patrik's stone, regardless of the grandmother's wishes, or of her own desire. A sense of loss still filled her without the halved gemstone on her person, but 'twas right to have returned it to the tower chamber early this morning.

The snort of horses echoed from below.

Emma looked out the window. Near the stable, a large bay stood readied, a roan mare nearby. How ironic that Sir Alexander would escort her to the abbey a day's ride north. She could live there in peace, could fulfill her dreams of helping the children whose lives war had shattered. Except, her heart would remain here with Patrik.

She fought back tears as she took in Patrik sleeping

peacefully upon his bed. He'd continued to improve since yesterday morning. With his fever broken, soon he would awaken. 'Twas best if she was long gone before then.

"The horses are ready," Lady Nichola said in hushed tones from the entry.

"My thanks, my lady," Emma whispered.

Alexander's wife stepped inside. "Once Patrik awakens, I will explain that you have left, and as you requested, I will not tell him where you are."

Emma swallowed hard. "I . . . Patrik's involvement in the plan to rescue Bishop Wishart will keep him busy."

"It will."

Would Patrik ever think of her? Yes, but anger would taint his thoughts, anger he would never overcome. With her heart breaking, she took one last longing look, memorized the merest hint of dimples, the scar across his brow, the shadow of a beard.

I will always love you.

"I am ready." Emma turned and walked to the door without looking back.

Emma set the woven laundry basket filled with clean clothes upon the ground. Wind whipped around her as she reached for the gown on top, secured it to the sturdy line of hemp. It was hard to believe a fortnight had passed since she'd arrived at the abbey, or how easy it had been to adjust to the simple lifestyle there. She reached for another gown.

The sounds of children playing prodded the emptiness within her soul. Though they were not her children, her life held purpose. Helping the orphaned children had allowed her to finally come to terms with her past and the death of the priest she'd adored. As for Patrik, however much she longed for him, at least here she'd found contentment, and here, she would live out the rest of her days.

She smiled at the sway of grass, the leaves clattering in the trees. None of the sisters had asked about her past, neither would she bring it up. Her desire to help was sincere, and they thankfully accepted it. For her, shelter and food was a fine exchange.

As Emma bent to retrieve the next sodden garment, a shadow darkened the basket. A smile touched her mouth. Which child needed her help now? She turned.

Hazel eyes pierced her.

She stumbled back. "Patrik!"

His warrior's frame towered above hers. "You thought I would not come after you?"

"I . . . No. You should not be here," she said.

Eyes blazing, Patrik caught her hand. "Come."

Panic built, the curious looks of the others flustering her further. "Let me go!"

"If I did, I would be a fool."

Unsure of anything, she followed as he strode toward the chapel. Once inside, he guided her to a pew. "Sit."

Frankincense and myrrh scented the air as she stared at the man she'd believed she would never again see. Heart pounding, she fought for calm, too aware they were alone.

"What are you doing here? You and your brothers are supposed to be planning to free Bishop Wishart!"

"Just sit."

Mouth dry, she sat. "But the bishop—"

"Plans have been made. Soon we will ride to accomplish the task." Patrik crossed his arms. Candlelight framed the anger slashed upon his face. "Why did you request I not be told where you had gone?"

Her chest squeezed. "Is it not obvious?"

A muscle worked in his jaw. "Tell me."

She clutched the time-worn bench, swallowed hard. "After you learned I was an English mercenary, you despised me. How could you not? I could not stay, my presence would only bring you more pain. Your having knowledge of my whereabouts would only upset you."

Patrik took her hand. "When I awoke and learned you were gone, I ignored the sense of loss, assured myself I should be relieved you were gone from my life." He curled his fingers over hers. "But with each passing day, the ache in my chest grew and I realized 'twas not from my wounds, but my heart."

"Patrik—"

"Nae, let me finish." He blew out a deep breath. "As I lay there healing, with time but a nuisance to endure, I realized I was wrong to cleave to my anger when you had sacrificed your life to save mine."

A tear slid down her cheek. "'Twas my treachery that endangered your life."

"It was, but a wrong you righted."

She withdrew her hand, lashed at the tear. "Do not

claim me righteous. 'Twas my greed for money, my craving for danger that guided me to deceive you."

"Mayhap then, but if now offered the same task by Cressingham, would you agree?"

Ire flared in her eyes. "Of course not!"

Patrik smiled, appreciating the fine indignation on her face. The lass was amazing, her passion and determination qualities he would forever savor.

"'Tis not a fact I find humor in."

"Nor I," he said, his words somber. "Over the weeks, you have changed. As I have. I realized that my anger toward you after your selfless act was wrong." Patrik exhaled. "After my parents' deaths, I held onto my anger, allowed it to sever my bond with the Mac-Gruders, men who had taken me into their home, had treated me like a brother. With your help, I recovered that bond. Nay, 'tis folly to cling to such darkness, a mistake I will not be making again."

Tears welled in her eyes. "You forgive me?" she whispered.

"Aye." Emotion welled in his throat. "With the passage of days, dreams invaded my mind, those of a lass afraid and alone, a lass who had borne the brutality of man. Also, a woman who sought forgiveness, a woman who wished to help children who'd lost their families as well." At the flush sliding up her cheeks, he smiled. "I believed the memories but dreams. When Nichola told me you'd remained overnight by my side during my fever, I realized 'twas you I had heard, not my mind's whispers."

"Patrik, I—"

"Was it not?"

Emma lowered her head.

Patrik caught her chin, raised her face until their eyes met. "And, in my dream, the woman told me she loved me."

Another tear wobbled, slid down her cheek.

"Do you?" he whispered.

"Yes."

"Thank God." On a rough exhale, he drew her into a heated kiss, one seasoned with passion, one delivered with desperation to have her in his life. Slowly, Patrik drew away, stared at the woman who had touched his life, the woman who had allowed him to heal, and the woman who had helped him regain his family. "I love you, Emma Astyn."

Tears flowed unchecked down her face. "I do not deserve your love."

"Aye, you deserve that and so much more." He hesitated. "Emma?"

"Yes?"

With his body trembling, Patrik knelt before her, withdrew the halved malachite dangling upon a chain from around his neck.

She glanced toward his neck. "The gift from your grandmother?"

"Nae." He withdrew the matching half from beneath his tunic. "This gemstone is the other half. I had it made into a pendant to give to my heart's desire, the woman I was destined to love." He brushed away a strand of hair from her face, the flicker of candles warm upon her cheeks as if a golden caress. "Emma, you are the woman who saved me when no hope remained, who taught me to love when I believed none existed. Within God's house I ask you to marry me."

Emerald eyes widened in wondrous disbelief. "You want me to marry you?"

"Emma, you are my life and the woman who fills my every dream. Marry me and I swear, I will show you only love."

She nodded, tears streaming down her cheeks. "Yes! Oh yes!"

He stood, lowered the matching pendant over her head and claimed her mouth, her love erasing the last wisps of emptiness within his heart. Nay, Emma was not a threat, but *His Destiny*.

If you liked this book,
pick up the rest of the series!

His Captive

Strangers

With a wastrel brother and a treacherous former fiancé, Lady Nichola Westcott hardly expects the dangerously seductive Scot who kidnaps her to be a man of his word. Though Sir Alexander MacGruder promises not to hurt her, Nichola's only value is as a pawn to be ransomed.

Enemies

Alexander's goal is to avenge his father's murder, not to become entangled with the enemy. But his desire to keep Nichola with him, in his home—in his bed—unwittingly make her a target for those who have no qualms about shedding English blood.

Lovers

Now Nichola is trapped—by her powerful attraction to a man whose touch shakes her to the core. Unwilling and unable to resist each other, can Nichola and Alexander save a love that has enslaved them both?

His Woman

Trusting Her Was Unthinkable

Lady Isabel Adair is the last woman Sir Duncan Mac-Gruder wants to see again, much less be obliged to save. Three years ago, Isabel broke their engagement to become the Earl of Frasyer's mistress, shattering Duncan's heart and hopes in one painful blow. But Duncan's promise to Isabel's dying brother compels him to rescue her from those determined to bring down Scottish rebel Sir William Wallace.

Resisting Her Was Impossible

Betraying the man she loved was the only way for Isabel to save her father, but every moment she spends with Duncan reminds her just how much she sacrificed. No one could blame him for despising her, yet Duncan's misgivings cannot withstand a desire that has grown wilder with time. Now, on a perilous journey through Scotland, two wary lovers must confront both the enemies who will stop at nothing to hunt them down, and the secret legacy that threatens their passion and their lives . . .

His Conquest

The Only Man Who Could Save Her

Linet Dancort will not be sold. But that's essentially what her brother intends to do—to trade her like so much chattel to widen his already vast scope of influence. Linet will seize any opportunity to escape her fate—and opportunity comes in the form of a rebel prisoner locked in her brother's dungeon, predatory and fearsome, and sentenced to hang in the morning.

Would First Need Saving Himself

Seathan MacGruder, Earl of Grey, is not unused to cheating death. But even this legendary Scottish warrior is surprised when a beautiful Englishwoman creeps to his cell and offers him his freedom. What Linet wants in exchange, though—safe passage to the Highlands—is a steep price to pay. For the only thing more dangerous than the journey through embattled Scotland is the desire that smolders between these two fugitives the first time they touch . . .